Adiós to My Old Life

Adiós to My Old Life

caridad ferrer

BOOKS

POCKET BOOKS
New York London Toronto Sydney

POCKET BOOKS, a division of Simon & Schuster, Inc.
1230 Avenue of the Americas, New York, NY 10020

This book is a work of fiction. Names, characters, places, and incidents are products of the author's imagination or are used fictitiously. Any resemblance to actual events or locales or persons, living or dead, is entirely coincidental.

Library of Congress Cataloging-in-Publication Data

Ferrer, Caridad.
Adios to my old life / Caridad Ferrer.— 1st MTV Books/Pocket Books trade pbk. ed.
p.cm.
1. Hispanic American women—Fiction. 2. Game shows—Fiction. 3. Women singers—Fiction. 4. Female friendship—Fiction. I. Title.

PS3606.E766A63 2006
813'.6—dc22

ISBN-13: 978-1-4165-2473-1
ISBN-10: 1-4165-2473-8

First MTV Books/Pocket Books trade paperback edition July 2006

10 9 8 7 6 5 4 3 2

Designed by Jan Pisciotta

Manufactured in the United States of America

For information regarding special discounts for bulk purchases, please contact Simon & Schuster Special Sales at 1-800-456-6798 or business@simonandschuster.com.

For Nate and Abby

Because dreams are beautiful, wondrous things

Acknowledgments

Wow, this is like the writers' equivalent of an Oscar speech, except we don't have the conductor in the orchestra pit playing us off the stage with some cheesy piece of music. Cool.

First off, to my agent, the magnificent, fabulous, and genuinely amazing Caren Johnson. To find an agent who shares your same demented, snarky sense of humor and just completely "gets" you is such a gift, and thank goodness I sent that first e-mail that read something along the lines of, "Look, do you rep romance or what?"

To my editor, Lauren McKenna, a fellow former South Floridian who understands all about beehive-driven Caddies. Thanks for taking a chance on me. And to Megan McKeever, who is absolutely great at soothing my frazzled nerves, thank you—I so owe you good chocolate.

To the Cherries, a more supportive, wonderful group of fellow writers and readers I've yet to come across. Finding out that I sold while at RWA Nationals was amazing. To have you be among the first to congratulate me, en masse, is a moment I will treasure forever. And to the Head Cherry herself—Jenny, your continued dedication to learning and the craft of writing is an inspiration. Thank you.

To Deb and all the Treehouse denizens, you guys rock like rocking things. Thanks for the laughs, the shoulders to cry on, and for being there, no matter what. Oh, and chocolate death-bomb cookies.

To Lani Rich and Michelle Cunnah, the literariest chicks I know. You guys have been so tremendously supportive through all the lows ("I'm never gonna sell!!"), to the highs ("You sold? Let's go to the bar!"), and all points in between. Thank you for all of it.

To Alesia Holliday, who is not just one of the funniest, best writers out there, but who is also one of the most remarkably generous, supportive people, period. To have you as a colleague is a privilege; to have you as a friend is a true, rare gift. Thank you.

This is where I geek out and thank the musicians who inspired me through the creation of this manuscript. Believe me, narrowing the list down wasn't easy! To Sting, for simply being Sting. My trip down your musical road began as an adolescent, may the journey continue until I'm a very cranky old lady, and to Dominic Miller, for providing a remarkably open, honest, and insightful peek into the world of musical creation. Plus, you're simply a kick-ass guitarist.

To Chris Botti, not just for the sheer command over your instrument, but also for your passion for music and for always imparting the importance of music in our children's lives. You are a valued advocate and an ambassador for the art form.

To Peter Cincotti, for providing an exemplary model of a young musician with his own unique vision—someone who doesn't allow others to set his boundaries or define his limits. May you one day become your generation's Ray Charles or Sting.

To my dear Torrie. None of this, and I mean *none* of it, would have been possible without you there nearly every day, cajoling me and IMing me with the expectant, "Have you perchance, something for me to read today?" You're not only a tremendous writer and critique partner, but my best friend, a true sister of my heart, and I love you dearly.

To Mom and Dad, thanks, and much love for not thinking I was nuts. I know it's not always easy.

To Mom and Maria, thank you for always, always supporting me no matter what I choose to do. Except for that wanting to run away to San Francisco phase when I was sixteen. I can sort of understand why you had a problem with that, Mom. But otherwise, you both have always been there, and I love you both very much.

To Nate and Abby, thanks for (mostly) learning to stay out of Mommy's office when she's staring at the big monitor. I love you both more than my luggage.

To Lewis, thank you. Anything else would take up a lot more pages than I have.

If you'd like to support young musicians like Ali, please visit VH-1's Save The Music Foundation, which supports music education in our schools at: http://www.vh1.com/partners/save_the_music/.

1

"Girl, you do realize you're crazy, right?" the voice hissed in my ear. "Like, as in, gone softer in your head than one of our nasty school cafeteria tacos?"

I didn't look up. "Would you shut up, Sosi?" I strummed a chord on my acoustic Bernabé. No, not yet. The humidity was so freaky high, I was probably going to have to adjust again, but I had to get it as close to perfect beforehand so I wouldn't waste time. I reached over to the tuners, making a few adjustments, even while my best friend kept going on. And on . . . and on . . . and on . . .

"Sos, I can't hear with you babbling, girl. Please—just for thirty seconds—zip it, then you can tell me again how crazy I am." I looked up for a second and grinned, even though I totally felt like I was gonna hurl. "Besides, you've been all over this from the beginning and don't even try to lie by saying you haven't. 'You should do it, Ali. Send in the audition tape, Ali. It'll be so cool to see you on TV.' You need to quit being all bipolar about this."

"Yeah, *mija,* but that was before we got down here." Sosi's voice was squeaking—a sure sign she was nervous. The nuns at school always knew when she was up to something because she'd start sounding like Mickey Mouse. "I haven't seen a single person go on out there who's not wearing spandex, rhinestones, leather, or some combination of all three."

After practicing a final run, I carefully propped my guitar against the wall. Sosi's round face looked seriously panicked as she kept reporting on what she'd seen during her "scouting mission," as she'd called it.

"And they're all out there shaking their asses like someone took DNA from Shakira, Celia, Selena, and Ricky Martin, mixed it up, and said, '*Oye,* here's the perfect Latin entertainer.'"

"Sounds like the perfect Latin nightmare to me." I stretched my arms above my head, trying to keep them limber, and took a drink of water so my throat didn't dry out. Deep, calming breaths were always good but had a way of leaving you parched.

"That's the benefit of playing an instrument, I guess. Can't shake my ass and play at the same time." *Mira,* I couldn't believe *I* was trying to keep Sosi calm. She was supposed to be keeping *me* from losing my mind.

"Besides, I'd never wear stuff like that." I nodded at the bleached-blonde chick who was stalking past us in a cropped black leather vest with laces that crisscrossed the front and wound around her waist to lace down the back of her silver-studded leather pants. Looked painful.

"As if," Sosi agreed as we watched the girl bend over and shake her corkscrew curls so they poofed out even bigger and wilder before taking the stage, all full of 'tude and what I'm sure she thought was street cred. Please. Girl looked like she had about as much street cred as Gwen Stefani. Bet she was from Kendall. Whatever. Wasn't my problem.

"Aside from the fact you've got much better taste, you'd never wear that because your father would kill you. As it is, if he finds out you're even doing this, he's gonna send you to the nuns in Spain like he's been threatening to, like, forever, and then where would I be? Who would I have to go to the mall with me? Help me with math?"

"Let me remind you one more time, Sosi Cabrera, that you're in this as deep as I am and *your* father might just send you right along with me to the nuns. So shut up, and let me get into my good head space, okay?"

"Pissy diva," she muttered, but she did pipe down, sliding a few feet down the wall and taking a swig from the gigantic Mountain Dew Code Red she'd been working on for the last hour. That was half the girl's problem right there. All that caffeine and sugar.

"Do I look okay?"

"I thought you wanted to get into your 'good head space,' *chica*?"

I just waited. She *had* to say something snarky, otherwise she would've exploded. She'd been like that since we were five. But she'd said it, now she was fine, and she could concentrate on the question I'd asked.

"You look fine, girl. Besides, how much of you are they gonna really see behind your guitar?"

"Yeah, but they're going to see me when I'm walking out onstage. First impressions count."

Sosi closed the distance between us and whipped my makeup bag out of her enormous tote. "Let's take the shine off and add a little more color." She used a big brush to dust some more powder and some of the Benefit Georgia she'd gotten me for my last birthday after convincing my father the peach shimmer powder wasn't at all slutty looking.

"Adjust the hair a little . . ." She pulled a couple of pieces free from my French braid with the skinny tail end of a comb so they framed my face and spritzed some hair spray over the whole mess. Thank God for Sosi, you know? Otherwise, I wouldn't have the first clue how to do anything with hair or makeup.

"And your outfit looks great, Ali. It really does." She dabbed on a little bit of lip gloss with her pinky, just a touch, right in the center of my lower lip. "It's going to flow while you're walking, but won't get in the way while you're playing." Setting the bag down, she reached out and adjusted the waist of the turquoise mesh sleeveless tunic I was wearing with a pair of dark-rinse jeans. No spandex. No rhinestones. At least my high-heeled boots were leather.

"Ali Montero?" A guy wearing a headset over his backward baseball cap and holding a clipboard stopped in front of me, looking at the plastic tag I had hanging on a cord around my neck. "Curtain."

Oh. My. God. That meant I had five minutes before I went on. Five minutes before I went on. And four minutes to prove myself. Oh. My. God.

"Hey, you can breathe. I'm harmless. The real vultures are out there." He cocked his head out toward the stage.

Okay, so he was right. I'd sort of stopped with the breathing action.

"Here."

I found a bottle of water in my hand.

"Don't worry, it's cool. It's unopened." He smiled—a really nice smile—and gestured to the messenger bag slung across his chest. "Been keeping a few stashed in case I come across someone who looks like they're about to pass out."

"Thanks," I croaked as I tried to twist off the cap, but my hands were shaking so much I wound up dropping the bottle on the floor instead. And nearly cracked heads with Mr. Sweet Guy as we both dove for it.

"Whoa. You really are nervous, aren't you?" Putting a hand beneath my elbow, he helped me back up and handed me the bottle, the cap loosened. "I heard you practicing. You're good." Another smile, bigger, that made his eyes go all crinkly at the corners. "If nothing else, you'll be a breath of fresh air. I mean, if I hear 'Suerte' one more time, I may just go postal, y'know?"

"I bet you're gonna hear it a lot more before the day's over,"

Sosi piped up with a wicked grin. I could not *believe* that girl. If the world was ending, she'd find a way to flirt.

"Yeah, that's what I'm afraid of," he said, rolling his eyes. "Huge catalogs of fantastic music out there and everyone thinks it's all about Shakira or Marc Anthony. Not that they're not great, but a little imagination, people." He winked at me. "Like you. Break a leg."

"Thanks," I called to his retreating back. *Ugh.* If I could smack myself upside the head without looking dumber than I already had, believe me, I would. This guy was being nicer to me than most of my male relatives between the ages of seven and twenty-three, and all I could manage was *thanks*? I had the social skills of a banana slug.

"Ali Montero, one minute." A woman this time, also wearing a headset and holding a clipboard, gestured from her position just offstage.

Handing Sosi the bottle of water and ID tag, I picked up my guitar and walked toward the spot the woman was indicating.

"Hey, watch where you're going, *niña.*" Miss Black Leather shoved past me, all sweaty and gasping like she'd just run the Boston Marathon or something. *Oye,* that leather must've been tighter than I thought. "Leave room for the people who're actually going to make the cut."

Next to me, Sosi muttered, "Ignore her. *Sangrona.* I hope that tacky outfit chafes—maybe leaves a rash."

But it wasn't really registering. I mean, I knew Miss Leather had been rude and I know Sosi was trying to reassure me, but none of it was really penetrating because I was already going into my zone, that place in my head I went right before I performed.

I waited in the wings while the woman who'd called me stepped out on stage and said, "Okay, next up, from Coral Gables, Florida, Ali Montero." She nodded at me. "All right, Ali. Come show us why you should be a finalist on *Oye Mi Canto.*"

2

As I settled myself on the stool, I heard one of the judges—a man—say, "Welcome, Ali. *Mucho gusto.*"

"Un placer," I replied automatically.

Another voice, female, also sounding nice. "Are you more comfortable speaking in Spanish or English?"

"Either."

"All right, then." A warm laugh—the nice man again. "We'll play it by ear."

The female voice asked, "So what are you going to be performing for us?"

Peering out into the shadows, I tried to focus on where I thought the voices were coming from. This sucked, not being able to see the judges. Had to rely completely on tone with no facial expressions to fall back on. They sounded nice, at any rate.

"'Bella Luna'."

"Doesn't sound familiar." Okay, mostly nice. Another woman. Sharper, not so friendly as either the man or the first woman.

"It's a Jason Mraz song. Off his latest release," I added helpfully.

"Jason Mraz." The same nasty, sharp voice. "Hardly a giant in Latin music. You *are* aware this is a contest to find the next big Latin star, right?" A few scattered laughs echoed around the interior of the Jackie Gleason Theater. Bitch.

Out of the corner of my eye I could see Sosi's face settling into that angry frown that was a sure sign she wanted to pound on someone, and with that much Code Red in her. . . . Next to her, Cute Helpful Guy was shaking his head. And I kept getting calmer. This was my turf. I knew how to work it.

"Last time I checked, *I* was Latin—and so is the way I play this," I replied, earning my own set of chuckles as I lowered my chin and lifted my guitar to my lap. After a last-second check on the tuning, I nodded at the sound tech, indicating he should start my backup disc. A nod and a thumbs-up; five seconds later, I heard the soft gong I'd added to the beginning of the track as a signal I should begin playing. I'd needed something, since it dove right into a guitar solo for the first eight measures—letting the judges see what I was about up front. It had taken me weeks, messing around with the music programs on my computer, to extract the guitar and vocals so I could play over what was left, but I'd finally gotten it right.

And it was a risk, using it as my second audition piece. I'd gone a lot more predictable with the audition tape that got me here in the first place, a Spanish-language version of Toni Braxton's "Un-Break My Heart." Yeah, yeah, I *know* it was cheesy, especially the L7 way it had been recorded by Simon Cowell's multilingual boy band Il Divo, but hey, it worked. Good showcase for my alto range, familiar without being so overdone it was *boring,* and in the end, it got me here, *verdad*? On the stage of the Jackie Gleason, where a couple hundred South Florida hopefuls who'd also made it to this point were going to give it their best spandexed, rhinestoned, and leathered shot to become contestants on a new show: *Oye Mi Canto,* aka "Hear My Song," aka the Latin American version of *American Idol.* And when I said Latin America, I meant *all* of Latin America, *mija.* The plans, according to the ad I'd seen, would be for the show to be broadcast from Miami and televised not only in every major

Spanish-language market in the United States, but throughout Mexico and Central and South America and the Caribbean. I'd heard some of the people talking backstage that they were even hoping to get a feed over to Spain.

It was enough to make anyone wanna hurl. Except I was concentrating on the music and when I concentrated on the music, that was it for me. Everything else fell away. Had always been that way for me, ever since I first remembered seeing my *papi* playing and teaching. Since he'd first put his hands over mine on the strings and showed me how to make the pretty sounds.

The strings of the Bernabé vibrated beneath my fingers, a soothing, familiar sensation. Adding a few flamenco flourishes, I continued getting more elaborate during the solo break, building emotion and intensity

It *was* a risk, because while the style had a definite Latin vibe, the lyrics were still in English. Because it was mellow and jazzy, not a big, energetic pop or rock number or some power ballad designed to show off the Mariah-style pipes. But while a relatively new chart, it was still totally the kind of stuff I'd grown up with—what I was most comfortable with. If there was anything Papi had taught me about music was that the time to push your comfort zone was in the rehearsal studio, not on the stage. You didn't take it out on stage until it *was* your comfort zone.

Now . . . I was in my favorite part of the song. More flamenco on the guitar, my fingers flying over the strings, alternating with the occasional percussive tap on the body, using my voice as a second instrument—*this* was what it was all about, baby. And then . . . easing back, allowing the song to cruise into a quiet, gentle finale, and one more time, just call me Risky Girl, because everyone knew you left 'em with a big impression—a big sustained, blow-out-the-windows note, or some kind of showy finish that had the audience imagining that fireworks were exploding on the stage beside you.

So not my style. Maybe Sosi was right. Maybe I *was* crazy for thinking I could do this. This kind of program was all about showy and letting it all hang out.

Applause.

I snapped my head up, my eyes opening. Hadn't even realized I'd closed them. Glancing toward the wings, I saw they were a lot more crowded than they had been at the outset of my performance. A *lot* more. Man, I felt like I was gonna hurl again, except . . . who could hurl when they were getting that kind of reception? I might be way crazy, but it was worth it for this kind of response. It's what any performer lives for.

Sosi's face was flushed as she stuck her fingers in her mouth and let loose with a shrill whistle that reverberated through the near-empty theater. Bobbing my head, I acknowledged the applause, then slid from the stool, figuring my five minutes were more than up.

"Wait a moment, Ali." A light snapped on in the center of the theater, revealing four people sitting a couple of seats apart from each other. Four. But I'd only heard three voices. The fourth judge, if that's who it was, was a man who was sitting there, his arms crossed, just . . . staring. I felt like one of those butterflies that Sister Constanza had pinned onto boards for us to study in biology.

"You performed 'Regresa a Mí' on your audition tape, correct?"

I looked at the woman with the nice voice who'd asked the question. "Yes, ma'am."

I watched, my stomach doing this painful clenching thing, as the four people leaned in toward one another. Finally they sat back in their chairs and the man who'd spoken before said, "Interesting selections. And you're only what, seventeen?"

"Yes, sir."

The nice woman spoke again. "You have a unique sound for someone so young."

The Bernabé was sliding in my sweaty grasp. I carefully propped it against the stool and tried not to look like a total dork as I wiped my palms down the sides of my jeans.

"Thank you." What was going on? Had they done this with everyone else? Risking a glance into the wings, I saw a bunch of confused expressions. I was somehow guessing not. And now the Hurl Fairies were making their presence seriously known.

My suspicions were confirmed when Nice Woman said, "We realize this is a little irregular, and we'd understand if you aren't prepared, but do you have something a little more up-tempo that you could give us a sample of?"

Something in my gut told me this was really, *really* important. As in could-determine-my-future important. And if I was going to be a performer, I was going to have to be able to handle stuff like this on the fly. As it so happened . . . I could.

"Yes, actually. I have another disc with me, if I could get it?"

"Of course." The two nice judges nodded while Cranky Woman just cocked her head, and the fourth guy just sat there . . . staring.

I controlled myself as I strolled to the wings where Sosi was already waiting with my gig bag.

"Oooh, girl. What're you going to sing?"

"Don't have much choice, Sos. Only have one other disc in here." I reached into the outside zippered pocket of the black nylon bag and pulled out the disc I had stashed in there. Quickly zipping my axe into the bag, since I didn't need it for this, I went back out on stage, forcing myself to maintain the stroll . . . casual, confident . . . yeah, right. Maybe on the outside.

I leaned down into the pit and handed the disc to the sound tech before moving the stool and microphone stand out of the way. Needed some room for this one. Nodding at the sound guy, my body automatically began moving to the rhythms as the quiet, insistent percussion started building—cowbell, maracas, the bongos. Four measures, then the guitar and finally, syncopated piano lead with a dramatic rest and right into—

"De mi tierra bella. De mi tierra santa."

The song that had put Gloria on the Spanish-language music map as a bona fide bilingual star; an homage to the country of her birth and one I'd learned ages ago, to honor Papi and our Cuban roots. If the jazz charts were my comfort zone, songs like this were my soul.

Plus, it went over really well with the older crowd at all the *quinces* and First Communion parties I got roped into singing at.

Another quick glance over to the wings revealed Sosi grinning like a fool, most everyone else bobbing and moving, and one really bored-looking chick. Miss Leather. Clearly no soul.

I was kind of surprised they let me go through the whole thing—I mean, it's a four-and-a-half-minute song and if the idea was to see if I could sing up-tempo, well, that should've been clear by the end of the first verse. But I went ahead and wound the song up with a flourish—not quite fireworks material, but still pretty spiffy, if I did say so myself, my head thrown back, the hand holding the microphone on my hip and my other arm thrust in front of me out toward the judges.

They'd never turned the light off, so I could see them as I replaced the microphone in the stand and retrieved my discs from the sound tech, putting their heads together and powwowing again. Finally, Cranky Woman lifted her head and said, all snotty-like, "Can you manage something that's both Latin *and* contemporary?"

Oye, what was this chick's problem? And why'd she have to take it out on me? Sosi may be the one who likes to pound on people, but it didn't mean I didn't have a temper.

"You mean something like 'Suerte'?" I bit my lip, trying not to smile as I heard a few laughs at my smart-ass response. Maybe I was screwing myself, but hey, I was probably already screwed. And while my *papi* went to a lot of trouble to raise me to be a lady, he didn't raise me to take no one's crap. Not even some judge who could ensure I never saw a single televised moment on *Oye Mi Canto* unless I was parked in front of my own television and catching it on Telemundo.

"Not a bad example." The crank seemed to have settled a little as she eyed me from her perch, uh, seat. I tried to clear images of her as a vulture from my head.

"Sure, I know it." I shrugged. "Just seemed kind of . . . common."

The laughs were louder and longer now. Even Cranky was allowing herself a small smile. Turning back to the wings, I grinned at Sosi, who was bent over with her hands on her knees, clearly laughing her head off. Oh well . . . at the very least, we'd have something for *chisme* time on the phone. For Sosi, reliving this would keep her going for the next three months at least. Behind her, Miss Leather looked seriously chapped. *Whoops.* Guess I know who one of today's versions of "Suerte" belonged to. Ah well, it'd been a thin slice of heaven, but I needed to quit hogging the spotlight. Lots of other wannabes waiting for their earned moment.

"Thank you for your time."

"No, thank *you*, Ali." The nice guy, the first judge who'd spoken to me, lifted his head from a sheet he'd been scribbling notes on. Or maybe it was just the *New York Times* crossword. "We'll be in touch."

I nodded and headed for the wings, where I collapsed into Sosi's arms. Adrenaline letdown, you know?

"Come on, *mija*. Have some more water." She shoved the bottle in my hand as she led us to a relatively quiet spot. I slid down the wall to the floor, taking huge gulps of water as I did.

"Guess the pressure's just too much for some people. Shouldn't even bother." Miss Leather wasn't bothering to keep her voice down as she oh-too-casually strutted past. If I wasn't so dry-mouthed, I'd have slung the water at that spiral-permed head of hers. *What* a poser.

Helpful Cute Guy suddenly materialized in front of me. "What a bitch."

Okay, bitch worked, too.

He rolled his eyes, a bright, streaky green, I noticed, now that I wasn't about to die from fright, before he leaned forward and lowered his voice. "I've been tapping into the main feed on my headset. Even though I'm not supposed to." He grinned and shrugged, totally not apologetic.

"They like you a lot because you're going to appeal to the older demographic—*chica* who can sing with the soul of La Reina, but who's young enough to be their daughter or granddaughter. Reassurance that there's still respect for those who came before, *tú sabes*? But at the same time, you're clearly hip and familiar with the current scene."

He eased back, saying more loudly, "You need another? Yeah, I think I have one." Rummaging in his messenger bag, he pulled out another bottle of water that he uncapped and handed to me.

Huh? Then I saw some people with tags around their necks who looked Super Important walking past, and I got it. He wasn't supposed to be telling me any of this. What was he telling me, exactly?

"What are you telling me?"

He leaned back in, his voice going even softer. "Don't you get it? You're in. No matter what happens here or in any of the other cities we audition in, they want you for sure. Congrats. You're going to be on *Oye Mi Canto.*" He rose and held his hand out to help me up. Once I was up, he still held onto my hand, shaking it formally.

"Since we're going to be seeing a lot of each other in the next few months, I guess I'd better introduce myself." The eyes—big and green, I did say that, right?—crinkled up again at the corners as he smiled. "I'm Jaime Lozano. College intern masquerading as an assistant director and all-around lackey."

"Ali Montero," I responded automatically. And automatically felt stupid.

"I know who you are, Ali." He turned to walk away, but stopped and glanced over his shoulder. With a wink he added, "And pretty soon, so will a whole lot more people."

Ay Dios mío. I was so screwed. I never expected to make it. There was no way I was going to make it. I was too young, too different, too innocent. I knew they wanted the Shakiras and Chayannes and Juaneses and Thalías. I still had two names, for God's sake! I only even do this for the experience, I'd told myself over and over. Just to get a taste of what it was like for when I really struck out on my own and tried to make it in the biz. Like, in ten . . . twenty years, or so.

"Oye, mija . . ."

"I know, I know, Sosi." I shook my head slowly, still watching Jaime as he moved easily through the maze of people and equipment.

Beside me, Sosi sighed, long and pained. "I wonder if the nuns in Spain will let me keep my iPod?"

"If we make it that far without getting killed."

"Right."

3

"Ay virgen santísima." It was so awful, I couldn't even be bothered to send up my usual silent apology for blaspheming. And anyway, if *la virgen* was looking down, I knew she'd understand. Sosi and I looked at each other, looked in the mirror, looked at each other *in* the mirror, then looked back at each other for real.

"What is she thinking?" Sosi groaned, scratching at her shoulders.

"Stop that, Sos, you're making me itch, too." Not totally true. The nasty tulle that draped across the neckline and evolved into poofy off-the-shoulder sleeves was the primo culprit. But it didn't help that Sosi was sitting there, in the same butt-ugly gown I was also trying on, squirming and scratching like a dog with fleas. Sitting through the *quinces* Mass in this getup was going to be utter hell.

Okay, *now* the silent apology for equating Mass with hell; more detailed penance would have to wait until the next time I hit Confession, whenever *that* happened. Look, I went to Catholic school, okay? Far as Papi and I were concerned, that covered the religious obligations. Sundays belonged to us and our music, no matter how hard the elder relatives squawked. That's how it had always been.

"What she's thinking, Sos, is that it's her official entrance to womanhood and polite Cuban society and she's going to *shine,* girl." I scratched some more and tried to find a place on my upper arms where these stupid poofy-sleeve thingies wouldn't itch so bad—or make me look like a linebacker for the Dolphins.

"But did she have to put the *damas* in aqua?" she whined. "I mean, come on, Ali. Tell me there's a Cuban girl alive who looks good in this color?"

"Probably not, and that's the point," I retorted. "Amanda wants to come off like she's Salma Hayek or Eva Longoria, and the only way she's even gonna come close is at our expense. So we get sick, faded Easter egg aqua and ruffles—" I glanced down at the organza skirt that was standing out about two feet on either side of me before glancing back at Sosi. "While I'll bet you a double scoop of Ben and Jerry's New York Super Fudge Chunk she's going to be wearing something sleek, sexy, and—once we hit the party—strapless, the little tart."

Sosi groaned and dropped into the dressing room chair, her skirt poofing up nearly to her ears. "Girl turns fifteen, she thinks she's all grown and shit."

"*Your* cousin."

"Don't remind me."

"Hey, how are you guys doing in there?" came a voice from just outside the dressing room. A second later, the door opened.

"Elaine, save us." *Ugh,* I was whimpering.

"Oh . . . boy." Elaine Garces, my father's best friend who'd accompanied us on the *damas* gown expedition, slid into the remaining available square foot of space in the room. Good thing she was so tiny. Which was just wrong for a Latin girl, but she was way cool, so we forgave her.

"Man, those are seriously awful, *mijas*."

"Not helping," Sosi grumbled as she struggled to get up from the chair.

"No, really, you guys look like malaria victims."

I held a hand out and hauled Sosi to her feet. "Tell us something we don't know, Elaine. This is suckagetude beyond all suckagetude."

"It's mondo enormous suckagetude," Sosi agreed as we faced the mirror once again, this time with Elaine between us, peering over our shoulders and shaking her head. I could tell by the expression on her face that nope, it hadn't been overwrought teenage imagination. These were truly the worst *damas* dresses in the history of the world. All icky aqua and ruffles and waterfalls of hanging beads.

Best of all—we got to *pay* for the privilege of wearing them, along with matching dyed shoes and elbow-length gloves, for several hours from Mass to the big, obnoxious party with five hundred guests. And in between, formal pictures, immortalizing Amanda on the occasion of her fifteenth birthday—and us in these butt-ugly gowns. Groovy.

This was my punishment for not telling Papi about *Oye Mi Canto* yet. It had to be. Three weeks on, and I still hadn't worked up the nerve to tell him. But you know, I pretty much had decided it was all a figment of my imagination anyway. Because think about it—all I had to go on was the word of some college intern assistant director who'd eavesdropped on a conversation he wasn't even supposed to have access to. And I was supposed to believe *him*? Shyeah, right. For all I knew, he'd heard wrong. Or he was getting his jollies off messing with the naïve teenager's head. Although he'd seemed super sincere. And very cute—too cute to be the messing-around type.

Yep. All a figment of my imagination.

"Why don't you two ditch those homages to flammable fabrics, and we'll go get ice cream—dull the pain some?"

Sosi was nearly contorting herself trying to get to the zipper. "You're a goddess, you know that?"

"Yeah, well, from your lips to some fabulous guy's ears, girl."

Turning first Sosi, then me around, Elaine pulled our zippers down. "Because the ones I been dating? Not so much with the fabulous or thinking I'm a goddess. Meet you out front." A second later, she ducked out, giving us room to lose the bad taste ball gowns.

As I changed back into my school uniform skirt and polo, which were tacky, but still better than the dresses, I couldn't help but think I knew just the fabulous guy—I *knew* he liked her and he probably already thought she was a goddess. He was just a pinhead—at least when it came to dating.

"Hey, we're back," I yelled out over Oscar Peterson's swingin' "'C-Jam Blues" that Papi had blaring from the stereo. What? You think just because we're primarily guitarists around here that we can't appreciate good piano chops? Good music is good music, baby, no matter the axe or the genre. One of the best concert experiences I ever had was Yo-Yo Ma. Another was Lenny Kravitz, although I thought Papi was gonna have a heart attack over how, uh . . . *suggestive* Lenny was up onstage. Thankfully, Elaine was with us and told him to get a grip and close his eyes and just listen to the music if watching Lenny was too much for his delicate constitution. Honestly. You'd never know the man had come of age when Prince and Madonna were in their heyday. First heyday, that is.

Tossing our butt-ugly dresses on the couch, we cruised into the kitchen for sodas and snackage.

"*Oye,* don't dive into the chips—they're to go with dinner," Papi scolded with his hands wrist-deep in a bowl.

"Hamburgers? Cool." I kissed his cheek and snagged a ring of Bermuda onion from a plate at the same time.

"Yeah. I figure we have a couple more weekends' use out of

the grill before it gets too hot to cook outside. Either of you staying?" he asked over his shoulder as he started forming patties and putting them on a plate.

"Thanks, but I can't—I have to babysit," Sosi replied, while Elaine looked up from where she was perusing the interior of the fridge.

"Sure, why not?"

"Thought you said you had a date tonight?" I popped the tab on my Diet Coke and dropped into a chair at the kitchen table, skimming through the pile of mail. Maybe some good catalogs with clothes Papi would never let me buy had come today.

"Total pity date, girl." Pulling a couple of bottles of beer out, she uncapped both and set one next to Papi. "Some guy fresh from the island who knows the family via one of my mother's cousin's *tías* or some such nonsense. My mother kept nagging me to make the date because he was going to be visiting Miami for a few days before he moves to New York. Which is code for 'Who knows? Maybe you two will hit it off and get married, so you can move back to New York and give me lots of grandchildren to fuss over like a good Puerto Rican daughter should.'"

She shuddered and leaned against the counter. "Hamburgers with you guys is definitely preferable. Robbie, how much pepper have you put in?"

"Enough, and hasn't your mother figured out you have no intention of moving back to New York? Ever?" Washing his hands at the sink and drying them off, Papi pushed his wire-rim glasses higher up on his nose and took a drink from his beer.

"'Enough' means 'barely a sprinkle' where you're concerned, you big wuss, and this is my mother we're talking about. She knows. She just refuses to accept it as a reality. Along with the fact that the likelihood I'll give her lots of grandchildren lowers every year. I'm so not pulling some Christie Brinkley, squeezing them out in time for me to go on Social Security."

Shoving Papi aside, Elaine picked up the pepper mill and started grinding . . . and grinding . . . and grinding some more. Good thing I loved spicy food. Papi not so much, which is why he snatched it from her after about the fifth grind.

"Ease up, would you? You can put more on your burger after it's cooked. And you're only thirty-seven."

"Wuss. And thirty-seven is ancient in the scheme of Latin motherhood, unless, of course, you're popping out the sixth or seventh *angelito.*"

"No, just still in possession of my taste buds, you freak, and six or seven? Is she insane?"

"You've met my mother, what do you think?

Sosi and I grinned at each other across the table. Over ten years Papi and Elaine had been fellow music professors and buds at Florida International and over ten years, they'd been perfecting this Abbott and Costello routine. Shaking my head, I looked back down at the mail, paying attention to the stuff in envelopes now that it had been ascertained that no catalogs of interest had shown up.

I picked up one such specimen, a stiff, cream-colored number with my name on it and a New York return address. No name, just an address. Probably just junk, but hey, it had my name on it. In calligraphy, no less.

Not junk. I about had my own version of Papi's Lenny Kravitz heart attack when I unfolded the single sheet of heavy cream paper and saw the big OYE MI CANTO blazing across the top in navy blue and gold lettering.

¡Felicidades!

Oh.
My.
God.

It's with tremendous pleasure that we're sending this letter. Congratulations Alegría Montero, you have been selected from over forty thousand applicants to be one of only sixteen finalists on Oye Mi Canto, *the search for the next great Latin superstar! In the coming weeks our production team will be in touch with details—*

And all of a sudden, my stomach was somewhere up in the vicinity of my throat. Then down by my feet somewhere. And my head was spinning.

"What's that, *mija*?" Papi squinted at the sheet as he passed by on his way to the refrigerator with the covered plate of burgers. But he wasn't really paying all that much attention, because if he'd actually picked up any vibe as to what it was, I'd be packing for the nuns, like, five minutes ago.

I passed it under the table to Sosi, who took one look at it and made some sort of squeaky noise that had Papi's head whipping around and Elaine glancing up from the newspaper article she'd been reading.

And, of course, that's when she tried to pass it back to me, under the table, which was totally obvious. Which made Papi give me The Look: eyebrows raised as his glasses slid down his nose and he stared over the tops of the rims.

"Ali?"

Oh man, showtime. Because how bad did I really want to do this? How important was it to me?

"Uh, Papi . . . there's something I sort of need to tell you."

4

Nope. *Definitely* not a figment of my imagination. Try horrible reality, facing Elaine, Papi, and Sosi's parents. Because after I'd handed over the letter and Papi read it and realized what it was, he'd also *known* I couldn't have pulled it off completely alone. Because while there haven't been a whole lot of them, Sosi's almost always been a part of every time I've ever gotten in trouble before. Please—Papi's no one's fool.

So here we were . . . Sos and I, sitting side by side on the sofa, feet together, flat on the floor, hands folded in our laps. Since we were still wearing our school uniforms, it gave a pretty decent impression of the good Catholic schoolgirls we were. Or . . . looking at Papi's face—at how narrow and dark his hazel eyes were behind his glasses as he turned on us—maybe not. I was kind of seeing a bullet train to hell in my future.

"So let me get this straight. You," Papi said, pointing at me, "saw the ad for this . . . this . . . *program,* where? A magazine? TV?"

"On television," I answered quietly.

"Saw it in the *Herald,* too, remember, Ali?" Sosi piped up. "That big article about the show?"

"*You* spotted that." I was totally unable to resist reminding her of that fact. *So* wasn't gonna get busted for the whole thing. As it was, my ass was probably going to be grounded until it wasn't firm and perky anymore.

"And *you,*" Papi shifted his attention to Sosi. "Beyond encouraging her, helped out by . . . ?"

He already knew exactly what she'd done. But he wanted her to say it in front of her parents. Big with the accountability, my father was.

Sosi stared down at her hands and mumbled something even I couldn't understand and I was sitting right next to her and had been interpreting her mumbles for most of our lives.

"Cecilia Josefina Cabrera."

Yikes. I cringed in sympathy. Sosi totally hated when her mom pulled out the dreaded middle name.

She still didn't look up from her hands and her voice wasn't a whole lot louder, but it was clear and didn't even squeak as she replied, "I forged Señor Montero's signature on the entry form." Then her head snapped up, and she looked my father dead in the eye. "And I'd do it again. Ali deserves this chance, Señor Montero, she really does and she was so good, I wish you could have seen how she totally owned those auditions. You'd have been really proud of her."

Holy crap.

Sosi's mom did one of those Cuban Mom gasps because her little girl had spoken to an adult that way, as her dad growled "Cecilia . . . ," and I just sat there, sort of stunned and horrified.

I had no clue what Papi would do—how he would react to that. I mean, this was completely new territory for us. Sure, I'd gotten in trouble before, occasionally talking back or not finishing homework or other dumb stuff like that. He'd raise his voice and do his Cuban Dad Thing and we'd be good. But this was way, way, *way* beyond getting in beaucoup trouble because we'd dug a big hole in Sosi's backyard trying to build our own pool the summer we were eight.

No yelling.

"I appreciate, *mija,* how you defend Ali, but I'm her father and I'm the one who's responsible for her. And for helping her decide what's best."

And still, she didn't back down. "You're not going to let her do this, are you?"

He glanced over at Sosi's parents. "I need to speak with Ali now. But thanks for coming over."

"*Seguro,* Roberto. Thanks for calling." Sosi's dad shook hands with Papi, her mom kissed his cheek, and then, like they'd choreographed it, each of them took one of Sosi's arms and marched her straight toward the door.

"I'll call you later, Ali," she called over her shoulder.

"You think so, *niña*?" I heard her mother say. "You're so grounded. No phone, no cell, and you're going to babysit your little brothers free for the next two months and that's just for starters." A second later the door slammed shut behind them, leaving me and Papi facing each other.

"You aren't going to let me do this, are you?"

Wasn't going to cry. Wasn't going to cry.

Wasn't.

Going.

To.

Cry.

But you know, scared as I'd been of this whole thing, of telling Papi; as nervous as I'd been during the audition, I still wanted to do this so bad it hurt. And I just knew I wasn't going to be able to.

"You aren't?" My voice was shaking and getting louder. "Are you?" Damn, I was going to cry.

Nothing. Just . . . silence.

Crossing to the bookcases that ran along one whole wall and held our music scores and albums and CDs, he leaned his forehead against the edge of a shelf. The one where all the family photographs—including the ones of my mother—were arranged. It was one of those pictures he reached out and touched—she was outside and holding me on her hip. I was two years old, both of us with our hair in ponytails, our faces covered in chocolate ice cream because it had been a superhot summer day and we'd both been desperate for something cold. No one told me I had to *eat* it—it had just felt good. Thought it would feel good to Mamá, as well.

At least that was the family legend. I had no memory of it. And a few days later, after feeling kind of sick for a few days and blowing it off, she'd been rushed to the hospital with a burst appendix that had gone septic. It had been Papi and me ever since.

"I don't know what to do."

Now I really felt like I was going to cry, but for all different reasons. He hadn't done this in a long time. Talked to her.

"Just tell me, Papi. Are you going to let me do this or not?"

He turned, his eyes back to being all dark and narrow. "How can I, Ali? How can I let you do this *now*?"

"Don't even." My hands were balled into fists and digging into my thighs. "Don't *even* try to act like if I'd come to you and asked, you would have even given permission for me to do this because it's bullshit. You know damn well you wouldn't."

"Alegría—"

"I know you don't care about performing. But *I* do."

"*Yo se,* Ali. And I have nothing against you performing."

"Yeah, right," I snorted and shook my head. "As part of a faculty ensemble—while I teach during the days. Then maybe I can join Los Gitanos and do the occasional weddings or club gigs with you on the weekends?"

"What's wrong with that? It's given us a pretty nice lifestyle, *mija*."

God, he just did not get it. "It's not about the money, Papi. It's about the performing."

"What? You think the faculty recitals or the club gigs or even teaching aren't performing? You're on a stage—you're playing and singing and there's an audience appreciating your efforts. It's no different, Ali, even if it isn't on television."

He threw an arm out, gesturing toward our guitars, neatly propped on their stands in the corner. "The size and nature of the audience—whether or not there even is one—shouldn't matter. *La musica viene de tu alma,* Alegría. When you play, it's for you. You're feeding your heart and your soul and that's what genuinely matters."

"You just don't understand!"

And silence—a total silence—fell over us.

Papi and I had a really good relationship. Probably because it had been just the two of us for so long, or maybe because we were both musicians, but we were usually on the same wavelength and even if we argued, we'd always been able to talk things through. Of course, we'd never actually *talked* about this particular subject because I kind of knew how he felt about it and, well . . . judging by this exchange, there just hadn't been any point in even trying.

Which brought us right back to, "You just don't understand, Papi." I was over the yelling thing. My voice just kept getting softer and softer. "What's worse—you don't want to."

"She's right."

Elaine. I'd totally even forgotten she was in the room. So had Papi, if the open mouth and dark red spots on his cheeks were any indication.

"*Ay,* Elaine, *disculpa.*"

She rolled her eyes at his apology. "What? Like I haven't

seen you guys argue before? I was front and center for the great Winter Ball Dress Argument, remember?"

Leaning back in Papi's desk chair where she'd been sitting for the floor show, she crossed her arms. "While I sided with you on the dress thing, I happen to think she's right on this one. And if you weren't so busy being bullheaded, you might actually see she has a point."

Whoa. But any sense of triumph was pretty short-lived because in the next breath she glared at me and said, "And you are being equally as bullheaded as your father, which doesn't come as any big surprise. However, if you want to be taken seriously, argue your cause like an adult, not a petulant brat, with all of this sneaking around and 'you don't understand' shit."

Whoa again, but even that didn't negate the truth of how I felt. Time to try this the grown-up way then.

"Papi . . ." He turned his gaze back from Elaine and focused on me.

"The music . . . it does feed my heart and my soul, in ways that no one but another musician can begin to understand or imagine, but . . ." I stopped, gathering my thoughts, because this was the part he'd never been able to get and I'd never been able to articulate all that well. I walked over to where my Bernabé was propped in its stand. Just picking it up and holding it—it felt like an extension of my body. Like a part of me that had been missing.

"When I perform, I feel . . ." I ran my hand along the long neck of the guitar, feeling the satin texture of the wood on the back, the subtle ridges of the frets on the front intersecting with the smooth, nylon strings. "I don't know—it's not about the applause or the audience. It's just this sense that when I'm up there . . . I feel alone, I *am* alone, but it doesn't matter because I'm more myself than at any other time. It's like . . . I feel complete."

"Sound familiar, Roberto?"

My head snapped up at the quiet words. Again, I'd totally forgotten that Elaine was there.

"¿Qué?"

"You don't remember?" One eyebrow went up as she continued to lean back in his chair, her legs crossed, like it was this casual thing, but I could tell . . . maybe it was the expression in her eyes . . . but there was definitely nothing casual about what she was saying. "I do. Some thirteen years ago or so, I think it was. A very idealistic, young music professor was describing what teaching was like for him, to another equally idealistic and young fellow professor who was scared spitless over teaching her first graduate seminar."

"Elaine, that was different . . ."

"How, Robbie? Tell me." Now she was leaning forward in the chair and pointing at me. "What Ali described may have to do with performing and not teaching, but with the exception of a few word choices, it's *precisely* how you described teaching to me all those years ago. Can't you see it?"

"See *what*?"

She rolled her eyes, looking like she was about ready to slap him. "Your disciplines may be different, but your feelings about music are exactly the same."

She gestured toward Papi's computer monitor on the desk. Even from across the room, I could see she'd pulled up the *Herald*'s website and I could just make out the headline, "Search for Latin Talent Comes to Miami." What the . . . ? She'd found the article Sosi had mentioned. But why?

"Do you even realize what she's done?"

"Aside from sneak around and lie?"

"Oh, don't worry," she shot back. "We'll get to that part in a minute."

Which worried me. Because trust me, I knew, no matter what happened, Papi wasn't going to let that little detail slip through the cracks. And when I wasn't busy feeling like my world was coming to an end, I knew he couldn't.

"All she's done, Robbie, is become one of only sixteen individuals to have beat out over forty thousand other people for the opportunity of a lifetime. Forty *thousand*," she repeated, crossing the room to stand in front of him. "Who would probably give their right arms to have this," she waved the letter I'd received, "in their mailboxes right now. Furthermore, how *dare* you even consider denying recognition of that kind of talent—especially when it's what you've dedicated your life to nurturing? It's good for your students, but not good enough for your daughter?"

Papi opened his mouth, like he wanted to say something. Elaine didn't give him the chance.

"No, it doesn't excuse the fact that she snuck around and lied to do this, but *think* about it. Think about how much it had to mean to her, that she *did* go to such lengths. When has Ali ever defied you like this?"

Try *never.*

Papi knew it, too, and so did Elaine, which is why a response wasn't necessary, not that she was waiting for one. And boy, was she working up a full head of steam. I'd never seen Elaine like this—she was usually so mellow, but there she was, glaring up at Papi and poking a finger in his chest to emphasize her points. I tried to feel guilty about being the cause, but I was too busy fighting off the nervous sensation that we were maybe close to some sort of breakthrough here.

"Just a couple more things, Roberto, for you to chew on. In case it has escaped your attention, Ali is only a few months away from turning eighteen. You can say no to her now, but what's to stop her from taking off the second she becomes legal? You heard her just now, saw her face—you think that kind of desire is just shoved aside because you want it to be? No, baby, something like that will eat at her and gnaw at her soul until she has no choice but to follow her dreams, with or without your blessing."

"She wouldn't—she has school still . . . then college . . ."

But his voice wasn't at all sure. And the look he gave me—it was like he was seeing for the first time how close I was to being an adult.

Not that I felt it. Right now, I felt about five years old and all I wanted to do was go crawl under the covers. But I wasn't five. And while Elaine had argued more—what was the word?—eloquently, than I ever could have, it was time for me to take back control.

"I wouldn't leave, Papi." He looked relieved. For about two seconds. Until I spoke again. "Not right away, at any rate.

"But even if you don't let me do this—" My breathing was shaky and it was hard to force air and words through my throat, which felt all tight and scratchy. "I'm not going to be a teacher. That's you. Not me. I know you want it for me, but I'm sorry—it will *never* be me. Not the way performing is."

Everyone remembers what happened after the signing of the Declaration of Independence, right?

A war.

5

"Ali."

"Don't." I stared up at my bedroom ceiling, watching the fan go around and around and around. Nowhere to go, just ending up in the same place, an endless journey to nowhere. Just like me. Okay, a little much with the drama queen routine, but I didn't indulge in this kind of self-pity all that often, so I figured I was entitled.

"Just . . . don't, okay, Papi?"

"*Mijita,* don't you think you're overreacting? Just a little?"

"No."

My mattress shifted as he sat on the bed. I glared at him through my lashes. Yep, just like always, perched at the foot, leaning against the solid wood footboard of the full-size sleigh bed I'd begged for when I turned ten. A grown-up girl bed. He'd grumbled and made all sorts of parental noises—didn't really need it, the bed I had was perfectly fine . . . Well, functional, yeah, but it was light pink wrought iron with bunnies perched on the posts. It was cute and adorable when I was three. But at *ten*? Come on.

But you know, after all the grumbling and groaning, on my birthday, after returning home from roller-skating with Sosi, there it had been, all set up and even made with new sheets and a comforter in all my favorite bright pinks and turquoises and purples. He'd even finally admitted he liked it better because it gave him more room and better support when he played music for me to go to sleep by.

While I'd outgrown the tucking-in and singing-me-to-sleep business a while back, it was still his fave place to perch when we had our little "father/daughter" confabs.

"I have no choice, Ali."

"I know, Papi," I sighed.

"But you're still upset."

Now I sat up. "Well, did you have to look so *happy* about it?"

He still looked happy, dang it, his eyes turning that bright green-brown they did when he was really juiced about something, although I had to give him grudging props for trying to hold back his smile, at least a little.

"Not so much happy as relieved." He brushed my hair back from my face and tucked it behind my ear. "Look at it as a win-win situation, Ali. You're still getting to do this. And I at least get some peace of mind."

Okay, I suppose he had a point. Especially since "this" referred to *Oye Mi Canto,* as in, I get to compete. Yeah, you heard that right. I get to compete. On television. In front of all of Latin America and select U.S. markets. Prime time and everything. Well, except for the U.S. markets. There, it'll all depend on where they want to put us. Some places it'll be right after *Jeopardy!,* some places it might be 3:00 A.M. after a Ron Popeil infomercial.

That's showbiz.

So we've fast-forwarded a little bit here. Here's the deal: After Elaine basically read Papi the riot act and I followed up with my proclamation, he'd looked at the two of us, then just . . . left. No outburst, no yelling, no war. Just went back to the kitchen and finished making dinner like nothing at all had happened.

Can we say surreal? Papi went outside, grilled the burgers,

came back in, heated the buns in the oven, grabbed the pasta salad out of the fridge, all the normal everyday stuff that went along with a normal everyday Friday dinner. And I'd wanted to totally scream in frustration. I'd wanted to go after him . . . get him to tell me one way or another if I had to shake it out of him. But Elaine had put a hand on my shoulder and shook her head.

"Let him work it out, girl. This is tough for him—figuring out when and how to let you go."

So I'd left him alone—acted like nothing big was up. Elaine and I set the table while Papi finished with dinner; after a mostly silent meal, she and I did the dishes while he wandered back into the living room. And while we were rinsing dishes and stacking them in the dishwasher, the sound of his guitar, sweet and melodic, began drifting in—joined a few measures later by his clear baritone, pitched low and soft as he sang the lyrics to "Cielito Lindo."

The first piece of music he'd ever taught me.

That song was such a part of me. Like no other song. All I had to do was hear a note or two and it was *there,* imprinted, just like endless hours of practice imprinted muscle memory, making the notes automatic, the flourishes an effortless extension.

The call of that familiar 3/4 was way too strong. It wasn't like it was even a conscious action on my part to go out into the living room and pick up my Bernabé. Settling onto a chair, I began strumming the counterpoint and singing the melody, Papi automatically dropping into the harmony.

Playing with Papi was comforting, like a familiar blanket is comforting. Going through the verses, trading off these jazzy/flamenco licks in between, before returning to the chorus one last time, easing down with a nice diminuendo over the last four measures.

"What did you sing for your audition, *mija*?"

Color me shocked. "'Bella Luna.'"

"You took a gringo chart into the audition for that show?"

"Yeah."

That made him smile, believe it or not.

"Show me."

And after the last note died away, we looked at each other and I knew. I knew what his decision was.

I also knew I was grounded until I was thirty, too.

But the bigger part, at least in the immediate, was that I was going to get to do this gig. My way.

Sort of.

"Knock, knock. Where y'all at?"

Another smile on Papi's face. Pinhead. "We're upstairs." He raised one of his eyebrows my direction. "Or if you're going to continue sulking I can take this downstairs."

Adult. I was going to treat all of this like an adult. Even if forces beyond my control were conspiring to keep me stuck in Nice Cuban Girl Land. Adult, adult, adult. Maybe if I kept repeating it like a mantra, or something, it might actually rub off.

"Not sulking." I flopped back onto my pillows.

"*Bueno, mija,* when you're through not sulking, feel free to join us downstairs, okay?"

Didn't get the chance, though, since right at that second Elaine appeared in my doorway, a bag of Tostitos in one hand and a Coke in the other.

Papi shook his head at her. "Don't you have food at your place?"

"It's been a couple of hours since lunch. I'm hungry."

"That metabolism of yours is just wrong, you know that?"

"Yeah, yeah, so you've been saying for years. However," she paused, taking a swig from her Coke, "I don't think you called and left three messages on my cell for me to get my butt over here so you could marvel at my metabolism. What's this about Ali needing a chaperone and that it's going to be me?"

"Yeah, that's right, and where've you been anyway?"

Coming all the way into the room and leaning against my dresser, she said, "Working with a student on research . . . are you serious about this chaperone stuff?"

"Which student? You aren't supervising any this semester, and yes, I'm serious."

Elaine shrugged. "One of Chandler's guys doing a section in his dissertation on ethnic music instruments and their inclusion and integration in modern digital recordings. Chan asked me to help him out. Professional courtesy. Now focus, Roberto. Chaperone?"

He looked like he really wanted to ask more about this professional courtesy gig for Dr. Chandler, who was new to the university, young, and way hot, but Elaine was pinning him with that Dr. Garces stare that demanded answers. Now.

"You're going to chaperone Ali during *Oye Mi Canto*."

I heaved a major sigh as Elaine shook her head.

"*Mira,* Roberto, I seriously think you're going over the edge here. You've already agreed to let her do this, but now you want her to have a chaperone?"

"Not me. The show."

"The *show* wants her to have a chaperone? Why?"

"Because I'm only seventeen," I grumbled.

Papi nodded and added, "Ali's the only minor who made the finals."

Elaine looked confused. "So?"

"So think about it, Elaine. This show is going to be primarily broadcast throughout Latin America and here, to Latin audiences. How would it look to have a seventeen-year-old girl in a house full of adults?"

"You have *got* to be kidding me. It's the twenty-first century."

"Not in parts of Latin America, it's not."

"Oh, for the love of—" Elaine slammed her Coke down on my dresser so hard liquid sloshed out over the sides. Using the hem of her T-shirt to wipe it off, she muttered, "Don't these people watch *novelas*? There are girls on those shows barely older than Ali, making the Desperate Housewives look like Joan of Arcadia."

"Doesn't matter," Papi shot back. "The producers know a large portion of the viewers won't like the idea of Ali on her own. They don't want to jeopardize her chances—or their ratings—by any appearance of impropriety. So she's going to live at home and when she's at show functions, they want her accompanied by a chaperone."

Now you understand why I was so royally pissed? I mean, all the other contestants were going to live in some big, fancy-ass house on Miami Beach, but *noooo,* I couldn't because I was only seventeen. And to top it off, this chaperone business.

Elaine stopped wiping and looked at him like he'd grown two heads. "Okay, but why me? You're her father, why can't you chaperone her?"

"Couple reasons." Man, talk about your evil grins. "One, you know I'm teaching a full load this summer so there's no way I can be at the beck and call of this crazy program. And two, in keeping with all those grand Latin traditions, they feel it best a young lady her age have a same-sex companion."

Elaine's jaw just dropped farther and farther while I shook my head and pushed myself back up to a sitting position. I mean, what was I going to do, right? Very "my way or the highway" this all was.

All of a sudden, Papi's expression segued from evil grin to something a lot more serious. "Elaine, look—I know I've got relatives who would be willing to step in, but that would go against everything I've done since Patricia died."

One of the things I loved him best for—he'd never *once* handed me off to any of the relatives. Not even right after Mamá died, and they were practically breaking down the doors to help. Twenty-five, a widower and suddenly single father? That he hadn't lunged for it like a drowning man for a rope was the real surprise and don't think I didn't know it.

Instead, he'd told them all to back off. Not like it stopped them from trying, mostly by suggesting he find a new wife and mother for me as soon as decently possible. Yeah, I know, but Cuban women have these weird notions about men and their abilities as parents. However, seeing as I got decent grades and didn't have any piercings I wasn't supposed to, they figured he was doing okay and left us pretty much alone.

Asking for help now, though, would be like waving raw meat in front of hungry lions. No way. I was with him there. I *liked* being left alone.

He looked away from both of us and out the window. His voice was really soft as he finally said, "You're the only one I can ask."

"Leave, Robbie." Elaine's gaze didn't leave my face, not for one second. "Go practice or grade exams or something."

"But—"

"*Now,* Roberto. I need to talk to Ali." Now she stared hard at him. "Alone."

Sheesh. No wonder her students didn't mess around with her. No wonder Papi didn't either. He just got up and left the room without another word.

She took Papi's spot on the bed. "All right, girl. Truth time. I'm fine with doing this, but are you?"

Adult, Ali. Act like an adult.

"You know I am, but I am sorry Papi blindsided you like this."

"*Pfft.* Don't worry about your father." She waved her hand in the air. "I can read him like a book. He sees this as justifiable payback for my arguing on your behalf."

"Yeah, well . . . I'm sorry about that, too." I stared down at my bedspread, tracing the gold ribbon trim. "You shouldn't have had to."

"Hey, Ali." Her touch on my hand made me look up. "I've been there, *mija.* I had to argue like crazy with my mother when I wanted to study music in college and then when I wanted to go to grad school instead of just teach at Performing Arts or some other high school. God knows, I wished I'd had someone to back me up. And you did good—made your point and he got it."

"Does it ever get easier?"

"No." Her brown eyes lit up as she grinned. "Not really. Not if you really care about the person you're arguing with."

She reached across and pushed my hair back and behind my ear, just like Papi had. "All right, then, I'm yours for the next—"

"Ten weeks—we get started next week."

"Okay." She got up from the bed. "Let me go grill your father on the details."

After she left my room, I sat down at my computer desk. Hitting a button on the keyboard, I waited for the screen to light up; a second later, my IM blinked to life and just that quick, a window popped up.

Sosi_C: Sooooooo???? How'd it go with the show people?
Sosi_C: Tell me, tell me, tell me!!!!
Jazz_Ali: Give me a chance and I will, girl. ☺
Sosi_C: Does the smiley face mean it's of the good?
Jazz_Ali: Good and bad, but mostly of the good.
Sosi_C: That sounds interesting. Do tell . . .

6

Holy Mother of—

This had to be the *biggest* house I'd ever seen up close in my life. Seriously. Well, maybe outside of Vizcaya—but former baronial estates-turned-museums so didn't count. This house was brand new, it looked. To one side I could see an enormous pool, sparkling in the sunlight, and not twenty steps past it, was, oh my God, the beach, with little yellow-and-white–striped cabanas scattered around and chaise lounges, just waiting for a cute bathing suit and some Panama Jack SPF 8. Okay, in the interest of preserving my youthful skin, SPF 30.

And I had to live in our cookie-cutter Coral Gables townhouse instead of here. This rotted big, hairy unmentionables.

"*Oye, mija,* what do you imagine the price tag on this bad boy is?"

I looked over at Elaine, who was eyeballing the place from behind the steering wheel of her Mustang convertible, then back at the big white McMansion. "Couldn't begin to tell you, but I don't think there's a tag big enough for all the zeros."

She snorted and shook her head. "Ain't that the livin' truth."

You know, though, the more I stared at it, the more it reminded me of a typically tacky *quinceañera* cake, completely over the top and dripping with crunchy, sugary icing. Still . . . wouldn't sneeze at living here for the next ten weeks. I mean, *look* at it—the pool, the beach, the brick courtyard with a big-ass stone fountain and the house itself, with no fewer than six, count 'em, *six,* balconies. And that was just on the outside front. Could you imagine what the back was like? Or the inside?

"Can I help you ladies?"

Holy Dude. In a former life, the huge blond guy approaching the car *had* to have been a pro wrestler. Crammed into a beige knit polo, his shoulders looked like two HoneyBaked Hams with his biceps straining at the cuffs. With the wraparound shades, earpiece, and walkie-talkie, he looked like one of those cats who followed people like the Hilton sisters around—you know, to keep the unwashed masses back and all.

"Yes, we're here for *Oye Mi Canto*—the young lady's a finalist." Elaine gestured at the island pass discreetly tucked into the corner of her windshield. Because we weren't actually on the beach proper, which I'd been kind of bummed about. But it wasn't all *that* bad—considering it was one of the little private islands between the mainland and the beach. I'm sure everyone's heard of Star Island where people like Gloria and Diddy have their spreads?

Not the only high-rent island in the 'hood. Elaine and I were going to be commuting daily to Palm Island, where Al Capone had once lived and where none other than Julio Iglesias owned one of his not-so-little haciendas. At least, that's what Sosi's determined Internet research had turned up.

Truly, I was amazed she hadn't sent me off this morning with the Little Black Book O' unlisted phone numbers. Chick was kind of scary like that.

"You must be Ali Montero."

"Yeah." I handed over my driver's license and show credentials. With his shades pushed up to reveal a pair of blue, blue eyes and an actual smile cracking that tough façade, he didn't look all that scary . . . much. And Elaine was sizing him up like she wanted him weighed and wrapped by the local butcher.

"They told us you'd be arriving this morning. I'm Derrick Hayes; I'll be working security." He reached across Elaine to return my stuff, but wasn't even looking at me. "And you are?"

Man, was she ready, with her driver's license and a cute smile. "Elaine Garces. I'll be accompanying Ali during the show's run."

"Yeah, they told us Ali would have a companion." He winked as he handed her license back and flipped his shades back down over his eyes. "Lucky Ali." Walking over to the gate, he punched a series of buttons on a pad; a second later, the wrought-iron monster parted in the middle and swung open. "You can go on in—they saved you a parking spot in one of the garages so your car wouldn't roast."

As we slowly glided past him, he slid his glasses down his nose and raised his eyebrows, giving us another shot of the potent baby blues. "See you around, Ali." His voice dropped, "You too, Elaine."

"Looking forward to it, Derrick." She fluttered her fingers as the gates closed behind us.

Now, how did she do that? It was like with Sosi—the flirting was this . . . natural thing. Whenever I tried to flirt, which had been maybe twice in my life, I'd felt like the victim of some neurological disorder. Just did not come naturally to me—probably something Papi had lit candles and prayed real hard for. I so needed to carry a pad of paper and take notes.

"Okay, Ali, you can get that look off your face." We cruised up and around the curving driveway toward a pair of buildings that looked like miniatures of the house, but had wide-open doors with several vans and cars already in them.

"But . . . that was—"

"Oh, please. Flirting is beyond second nature to guys like that. Someone like me, they look at just as practice. I guarantee you, I'm at least ten years past the sell-by date on his usual honeys." She wrinkled her nose. "Besides, not that he isn't cute, but he's so not my type."

She pulled into an empty spot in the smaller of the Monster Garages and turned the car off. Lifting her Ray-Bans to the top of her head, she glanced over at me. "Probably uses steroids to get all bulked up and you know what that does, right?"

I shook my head. Not a clue.

"Makes the little buddy more like Silly Putty." She grinned and wiggled her pinky finger, then let it droop.

Learn something new every day.

"And you are *not* to tell your father I told you that."

"Silent as the grave."

I propped my chin on my lowered window and looked toward the house.

"Ali."

I couldn't look away from the house. "Yeah?"

Elaine's voice was quiet but firm. "Be friendly, but . . . be on your guard, too." Her hand was warm on my shoulder—reassuring. I knew she'd have my back, if needed.

"I'm not here to make friends, Elaine." I took a deep breath and glanced back over my shoulder at her, at the serious expression in her dark brown eyes. "I'm here to win."

Her hand tightened on my shoulder as the corners of her mouth curled up. "That's right, *mija*. It's your time."

"Let's go." All of a sudden, I felt like Dorothy about to go skipping down the Yellow Brick Road toward my own personal Oz. 'Cept even I knew better than to mix blue gingham and red sequins. I got out of the car and reached into the backseat for my gig bag and backpack. They'd said come casual, this was just an organizational meet 'n' greet, but I still brought a change of clothes just in case and a few other essentials. Like blank staff paper and my iPod. They were like my version of an American Express card—never left home without either. Of course, having an actual American Express card would be pretty sweet, too, but Papi drew the line there.

Grabbing her own backpack and purse, Elaine joined me as we made our way to the front doors, where even the doorbell was over the top, a huge, fist-size brass dome that cued chimes that resonated like the bells at Westminster when I pressed it. Half a second later, the door flew open, revealing . . . a pixie? Not like I was tall, but if she was hitting five feet, it was only because the atmosphere was thin.

"Ali, *hola, qué tal, cómo estás*—we've been waiting for you, it's so great to finally meet you, we're so excited that you're competing, another local girl, it's going to be so fabulous—"

Would've answered, except I was being squashed in a bear hug that kept breathing from being an option, forget speaking.

"Let's look at you—" Just that quick I was shoved back to arm's length as a shrewd, black-eyed gaze looked me over, top to bottom.

"Oh, wardrobe is going to have such a blast with you—you're totally adorable!"

Adorable? Me? I looked over at Elaine, who looked like she was trying not to laugh. Of *course* she was trying not to laugh—you just never knew what might provoke a psychopath.

"And you must be her companion, of course you are, and I'm *so* sorry about that, but you know, some of the sponsors are really old-fashioned and just the idea of Ali in this 'den of iniquity'—can you believe they actually *said* that?—I mean, in Spanish, of course, but that they even said it because who says stuff like 'den of iniquity' these days anyway—"

I reached out and snagged Elaine's backpack, which I knew had her laptop in it, just before it landed on the floor as she was treated to her own bone-crushing hug. Ha. The expression on her face was totally priceless. Now she knew.

"And ohmigod, the two of you must be related, right?" She shoved Elaine back and did that same head-to-toe thing. "I mean, I know you're not Ali's mom, I already know about that and I'm so sorry, but really, you two look so alike—"

Whoa. I'd never heard that before, but then again, first time in, like, forever that I'd met someone who didn't know Elaine as Papi's best friend or colleague, at the very least.

An annoying chirp echoed through the huge foyer. "Yeah. Yeah. She's here. We'll be there in a second. Tell the natives to chill, we're still ahead of schedule, I intend to stay there."

As she spoke into her cellphone, she turned and started walking away, then paused, turned back, and waved that we should follow. As I handed Elaine her rescued backpack and readjusted the strap of my gig bag across my chest, I studied her. Related, huh?

Both her eyebrows rose and she crossed her eyes. "I should only be as cute as you when I grow up."

I laughed as we followed the crazed pixie at a safe distance. "Nah, I think you scored all the cute points."

"Don't start selling yourself short, Ali. Not now. Not even joking."

"But—" I knew what she meant, but let's be real—wasn't my looks that had gotten me here.

"Yeah, yeah, you've got talent oozing out your little finger, girl, but these days, it's as much about the looks and selling yourself as it is the talent. You know it and don't ever fool yourself into thinking different because this business will eat you alive otherwise."

First impressions count.

It's what I'd said to Sosi back at the auditions.

So yeah, on some level, I did know it. But it was a good reminder. Especially as we followed the psycho into a room that I'm sure seemed huge when it was empty. Right now, though, it felt like one of those teeny cars at the circus that the clowns just kept pouring out of. How many people were in here anyway, and why did they all have to turn and stare at me? At least they were mostly curious stares, except for the one that looked more like I was something that should be scraped off the bottom of a shoe. What the hell? Then I recognized her. The hair was a brighter platinum and ironed straight, but yeah—Miss Leather from the auditions. Looked like her mood hadn't improved any.

The pixie made a sudden reappearance. "Just take a seat or grab a slice of wall anywhere you can find a spot, Ali, we're about ready to get started, or if you want to get yourself something to eat or drink first, you can do that, the kitchen is right there and we've got all sorts of stuff, just help yourself, even if you're not living here, you're to treat the house as if you are—"

Then, just as quick as she'd appeared, she poofed, leaving me sort of dazed and looking around the room, sizing up the occupants. Now that I more or less had my bearings, it was easy to pick out the other competitors—for one thing, they were the ones still glancing over in my direction and at one another.

"Just like the playground on the first day of school, isn't it?"

I glanced to my left and found a girl about my same height, with superlong black hair with heavy bangs, and blue eyes, standing beside me.

"Yeah, it is," I laughed, knowing exactly what she meant. Just like at school, you could pick out the different types with one glance.

"Let's see . . . he'll be the *cholo* Eminem," she said, nodding at the tattooed guy in baggy khakis and wife beater.

"Beauty queen with Vanessa Williams dreams," I added, tilting my head toward the chick who was staring into a mirror, fluffing her hair and applying lip gloss.

A gorgeous guy in a track suit and Adidas sauntered past, sliding his shades down his nose so we could get the full effect of sexy, dark brown eyes.

She and I stared at each other. "That's just *caliente,*" she whispered after he was out of hearing range, making me giggle. "And since I'm from Texas, I'll be the big-haired Selena wannabe." She grinned and held out her hand. "Monica Sanchez."

"Ali Montero." I carefully set my gig bag against the wall and took her hand. Not here to make friends, but didn't hurt to play nice. Get to know the competition a little. "Local girl or the baby of the group, take your pick."

"Baby," she replied with another smile, clearly not meaning anything bad. "Since I think there's some other chick who's from Miami."

"Yeah, the fake blonde."

"Oh, her." Monica wrinkled her nose as she glanced over her shoulder to where Miss Leather was studying her nails. "Never mind, you can be the local girl. She'll be the diva bitch."

Well—guess she'd already made an impression.

"All right, everyone, *su atención, por favor—*"

Santa María. That amplified voice—it was the pixie's voice. But slower, authoritative . . . pausing for a breath, even. Man, talk about a virtual whiplash. I blinked, as she stood on some sort of step stool that elevated her above the rest of us and made her a natural focal point of attention. No . . . it wasn't just that—it was like her entire demeanor had just totally changed, and there was no doubt. The pixie was completely in charge.

She smiled from her perch on high, and waited for the extraneous chatter to die away. Lifting the wireless mic, she continued in Spanish, "*Bueno,* now that we're all here we can get started. First things first. I'm Esperanza Villareal and I'm your stage director, which means in the coming weeks I'm going to be either your saving grace or your worst nightmare. Let me be clear—how well you listen is going to be the primary factor in dictating whether you think I'm the most fabulous thing since my *abuelita*'s flan or the biggest bitch you've ever met."

Another pause as she scanned the room with a narrow gaze that made it clear she was sizing all of us up, trying to figure out who was likeliest to score high on her Bitch-o-meter. Tell you what—aside from the fact that I'd been well-trained by both my father and nuns, I was planning on listening as if every word that fell from her lips was pure gold.

"Now that we've got that out of the way, let me just say how thrilled I am to be here with you all on what I hope is the beginning of a *lot* of bright careers. *Bienvenidos al primer día de* Oye Mi Canto."

I exchanged a glance with Elaine. Oh yeah. This was gonna be good.

7

"I should call your father. He's probably having fits by now, even though he'll completely deny it."

"Yeah, sure. I'd love one."

"One what? Ali, I said I was going to call your father."

"Whatever, Elaine. Chocolate's great."

"Ali!"

"Huh?" Chocolate really was fine and I was *trying* to commit to at least partial memory the rest of today's schedule. After her rah-rah, "listen to me or you'll so live to regret it" spiel, Esperanza had handed them out, informing us that first thing every morning, we'd be receiving individual schedules for that day's activities. Some of those activities we'd all be together, like press appearances, but mostly we'd be on our own or with only one or two other contestants. Worked for me.

"Ali." Elaine was laughing. Why was she laughing? What was so funny about chocolate? She'd been discussing chocolate, right?

"What?"

"*Dios mío*, girl. Get your head together." Elaine shoved my plate closer to me. "And make a dent in your sandwich. You've been staring at it for twenty minutes, and you only have another twenty-five for lunch. You don't want to piss off Esperanza by being late to your first appointment."

God *no*. Last thing I wanted to do. Grinning, I shoved the corner of the schedule under my plate so it didn't blow away and picked up half of the gigantor *media noche* sandwich I'd selected from the poolside lunch buffet. They weren't doing anything small or halfway around here, baby. The house was big, the pool was big, the food was big—

"Oh, look, how cute. It's the *nenesita* and her *dueña.*"

The egos were bigger.

Just my luck. Miss Leather. After the morning intros, I now knew her name was Fabiana. *Just* Fabiana, like she thought she was all that and could go one-named. Just like Monica had said—diva bitch. I guess the judges had needed at least one mass-produced, pop-star wannabe.

A finger with a long-ass acrylic nail painted purple-black and pierced with a tiny rhinestone reached out and tapped my schedule. "And, *mira,* makeup and wardrobe's first for you. They must have known."

Don't do it, don't do it. "Known what?" Shit, I did it.

"How much help you'd need."

She laughed, but trust me, nothing friendly about that sound.

"Why don't you back off, okay?" Elaine's voice was mild, but the expression in her eyes was anything but.

"Back off yourself, lady. You're her babysitter, not mine."

Oh, that royal bi— Finally finding my voice again, I snapped, "Hey, what's your problem anyway?"

She leaned down, her breath sort of hot and uncomfortable on my face. "I don't have a problem, but you will if you don't understand how things are. *I'm* the hometown favorite, not some *nenesita* who's barely out of diapers. You're nothing more than a novelty, so I'm telling you right now—stay out of my way and we'll all be fine."

Spinning on insanely high wedge heels, she stalked off with her plate of carrots and bottle of Pellegrino, ironed hair swinging in a platinum-and-pink-streaked sheet against her back. Would it be courting bad karma to hope it all fell out from overprocessing?

And what *was* it with her and leather? Come on, it's Miami, it's June, and Miss Thang was in a lace tank top with a leather corset-bustier thingie that had to be hot and not for any of the good reasons, either. At least the lowriders (complete with tacky thong peekage over the top, of course) were providing ventilation.

Still a total poser.

"Still a total bitch."

A bottle of water appeared at my elbow. Only one person that could be. I'd wondered if I would see him. I turned in my chair and, well . . . there he was. Still with his messenger bag. Still with his backward baseball cap. Holding a plate loaded with food and still totally cute.

"Hey."

"Hey yourself, Ali. May I?" He looked at Elaine, rather than at me. Like she was going to say no? But it was nice of him to defer to her—those were the kind of manners even Papi would approve of.

"Of course." She waved at one of the free chairs and as he settled himself, took a split second to look at me, eyebrows raised, and mouthed, *He's adorable—who is he?*

"Elaine Garces, may I introduce Jaime Lozano."

A quick glance my way that did whirligig things to my stomach. "You remembered my name."

Uhhh . . . *duh*? Of course, I remembered. But for once in my flirting-impaired life, I actually came up with the perfect thing to say.

"How could I forget the name of my chief water supplier, not to mention the first person to tell me I was going to make the finals?"

"Shhh . . ." He leaned closer; not Red Alert Territory by anyone's stretch, but enough that I caught a whiff of something nice. "That's our little secret. No telling." Leaning back in his chair, he grinned and oh yeah, the eyes still did that adorable crinkly thing that I remembered.

"And jeopardize that special bond we have? Never." Was this really me? Sos would be so proud.

Laughed. He laughed. And not in some "what a dweeb" way. I started to breathe again, as Jaime turned to face Elaine. Reaching across the table he offered his hand. "*Mucho gusto*, Ms. Garces."

With a frown that was totally fake, because, well, I knew Elaine, she shook his hand. *"Igualmente,* and child, the only thing that just saved your butt is the fact that you went straight to 'Ms. Garces' and didn't do the awkward fumble between *señora* and *señorita*."

He shrugged as he released her hand and lifted his Cuban sandwich. "What can I say? There's just no happy substitute in Spanish for 'Ms.' and who knew which title you might prefer? Ms. is the safest option and I'm big on taking the safe options."

"Can't fault that logic." The fake frown gave way to a smile as she added, "Elaine's fine."

Swallowing a bite of sandwich, Jaime glanced over at the schedule beneath my plate. "Did I hear Brunhilda saying you had wardrobe and makeup first today?"

Dang, but Diet Coke bubbles up the nose stung. "Brunhilda?"

Again with the slight lean toward me. "Her real name is Hilda," he mock-whispered.

"Fabiana's fake?"

Jaime just stared at me. Rolling my eyes I clarified, "Well, *yeah,* she's completely fake, except for the bitch part which is all too real, but the name?"

"Is really and truly Hilda."

"And she couldn't come up with something better than Fabiana as a stage name?"

"Actually, it's her middle name."

"Jeez, her parents must really hate her."

This laughing with a guy stuff was *really* nice. Especially when the guy in question was a total cutie with streaky green eyes and reddish-brown hair that was long enough to brush the collar of his black T-shirt. You know, maybe it was the looks or the confident, yet not in your face about it 'tude, but he sure wasn't like any Latin boy I'd ever met—not that this was a bad thing—although with a handle like Jaime Lozano, what else was he going to be?

"So, Jaime, what's your gig with the show?"

She had to. Just in case any questions came up with Papi, Elaine had to make sure she had the pertinent info.

"Well, I started with the show last spring as an intern—I'm a film and television production major at NYU. Technically, my official designation is something like Twelfth Assistant Director." Laughing, he added, "Although as I told Ali at the auditions, what that translates to in my case is all-purpose lackey."

"But even at NYU, it's not spring semester anymore." Said with a smile to soften the edges.

Had to hand it to him. He took the mini-interrogation real well—the *real* proof he was Latin. Because only a Latin guy would understand what she was going for and why she was doing it, and go with the flow without so much as a WTF glance and scurrying off to a safe distance. Just finished off the first half of his sandwich, even wiped the corners of his mouth before he finally said, "With the show running through August, it became my summer gig and as a choice bonus, I'm earning more college credits. Good for the résumé and for getting out of school that much sooner."

He didn't even wait for Elaine to find a way to ask, just answered the next inevitable question. "I'm already halfway through my senior year even though I only turned twenty last January." He winked at me. "I'm ambitious—graduated high school a year early, too."

Just as my heart had nosedived toward my stomach at the mention of "senior year," it skidded to a stop and reversed right back to its normal position—albeit with a little faster heart rate. He was only twenty.

Thank goodness. Because no matter how nice he was, if "halfway through senior year" had meant even an hour over twenty-one, Elaine would've had no choice but to shoo him off and watch me like a hawk, much as she and I would've both hated it. No way Papi would ever condone my hanging out with a twenty-one-year-old guy in any way, shape, or form unless he was a close blood relative; not with me still under eighteen. Okay, let's be real: Pigs would have to take to the friendly skies before he'd condone any kind of hanging out anyway, but with Jaime being only twenty, there was less reason for—

For what? *Ay Dios mío,* I was being such a twit. He was probably just being nice and here I was, acting like a total dork. A total dork who was going to be late if I didn't get a move on.

"Gotta go." I shoved a final bite of sandwich into my mouth and washed it down with the last of my soda. "After all, lots of work to be done." Sighing, I folded my schedule and shoved it in my shorts pocket.

"Ali, *mija* . . ."

"*Mira*, don't let Brunhilda get to you."

Couldn't look at either Elaine or Jaime as I stood and gathered my stuff. Too late. She'd gotten in my head—at least a little. I mean, yeah, maybe she made the hookers on Biscayne Boulevard look classy, and I had no clue as to her level of talent, but hey, she was good enough to have made it to the finals and had obviously mastered the trick of always being "on." Me? Outside of performing, I was pretty low key. I didn't know if I could sustain that kind of "on," you know? Or if I'd even be able to learn.

Truth time, too, I was probably also reacting—okay, most likely *over*reacting—to my realization that Jaime was just being nice to the little girl. And I kind of wished he wasn't. Because he was really cute and clearly smart and . . . well, he was probably just being nice and that kind of sucked.

Just as well. I didn't have time if I was going to work on learning how to be "on." At least, "on" enough to win this bad boy.

"Hey."

I blinked down at his hand on my wrist, noticing his dark tan, then looked into his face. "Yeah?"

He nodded toward the remains of my *media noche*—sucker had been so big I'd only managed half. "You gonna eat that?"

I blinked some more, this time at his empty plate, which, when he'd sat down, had been loaded with an enormous Cuban sandwich, a mountain of *mariquita* chips, and a couple kosher dills. Not to mention, he had yet another plate waiting piled with *pastelitos* and a few huge chocolate Deathbomb cookies.

Corner of his mouth turned up. "Hey, I'm a growing boy." He held out one of the Deathbombs. "Trade you a cookie?"

Totally couldn't help laughing at that puppy dog expression as I lowered my plate to the table and took the cookie. "Thanks." *Such* a nice guy. Since this so wasn't about sandwiches. He was trying to make me feel better about Brunhilda. Gah—did he *have* to be so nice?

"Catch up with you later? See how things went?"

Okay, now maybe I was embarrassingly inexperienced, but even I knew this went beyond simply being nice. Swallowing hard, I reached for the bottle of water Elaine was holding out.

"Sure, that'd be cool," I finally managed to choke out before pulling an about face and quick retreat before he or Elaine could see the color my face was turning. Honestly. You'd think a guy had never touched my wrist or offered me a cookie.

Or said they were going to catch up with me later. *That's* more what was on my mind as I climbed the stairs to the second floor of the garage, where wardrobe and makeup were being housed. How much did he *really* mean that? If at all? So color me a little unprepared for what met me when I knocked, then opened the door.

"Ay, mi vida, we've been waiting for you. Aren't you every bit as adorable as Espie said, and *Santa María purísima*—what on earth are you wearing?"

8

"*O*ye, Andre, let the girl catch her breath first."

"I can't wait, B. I've got to get the complete picture here."

Like I was immobilized in some weird sci-fi movie-worthy fog, I stood frozen as my hair was loosened from its clip and my backpack was slipped from my shoulder. However, the nanosecond that well-manicured hand reached for the strap of my gig bag, the fog broke.

"Relax, sweetie."

My grip tightened on the strap.

"Andre . . ."

"Ohhh-kay then." Andre held his hands up. "Backing away slowly, precious. You take care of your guitar."

"Hi, Ali. I'm Bianca." The tall and incredibly gorgeous woman who'd told Andre to let me catch my breath introduced herself. "I'm heading up hair and makeup. The lunatic beside me is Andre and he'll be doing wardrobe."

"Hi." I eased the strap of the gig bag over my head and carefully set my guitar in the corner farthest from the lunatic. But to be fair . . . I knew I was crazy-possessive about my axe. Hey, it wasn't just the means by which I made my music, it was . . . well, *more*. "Sorry about that. You just freaked me a little."

Paid to be nice to the hair and makeup people so I didn't go out onstage looking like a troglodyte. Which was a distinct possibility if I were to be abandoned and left to my own devices.

"It's okay, honey. I know I can come on a little strong. Not that I'm going to come on to you, cute though you may be."

"Like this is supposed to come as a surprise?" Tall, thin, sporting a spikey black coif with frosted tips, and, of course, dressed like something straight out of *Ocean Drive* magazine. For God's sake, there was even bronzer across cheekbones that were high and perfect and that most chicks would commit murder for. I mean, really there's naïve and then there's completely clueless.

"Wait a minute, aren't you supposed to be this innocent Catholic schoolgirl? And I was so looking forward to corrupting you." He actually pouted. Right before he winked.

"Don't worry." Now that he wasn't threatening my guitar, I was loose enough to wink back. "Plenty to corrupt. But if you're single, remind me to introduce you to my cousin." Who was flamier than a Homecoming bonfire to the never-ending despair of my *Tía* Bernice.

Interested eyebrow arch. "Is he cute?"

"Only if you like tall, dark, and looks just like a buff Orlando Bloom."

"*Ay, mi corazón,* I'm saving all the best wardrobe pieces for you."

"I think you have your first fanboy, Ali." Bianca smiled at me from where she was sitting on the mirror-and-light-lined vanity that ran along one long wall.

"First?"

"Precious, if what we heard about you is true, you're going to have a score of fans, ladies and gentlemen, boys and girls, children of all ages," Andre sing-songed, just like a circus announcer.

What they've *heard* about me? This was starting to border on Twilight Zone territory—everywhere around this barn, it seemed, I was getting that people had "heard" about me. What was there to hear? I'd made the finals. So had fifteen other people. Impressive on some level, maybe, especially compared to the thirty-nine thousand, nine hundred eighty-four who hadn't, but dude, other than that, what made me any different from anyone else around here? I just did what I loved doing. I did it very well but so did a lot of other people.

Andre was staring at me with another arched eyebrow expression, but this one was more like he should have an accompanying lightbulb above his head. "You really don't get it?"

I shook my head. "Not really."

"I think we need to leave it that way. At least for a while. It's special, don't you think, B?"

"Yeah. It is." She hopped down from the vanity and came to stand next to Andre. "And it's going to help. Especially in these first rounds."

Naïve and in this case, *definitely* clueless.

"Okay, let's crank some tunes and take a good look at this baby girl." Andre took a few steps back and looked me over top to bottom, just like Esperanza had this morning. God, was it only this morning? I was already exhausted. But then—the music drifting from the boom box in the corner canceled out exhaustion and brought on a smile from the sheer unexpectedness of it all.

"Joss Stone?" Totally high on the cool factor. I mean, anyone who could take a hip chart by the White Stripes and make it hipper still—and I loved that she wasn't a whole lot older than me.

"Natch, *mija*." Andre kept stalking around me like I was prey. "Gotta keep from overdosing on the salsa and merengue and if we want the club mixes, we'll go to the clubs. In here, we'll go for the relaxing vibe. Keep it Zen."

I could completely dig that.

"Now—much as I'm loving this vintage tee and jeans shorts look, from this second on, it is *just* not going to do."

I glanced down at my battered T-shirt, so old it had long ago ceased being black, devolving into a gnarly gray-green. But Andre was right—truly a vintage piece, one of Papi's Police concert shirts from back in the day that I'd absconded with ages ago and if he thought I was getting rid of it . . .

"You'd better not be coming at me with those scissors."

"Relax, *mija*. I'm going to use them to cut tags off some stuff I want you to try. Size ten?"

"Depends," I mumbled. Sometimes higher. Not that there was anything wrong at all with having a Cuban butt. Nope. Nothing at all. Just wish I had the Cuban boobs to balance it out.

"Oh, don't worry, you've got an adorable figure and I've got some great jeans and a bra that's going to do absolute wonders for you."

What was he, a mind reader?

"B, why don't you get started while I ponder?"

"Come on, Ali." Bianca led me toward the vanity. "Let Dr. Frankenstein *ponder* while we see what we've got here."

"Not much," I automatically responded, even as Elaine's "don't sell yourself short" and Jaime's "don't let Brunhilda get to you" reverbed through my mind.

"Oh, stop it." Bianca pushed me down into a chair and walked around to face me. "Obviously, you don't do a lot with makeup and hair—" She took a polite pause, waiting for the nod she didn't really need.

"I prefer that, actually. Gives us a clean slate to work with." She leaned forward and with both hands felt my hair and ran her fingers through it, fluffing it out before taking my chin in her hand and tilting my face this way, then that . . . reaching behind herself to shine a gooseneck lamp right in my face. Felt like an interrogation.

"Any objections to cutting your hair? Nothing drastic," she

added when I must have given her the look o' horror. "I think the overall length is great, but the nonlayered, flat look doesn't do a thing for your face, angel."

I leaned to one side and looked in the mirror. Just past my shoulders and all one length. Easy enough to put back in a headband or up in a ponytail for school, yet not so long it got in my way when I played. Shrugging, I glanced back at Bianca.

"Okay, so long as I don't end up with something I can't take care of on my own."

"Don't worry, I'll teach you how."

"Famous last words."

"Come again?" She pushed me forward far enough to snap a smock around my neck.

"It's what my best friend keeps saying." I sighed and leaned back in the chair. "She just goes ahead and does my hair and makeup herself when it's necessary."

Bianca began spritzing water over my hair and combing. "She interested in hair and makeup?"

As she went to work, we chatted about Sosi and how long we'd been friends and how she'd been trying since seventh grade to teach me how to put on eyeliner. Always complaining that she couldn't understand how someone who could play a musical run loaded with sixty-fourth notes and embellishments out the wazoo couldn't draw a simple straight line with what basically amounted to a crayon.

What's the point? Not like we could legally wear makeup to school, and I'd only rarely been asked on dates that I had to dress up for. Trust me, Papi was *real* good with both the no-makeup school rule and the essential non-dateageness of my life.

Truthfully, and it was the only secret I'd ever kept from Sos, I was fairly certain I'd never learned any of her beauty tricks because I enjoyed her makeup experiments and I *loved* having my hair played with. Like now. I fell into this nifty trancy state that didn't break until Bianca asked me to bend forward so she could dry the underside, running her fingers through, presumably for some fluffy goodness.

"Now up and flip your hair like you're fabulous."

The flipping brought on a head rush, but when my vision cleared—*whoa.*

"But . . . you didn't even use a brush." I reached up and touched the tousled bangs and waves around my face and brushing my shoulders. My boring dark brown didn't even look so boring—it looked shiny and bouncy and disturbingly cute in a Eva Mendes sort of way.

"Didn't use a brush because I wanted to play up the waves, although when we go to give you a sleek do, we'll go complete blowout." Bianca's jet-black ponytail and hoop earrings shimmied in perfect synchronicity to Joss's "You Had Me" while she rummaged through what had to be the World's Biggest Makeup Case.

"Andre?" she called over her shoulder as she pulled a palette of purple shadows from the case.

He poked his head out of a doorway. "Yes, my lovely?"

"Jewel tones."

"You read my mind." I saw his eyes go saucer-wide as he looked at me. "Oh—"

"I know, isn't it fantastic?"

"Outrageously so."

I swear, he was practically rubbing his hands together as he nodded his head and ducked back into the room. Dr. Frankenstein, indeed.

Since I was so used to having Sosi messing around with my hair and face, it was no big to sit still while Bianca did her thing—until she got to the eyebrow wax.

"Yow!"

"Sorry, *mija,* but no pain, no gain." And ruthlessly yanked at my other eyebrow while I clenched the arms of the chair in a death grip.

She didn't *sound* sorry. And it stung like a mother, although the cream she was rubbing in was feeling pretty good. The brow massacre was the worst of it, though, and afterward it seemed Bianca finished in record time—then wouldn't let me look when she was done, the evil woman.

"Nuh-uh, girl. Let's let Andre get to work with you, then we'll look at the complete package."

"But, Bianca—"

"Relax, Ali. It'll be fine." Her voice was gentle as she steered me away from the mirror and toward Door Number One where Andre'd been hiding. I swear, I'd even heard him cackling a couple times. Was it possible to be scared in a good way?

Oh . . . oh, *wow.* The door I walked through was like the difference between pre- and postcyclone head thwackage for Dorothy, keeping with the cheap *Wizard of Oz* references. Lining the perimeter of the huge room were racks and racks of clothes and shoes and accessories in every color under the sun and even some that were definitely not found in nature. It was like the contents of every store on South Beach and CocoWalk crammed into one space.

"Time for looking later, precious. I want to see the finished product." Before I had a chance to take more than a quick look—and oh, hella cute pumps sitting on a long table!—I found myself steered to a space in one corner that was blocked off by a couple of Asian-looking screens.

"Go. Try. Come out fabulous."

And there was that fabulous thing again. But again, thanks to training from nuns and Papi, I simply went behind the screens and surveyed what Andre had left out for me and dang, if he wasn't good. Everything fit. Including the wicked-hot black lace bra that probably cost more than six months' allowance and pushed stuff in directions they'd never been pushed before.

"Shoe size?"

"Eight and a half."

"Your lucky day."

I nearly squealed as the hella cute pumps appeared through a crack in the screen. Slipping them on, I took a deep breath and pushed aside the screen to face my judges.

"Oh, *mija,* yes." Bianca was grinning and nodding while Andre put one hand over his mouth and pretended to wipe away a stray tear with the other. At least I think he was pretending. Reaching out, he grabbed my hand and pulled me toward a small raised pedestal with a huge three-way mirror wrapped around it.

"Look."

Holy Sainted Mother of . . . All I could do was stare . . . blink . . . stare some more.

"Ali, I'm sorry it took me so long to get up here, I got caught up talking to Esperanza and then your fa— Oh, *Ali* . . ."

Behind me in the mirror, Elaine had that whole "Holy Sainted Mother of . . ." expression going on, too, so no, wasn't just me.

"*Ay,* Alegría, you look—"

"Like a star, baby," Andre interjected.

Really? Is this what a star looked like? I mean, I looked like me, just . . . different. The jeans and deep purple peasant top with the beaded neckline were definitely things I'd choose for myself if I could; the cute pumps and big, swingy silver hoop earrings, for sure. But the rest—the hair and the makeup—took me from being Ali to . . . whoever the heck it was I was staring at in the mirror. Not that it was garish or slutty or anything. Just . . . mouth fuller, cheekbones higher, eyes bigger; it was like me, exponentially squared, or something.

"You've got great eyes, Ali—the camera's going to love them. I tried to play them up without going overboard."

I leaned closer to the mirror at Bianca's comment. Hazel. That catchall name they gave your eye color when you couldn't lay claim to any one color. Like Papi. His eyes were hazel, too, but more distinct, with a ring of green surrounded by light brown. Mine, on the other hand—mine went beyond hazel and verged on, I don't know, multicolored mud, maybe.

Except with the dark gray eyeliner and purple shadows that Bianca had used . . . not so much mud, but more . . . kaleidoscope. *Très* cool. I leaned away from the mirror and took in the whole package again, shaking my head. The person looking back at me was shaking her head, too, and reaching up to touch her hair, just like I was.

Forgive me for just a sec, but I was having a hellacious time wrapping my brain around the idea that we were the same. That it was me.

It was. But so very different.

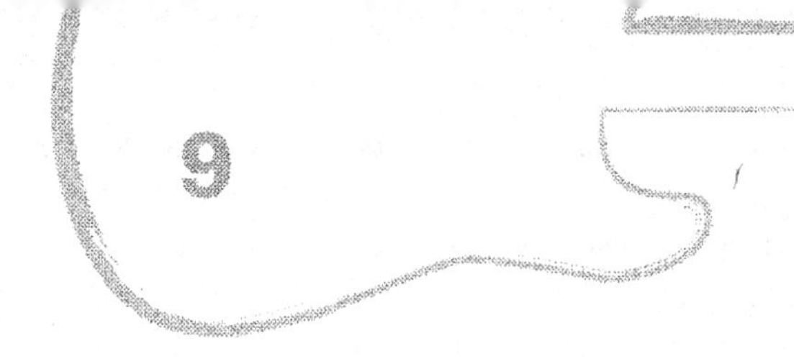

9

"Augh!"

"The life of trying to become the next great Latin superstar taking its toll on you already, *mija*?"

It would be so much easier to keep my head buried in the nice, soft leather sofa cushions where I'd flopped. But I couldn't let the snarkism pass without comment. Besides, my breathing was making the leather kind of moist and sticky and *eugh.* So I turned my head, just enough for fresh air and to be able to stick my tongue out at Papi.

'Cause that was all the comment I had energy for.

He propped my gig bag, which I'd pushed into his hands the second I walked through the door, against the coffee table—a second later, I felt the cushions down by my feet give.

"¿Qué pasa, mi vida?"

Slipping off my sneakers, Papi propped my feet on his leg. Shades of elementary school.

"Papi, nearly a week we've been there, and I haven't so much as played or even sung a note that hasn't been along with the radio on the morning drive." I rolled over onto my back and stuffed a throw pillow under my head.

"It's been all makeup and wardrobe and pictures—" Okay, so the wardrobe was cool, especially since Andre said we'd get to keep a lot of it as a bonus and I *was* a little curious to see my headshots, but still—

"Practicing with publicity people, because *Dios mío*, I actually had an interview today with some guy from the *Herald*."

Which in and of itself was enough to bring on the Hurlie Whirlies, but then my publicity coach had cheerfully said, "Here's to the first of many successful interviews."

Many? Could've cheerfully strangled her. All I wanted was to perform. And *not* just this trained monkey crap that took up so much time I wasn't even able to go sneak off into a corner to practice so much as "Mary Had a Freakin' Lamb."

"And how did that go?"

"It was okay, I guess." I flexed my feet back and forth, studying the light pink polish the manicurist had put on this morning while Bianca did my hair. "He started out with stuff like what's it like to be the youngest contestant, were we all getting along, blah, blah, blah, how did you get into music, bladi*blah*—"

My fingers twisted the hem of my T-shirt. "Then he came out of nowhere and asked stuff about Mamá."

As private as Papi had always been about her, except with me, I'd have expected him to maybe blow a gasket, but all he did was ask, "Like what?"

"Oh, stuff about what was it like to lose her when I was only two, and was the pain of the loss what fueled my artistic ambitions?" My chest was burning and my throat felt tight, just like earlier.

"Like it's not bad enough I lost her, but I'm supposed to remember and share the most private parts of my life with a total stranger?" It was one thing when family was creepy and invasive and asking about stuff that was totally none of their business—that was sort of expected, especially from a Cuban family. But some chump I'd met two seconds ago? As if. This was my life, not a Hallmark card. And, no matter what his twisted little brain had cooked up, really had zero to do with the music.

"It's like the music is almost the least of it. What's *up* with that?"

"It's a price you pay, *mija,* if you want to perform at this sort of level."

I sighed and reached for another throw pillow, hugging it to my chest. "That's fine, Papi, I get that it's a trade-off and actually, most of it's pretty fun—" Except for the interviews. "*Mira,* Papi, I just want to play . . . sing . . . *some*thing."

"Hmm."

Damn. I wondered if I'd gone too far with the whining. After all, wasn't I just begging for a "you wanted this"/"this is what you asked for" lecture?

No lecture. No told you so's. Just Papi making with the thoughtful expressions before he patted my leg.

"Come on, *levántate.*"

Curious, I set aside the pillow and pushed myself up to a sitting position watching Papi cross to the bookcases—and the stereo. Glancing over his shoulder, he asked, "What are you waiting for?" while nodding at my gig bag. "Warm up."

I could feel myself smiling, leaning forward, unzipping the bag and extracting my beautiful Bernabé. Giving the rosewood back and spruce front a quick polish with a chamois and plucking each of the strings, adjusting the tuning and stretching my fingers before—oh God . . . yeah, a nice easy run, the nylon strings vibrating under my fingertips and against the fret board. Coming home.

Already, I felt something hard that I hadn't even known was in my chest start to loosen.

"You warm enough?"

I glanced up to see Papi holding the remote. "For?"

"A little 'Aranjuez' . . . segueing into 'Spain' maybe?"

Oh. Oh *yeah*. I nodded and waited for one of my patented

gongs to signal I should begin with the simple strummed chords that four measures later would lead into Michel Camilo's slow, seductive piano. Yeah, another one of those recordings I'd performed computer surgery on, sending up a little apology to flamenco guitar god Tomatito as I worked to remove his kick-ass stylings from the chart so I could impose my own.

Personally, I thought I did it pretty decent justice. But then again, I had great material to work with, thank you, Joaquin Rodrigo and Chick Corea. Not to mention, an awesome teacher.

"Slow down, Ali. You were sloppy on those last two runs. It's adagio, not allegretto, *mija*."

I spared a quick glance and nod, to let him know I'd heard, then let myself sink further into the music. He was right—I was so anxious to play, had been feeling the deprivation of not having played for so many days, my precision was screwy and I was trying to overcompensate. But the music wasn't going anywhere. At least, not anywhere I didn't take it . . .

Relax, relax . . . *there* it was. The subtle rhythm of the adagio, then pause and *whammo*—into the tricky syncopated run that was "Spain's" signature riff. After that, it was off-to-the-races time, alternating between providing the rhythm and taking the melody, as Camilo's thundering chords and resonant bass line became counterpoint to my improvisations.

Really. Were there any two more perfect instruments than the guitar and the piano? How could any other instruments lay claim to such versatility? And together—they were absolute magic and this—*this* was the kind of playing that never failed to leave me feeling peaceful. That transported me.

"Well done, *mi niña*."

Seriously transported me. I blinked at Papi, who was sitting just across from me in his fave leather chair. No clue when he'd moved. When I'd glanced up at him before, he'd been leaning against the bookcase, listening. Kind of scary sometimes, how lost I could get in the music—in a weirdly reassuring way.

"Feel better?"

Breathing was easier, that's for sure. "Yeah."

I placed my guitar in his outstretched hand and sank back into the sofa cushions while he rose and placed it in its stand in the corner. Which meant he wasn't even facing me as he oh-so-casually asked, "Elaine didn't want to come in when she dropped you off?"

"Uh, she said something about running past her office at school and checking messages, then going home to see if her house plants had committed suicide yet and what kind of biology experiments might be growing in her fridge."

He dropped back into his chair with a monster sigh. "*Dios mío,* Ali, I honestly had no idea this thing would suck up quite this much time. This is the first night since you started that you've been home before dinner." Running a hand through his hair, he amended himself. "Forget dinner—it's the first night you've been home before midnight."

And would you believe he actually looked a little guilty?

"She's been digging it, Papi, for real."

Sign of how guilty he *did* feel that all he said was, "Really?" without even attempting to backpedal and make it more about me.

"Really—a lot of it's actually been fun." Even though we'd both been kind of relieved at the early dismissal today. "Honest. Come on, you know she'd tell you if she had a problem."

He laughed at that. "Yeah, true. Probably in really vile language."

"Can't be any worse than what I've been hearing." In multiple dialects, no less. Chelo, who was from Tijuana, and Tonio, the *caliente* Puerto Rican boy from the Bronx, were educations all by themselves. Who knew there were so many different terms for a guy's—

"You can stop right there." He held up his hand, but was still smiling. "I think this falls under the heading of what I don't know can't keep me awake at night."

"Like you go to sleep before I come home anyway," I half teased, half grumped.

He shrugged, but no apology there, no sir. "I'd be derelict in my duty as a father if I didn't stay up."

"Heaven forbid you should be a derelict," I joked, making him snatch a pillow from the end of the sofa and toss it at me.

God, this felt good. Joking and teasing with Papi like this. Hadn't been this way for weeks. Mostly because he was so pissed and disappointed with me about the audition. There was more, too, and not like I was so head-in-the-sand I couldn't see it. He was still worrying whether or not he'd done the right thing by letting me go through with this gig. Especially now that I'd started, I'd hardly been around. Considering I'd never even gone away to summer camp— Very weird, this new distance. A little scary, really. But the old routines weren't gone. They were still there. Thank God.

"So what do you want to do with this rare night of freedom, *mija*?"

I turned and stretched out on the sofa again, pulling the pillow against my chest. "Aside from sleep?"

"I think four-thirty's a little early for your bedtime, even if you are still grounded."

"Doesn't feel like it," I mumbled around a yawn. Everything hurt, all of a sudden, and I was *so* tired.

"Do you want to go to a movie, maybe get something to eat after? Granatello's or Wing Heaven?"

Oh yeah . . . food. Now that I could get into. Nothing but coffee and bottled water since breakfast because the interview with the creepy reporter had completely bogarted my lunch break.

"God, I'd love something to eat, Papi, but a movie . . . I don't think so. I'm so unbelievably wiped, if I even make it back up to an upright and seated position, I'll consider it an accomplishment worthy of applause."

"Ah, well then, takeout and TV for us. We can figure out what we want now; I'll order and go pick it up in a while." He grinned at me and ducked into the kitchen to go find the takeout menus.

Oh yeah, he was my *papi* and he loved me. I was a lucky girl. I should do more nice things for him.

"You want to call Elaine and see if she wants to eat with us?"

Didn't even bat an eyelash as he played Peruse the Menus. "She's probably enjoying the chance to be home as much as you are, *mija*."

Pinhead. "Won't know unless you call, will you?"

Now, he looked up. With this odd expression on his face. "No . . . no. I don't think so. Not tonight, Ali. Tonight, I just want *us* to have a quiet night. That okay?" That odd expression deepened, and his eyes went dark behind the lenses of his glasses.

That something hard that had been in my chest loosened even more. "Yeah. Very all right."

"Okay, then." He lowered his gaze back to the menus. "I suppose if we go with wings, you're going to want something unbearably spicy?"

"Duh."

"Figures. Good thing they have the variety buckets."

"Um-hm . . . yeah." I rolled over onto my side. Maybe too early for bedtime, but not for a nap. Something warm and soft floated over me, then tucked around my shoulders. A hint of Polo . . . a light scratch of stubble against my cheek.

"Te quiero, mi niña." Soft . . . like a dream.

"Love you, too, Papi."

As I drifted off, I heard the faint beeping of the kitchen phone being dialed, and then Papi's voice—

"Hey. No, she's fine. I just wanted to make sure everything was good with you."

10

I studied my printed daily schedule as I sipped from my *café con leche,* heavy on the *café* this morning.

"Hey."

Jaime stood beside me, holding a mug and a plate like the one I had in front of me, except mine only held one *pastelito,* not . . . I counted one, two, three, *four* of the bad boys on his. Jeez, to be tall and lanky with hollow legs.

"Please . . . sit down before your arm falls off from the strain of holding all those carbs." Gads, it was funny how this flirting stuff came so easily with him. Except it wasn't really flirting. It was just natural. Easy to talk to him. And got easier every time I saw him.

He laughed as he settled himself at the poolside table. "Good morning to you, too," he said before turning to Elaine. "Morning, Elaine."

She grunted something that sort of sounded like "morning," but didn't bother looking up from her laptop.

"Don't mind her." I waved her off. "She's all excited because she's unearthed some ridiculously obscure articles from long-lost musicology journals."

Hadn't been lying when I told Papi she was digging hanging out here with me. What was not to like? She had wireless Internet for the research she was doing for a journal abstract, got to flirt with Derrick the Security Hottie, even if she had no intention of getting close enough to find out about the Silly Putty thing (the thought of which still gave me a major case of the wiggins), *and* got to do it all in the McMansion by the Sea with every amenity known to man and then some. Plus, endless coffee.

"Forget it—she's as much as gone for the next few hours."

Since Jaime was already used to Elaine in academic guise, he just nodded and went to work on his breakfast, while I returned to my yogurt and granola. Had to eat fast because while the alfresco dining with the ocean view was dandy, it did pose the danger of food that was meant to be eaten cold going warm in a hurry. However, that particular hazard was held off some in spite of the ninety-degree temps because whoever built this barn had the foresight to put giant cooling fans disguised with artistic landscaping around the patio's perimeter. Kept those constant cool breezes floating over our skin even when there wasn't a breeze to be found for miles. Because God forbid the über wealthy do anything as pedestrian as, you know, *perspire.*

Some of the oversize fans even had attached water pumps that blew the occasional cool mist over the patio. So to recap—dewy sheen to the skin, acceptable, sweat, not so. We didn't sit anywhere near those, though, because of Elaine's laptop. Fried to a crisp due to electrocution so not a good look for her.

"You're here early."

I swallowed the last of my yogurt and reached for my *pastelito.* "Not any earlier than usual." Tearing off a corner of the guava-and-cheese pastry, I popped it in my mouth.

"Early enough. Everyone else is still sleeping off last night."

Totally hyped about the night off before we "get down and dirty with some serious work, *mis angelitos,*" according to Esperanza, a bunch of people immediately made plans to go "bond" by hitting some clubs on SoBe. Guess it had been some big fun time if they were still sleeping it off.

"Didn't you go?"

"I'm a lowly, underage AD." The shrug and snort sort of suggested he really didn't care, either. "You?"

"Are you insane? I have to have a chaperone just to be *here.* Can you imagine what a South Beach nightclub would call for?" I laughed. "Besides, right there with you in Underage Land and hello—still very grounded."

Jaime chuckled a little, but it was sympathetic "with you" chuckling, not "you la-*hooser*" mean laughter. Don't think the boy had a mean bone in his body. Which was why I'd already 'fessed up about the whole audition subterfuge and ensuing messy aftermath.

"I'd forgotten you were grounded until you were thirty."

"Yep."

"You don't sound all that broken up about not having gone."

"I'm not." I shrugged and pushed some crumbs around on my plate with my fingertip. "I'm not all that big on the bonding thing." I mean, chatting with Monica in makeup or learning new curse words from Chelo and Tonio didn't exactly qualify as bonding.

He leaned back in his chair, having inhaled his pastries in record time. "I've noticed you sort of keep your distance."

Ya *think*?

Look up "loner" in the dictionary. Might find a picture of me.

Not like I don't know where it comes from. I've hung at Papi's classes and gigs since I was old enough to sit still, talking and learning music with people twenty or more years older. Never seemed weird to me—not like I saw any big differences other than I was, well, shorter than everyone else. And once they realized I was on the same wavelength with the music, I was accepted. Was one of them. But at the same time, not like I could go grab a brew with them after rehearsal, either.

The only real friend I had my own age was Sosi. Don't get me wrong, I'm friendly enough with kids at school, at least, the ones who even bother to speak to me, but Sosi and I have been so tight for so long, know each other so unbelievably well, I think we must have this wall o' invisibility thing going that doesn't invite other people to get close. Which was cool by both of us, but it did add to the whole "not a lot in common with my peer group" syndrome.

"I just don't make friends easily, Jaime." So I was breaking Rule One of *How Not to Commit Social Suicide.* The one where you never, ever admitted what a total dweeb you were. But again, not like it wasn't the truth. "And around here, it doesn't seem like it really pays to. Some of these people aren't going to be around for very much longer."

A small smile curled the edges of his mouth. "You've been making friends with me."

"You're part of the show." And the one person I'd really connected with. I enjoyed hanging with Bianca and Andre well enough, but Jaime and I just . . . clicked. Had since that first day.

"Meaning I'm going to stay around?"

Whoops. There went Rule Two on the *Social Suicide* manual. Never let a boy see your ego or ambition—it's just not feminine, *mija,* and you don't want to emasculate the poor dears. Couldn't tell you how many times I'd been fed that line of bullshit, word for word, by more than one female relative.

"Yeah," I admitted. "You're going to be around." And so am I, was what we both knew was left unsaid.

"You know, most of these guys," I made some vague gesture to the still-quiet house behind us, "they're not so much musicians as they're all about being *stars.*"

"More style than substance?"

"Exactly." And how far was *that* going to get them? I know, I know . . . the music biz is littered with great pretenders. Hello, Milli Vanilli winning the Grammy ring any bells? Remember though, they *did* eventually get busted for not having the goods. Not an issue for me.

What Jaime asked next, though, threw me—big time. "Why are you even here, Ali? You had to know what this was going to be about."

It took me a while to answer. Staring out at the sailboats dotting the bay, I finally said, "It's about the music. I love *everything* about it—learning new charts, playing by myself, impromptu jams— Performing, though, it's like . . . nothing else for me. I don't have to be Britney Spears or Celine Dion, doing her Vegas gig for a gajillion dollars a week." I met his gaze head on. "But I have to perform." And having said all that, *now* I had to go and decide I couldn't look at him anymore.

"Whoa."

Cue the warm flush—up my chest, my neck, and all the way over my face. Even my scalp was all itchy and prickly. But when I snuck a look at him through my lashes, he didn't look freaked or scared by the crazy, intense music nut. Actually, he sort of looked . . . impressed. Which gave me the metaphorical *cojones* to keep going.

"I want to perform professionally, Jaime. *Oye Mi Canto*—it's a stepping-stone." I laughed. "A *really* unexpected stepping-stone since I never thought I'd actually make it this far."

"But now that you're here, you want the whole thing?"

"You got it."

11

Good head space, good head space, good head space.

Maybe if I kept repeating it, I could make myself go there . . . get into that famous good head space that Sosi loved to tease me I was such a pissy diva over. Man, Sosi. What I wouldn't give for her to be here right now. Soothe the opening night nerves. But thank God I had Elaine. Who was sitting off to one side, not hovering or anything, but she was there and her little bits of conversation and the occasional light touch were really soothing and really needed.

"Relax, *bella.* All that tension's going to add wrinkles."

I glared in the mirror at Andre. "How the hell can I add wrinkles to clothes I'm not wearing yet?"

Reaching past Bianca he tapped between my eyebrows. "You're far too young to be working on a set of these. And Botox is so . . ." He shuddered delicately, which, damn him, made me laugh.

"All right, you two take the comedy routine to the dressing room so I can keep working." But Bianca was smiling as she put a mist of some spray over my hair that gave it this silky, glossy sheen that just about reflected the vanity lights.

"About time. And make sure you don't waste too much time with the *nenesita,*" Fabiana snapped at Andre, looking down at her talons, er, nails. Painted a really festive teal with hot pink swirls and little gold microphone charms dangling from each pinky. How classy. *Not.*

"Get her little party dress on, then I want my clothes ready to go, Andre. Some of us," making it clear I wasn't one of the "us," "may have to meet press beforehand."

"What bullshit," I muttered under my breath to Elaine as we walked with Andre toward the dressing room. "No one's meeting any press until after the show's over. She must think I'm fatally stupid."

"Don't sweat it, Ali," Elaine said. "That chick's got a stick shoved so far up her ass, by all rights you should see it every time she opens her mouth."

I giggled at that image. "Which is entirely too often."

"And screw subtle with the makeup, Bianca. I want people to be able to *see* me."

It was kind of reassuring to realize she was that rude with most everyone. Still, she seemed to reserve a certain amount of extra venom for me. You know, though, the more she tried to get in my face with her nasty 'tude, the easier it got to ignore her ass. Sort of like the teachers in the *Peanuts* cartoons. Nothing more than gibberish you could tune out at will.

Andre closed the door behind us. "*Dios mío,* I wonder if it's possible to Botox a mouth shut."

I collapsed against the wall, giggling wildly. "Duct tape. Gets the job done and a lot cheaper."

Andre looked thoughtful. "Maybe itching powder in the bitch's thong?"

"Oh stop . . ." I carefully wiped tears away. "If I mess up my makeup, I'm telling Bianca it's all your fault."

"Tell her about the itching powder. She'll not only forgive you, but knowing her, she might decide to get some and add it to Fabiana's makeup," Elaine said with a nasty chuckle.

Maybe not my traditional good, *quiet* head space, but laughter was definitely good for loosening up. And God, did I need to be loose tonight.

"That's it, baby. We need to keep you relaxed. Come on." Andre helped me up off the floor where my giggling self had collapsed. "Come see what your *Tío* Andre has for your big television debut."

As he led me to the screened-off area that was a twin to the one back at the house, I chanced a look up at the clock. An hour. Plenty of time to curtain. I could do this. If I didn't hurl first.

Ten minutes later and I was dressed, out of the room, and looking for that quiet spot I needed to warm up and get into the head space.

It was kind of tough, because Venezia wasn't a true theater, but a nightclub—one of the hottest nightclubs on Miami Beach—home away from home to people with bank accounts bigger than *Tía* Bernice's ass. Normally, my chances of ever seeing the inside of this joint would've hovered somewhere between slim, none, and "in your dreams," but here we were. *Oye Mi Canto*'s broadcast home for the duration.

"Are you okay, Ali?"

I blinked my eyes and looked down into Elaine's concerned face. Down, because Andre had given me these ridiculous four-inch heels that were like works of art to look at, but walking in them was a total bitch. Short distances were my limit.

"Yeah, I'm good." Had a nice, reasonably quiet spot staked out against a wall where I could warm up and keep an eye on the wings for my cue without being in the way or seeing what was happening onstage.

"*Mira,* here's a bottle of water and your chamois. I'm going to see if Robbie's here yet with Sosi, but I'll be back in plenty of time, okay?"

Barely heard her. It was already starting. "Okay." Felt the brush of her hand against my cheek as I let my eyes drift shut again. Didn't need them to be open just yet. Easing the leather strap over my head, I settled my guitar in place and strummed a few experimental chords. I'd done a full vocal warm-up already, and tuned and adjusted my guitar, but it didn't hurt to do it again. A slight tweak on one of the tuners . . . a light run on something familiar. "Bella Luna," of course.

Seeing as it was now officially my good luck song.

A few more runs, then I eased the Bernabé off, propping it against the wall beside me and closing my eyes again, humming to keep my vocal cords warm and visualizing my performance for what seemed like the one thousandth time since Gabriel, the show's music director, and I had begun working on my piece for the first round. Wasn't entirely sure it was completely in my comfort zone yet, but I had no choice. Rehearsal time was over.

Applause . . . yeah, *applause.* It was just as important to visualize the reaction you wanted as it was the performance you wanted. Lovely, lovely applause and lots of it . . .

"There you are, Ali, you've got ten minu— Oh, wow."

My eyes snapped open.

"What? Is something wrong? Is my makeup messed up? Oh man, did you just say ten minutes? Do I have enough time to get Bianca to fix it? *Ay no . . . no, Dios mío—*"

Jaime reached down at the same time I did to save my guitar from toppling over. Oh God, *no* . . . not my guitar.

"No, no . . . hey, I'm sorry. I'm *so* sorry. Totally didn't mean to startle you."

He had. And in more ways than one. For one thing, his hand was still over mine on the head of my guitar, which was startling, but . . . nice. Then there was the way his other hand was wrapped around my upper arm, kind of holding me steady. Also nice. And a Very Good Thing. Oh boy, I *had* to find out what cologne Jaime wore. Didn't smell like he bathed in it, like most Latin guys of my acquaintance; more like just enough to make me want to get closer. Way closer. And *now* was so not the time to be thinking this way. I had a performance to get ready for and I had to go out there thinking of nothing but the gig, or I'd be packing my bag a whole lot sooner than expected.

"You look amazing, Ali."

Jaime said I looked amazing.

Ohmigod, there went Sister Constanza's butterflies again. "Th-thanks." Deep breath. "Ten minutes?"

Releasing my arm, he looked down at his watch. "More like eight now."

Deep breath. *Whoa.* Not that deep. Hyperventilation and ensuing head rush, bad. But as Jaime and I just stared at each other—definitely a little head rush action going on, complete with some light buzzing in my ears and who knows if it was due to the deep breathing or not and *dang* it, I needed to be thinking. About. The. Performance.

A nasty squawking noise that sounded sort of like Jaime's name startled both of us out of the mutual stare.

"Ow, *shit.*" Jaime pulled the earpiece of his headset away from his ear and shook his head, before gingerly sliding it back into place. He looked at me, eyebrows raised. After I nodded, he moved his hand from over mine on the guitar and pressed a button on the monitor clipped to his belt. "Yeah, boss, I've got her. No, don't know where she is. Yes, I'll make sure they're both in place. Yes, I know we're down to six minutes."

Releasing the button and shoving the mouthpiece out of the way, he asked, "Where's Elaine?"

"Right here."

Had she been standing there long and if she had, what had she seen? Not like there'd been anything to see no matter *what* it felt like.

"What do you need from me?"

Indicating that we needed to be moving toward the stage, Jaime explained, "They want you in the wings, as visible moral support for Ali."

"Well, duh, where else would she be?"

Jaime grinned over his shoulder as he walked a couple steps ahead. "Ah, but they want her strategically placed where the cameras can get suitably dewy-eyed shots from your support system."

"You have got to be kidding me." Dewy-eyed shots? Were they serious?

"Not a surprise, *mija.* While I was talking to your father and Sosi, some of the cameramen were staking out where he was seated so they could get shots of him during your performance, and Esperanza mentioned something about maybe a quick interview with him from the audience afterward."

I rolled my eyes. "Oh, he'll *love* that. Get to tell everyone what a juvenile delinquent I was in even getting on the show."

Elaine patted my back. "He's very proud of you, Ali."

"He thinks I'm very nuts."

"That, too," she chuckled. "He'll get used to you making your own decisions."

"By the time I'm forty-six maybe."

"Maybe."

"Shhhh!"

I bet I chipped some enamel off my teeth, hard as I snapped my mouth shut. Not pissing Esperanza off. Not now.

"All right, Ali, you're first up, the intros are finished, we're almost done with the rehearsal/prep-week video montage, two-minute commercial break, Chianna and Fredo do their little shtick, then they intro you, you ready?"

"Uh-huh." *No* idea what she'd just said. Not a single clue.

"You'll be fine, *mija*. We're all with you." *Santa María*, was Elaine's hand warm. Sort of needed that, because it was tough to play with blocks of ice for hands.

A few strands of hair tickled my ear along with a warm whisper of breath. "Break a leg, Ali."

Touching my cheek, I turned, but he was already gone, shouldering his way through the people crowding the wings.

"All right, Ali, it's time, it's time, here we go—"

Everything sounded like I was hearing it underwater and at really slow speeds. There was Elaine nodding, Esperanza smiling, looking calm and in control and stressed all at the same time, saying "break a leg" while one of Bianca and Andre's assistants applied a final dusting of powder over my face and brushed on a fresh coat of lipstick. Then—the dulcet, all-the-accent's-been-trained-out-of-them tones of the two young *telenovela* actors they'd brought on as hosts because they were hot, hot, *hot*, bay-*bee*.

"¡*Bienvenida* Alegría Montero, *a Oye Mi Canto*!"

Showtime.

12

"It's okay, *mija,* it's okay, you're fine, it's okay . . ."

Thank God I hadn't eaten. So there wasn't a whole lot that was coming up, but I just couldn't stop heaving and shaking and crying.

"*Shhh,* Ali, you're fine. You're fine, it's okay, really, it's okay."

"It's n-not okay, Elaine. It's not," I managed to gasp out before another round of heaves took over. "I can't do this. I *can't.*"

Elaine rose and left me there, collapsed on the floor of the oversized bathroom stall, hugging the sleek, high-tech toilet. I didn't give a rat's ass that it was sleek and high tech. It was a toilet. I'd lucked out, actually, since there were also bidets in here, as well. Which would've been par for my course tonight, my hurling into something that would hurl back at me.

God, Andre was going to kill me if I messed up my clothes. Just kill me. And I couldn't blame Elaine for leaving. It was nothing less than I *deserved,* to have my sorry ass left, all abandoned on a cold, high-class marble floor. I was the saddest of the sad, a miserable, loser excuse for a human. A second later, though, she was back and I felt a towel, damp and deliciously cool, against my overheated skin.

"You *can* do this, Alegría. If only to prove to yourself that you made the right decision."

Finally the world—and my stomach—quit spinning and twirling like the Tea Cup Party ride at Disney. Papi never would take me on that ride as a kid. Now I knew why. Pushing myself up, I staggered out of the stall and to the sink where I rinsed my mouth. Oh, and look, wasn't I lucky? Only a few steps away, a huge purple leather couch, one of a pair that were stationed in the ladies' lounge that was bigger than the second floor of our townhouse. God, this was surreal.

"I can't take another seven weeks of this, Elaine. Good thing I won't have to." A couple slow tears, aftermath, I guess, trickled from my eyes and down into my hair as I stared up at the ceiling.

Elaine dropped down next to me and resumed wiping my face. "God, girl, you are so full of shit. 'Won't have to,' indeed. You know you were good out there."

I lifted my head just far enough to meet her gaze. A long, long silence hung between us, then her eyes widened.

"*De verdad,* you really don't know—do you?"

"Elaine, *te lo juro,* my last memory is of that chump, what's his name—Frodo?"

"Fredo."

"Whatever. Calling my name, and next thing I know, I'm here, paying homage to the porcelain god."

"Nothing?"

"*Nada.* Which means I'm clearly trying to block out the horror of it all."

Couldn't blame her for the disbelieving stare. It was pretty freakin' unbelievable. I'd somehow lost over five minutes of my immediate past and illegal substances weren't even involved. If I could package that, I'd make a fortune and get to perform just for fun. But how do you package pure fear?

A knock sounded at the door. "Everyone decent?"

"Yeah, Andre."

At Elaine's answer, he breezed in, clearly not caring that he was in the ladies' lounge.

"Uh, you do realize—" I started, then stopped as one eyebrow that was prettier and even more well-groomed than mine went up.

"Never mind, you realize and you don't care."

"God no," he snorted. "Sometimes the little gay boys' room is just too skanky for words, precious. And I've had some of the best se—"

Hey, why'd he stop? Then I saw that Elaine was laying the patented Dr. Garces professorial stare on him. The one that reduced most Ph.D. candidates to spineless goo.

"*Oye,* I'm beyond open-minded, but I also have to answer to her father. Don't make me have to lie."

"All right, then. Story for another time." He winked and grinned and looked entirely too cheerful for my current mental state. Couldn't he see my pain? Wasn't it obvious?

"And anyhow, I only have a couple minutes before I have to go beautify Tonio. Not that he's not pretty already."

I sighed. Had to cut this off or it was five minutes of how adorable Tonio was and have you *seen* those abs? "Was there something you wanted to tell me?"

"Just wanted to check on you, *mi vida.* And to make sure you didn't miss it." While he spoke, he leaned over me, blotting my forehead and cheeks with some little papers he pulled from his pocket.

"Open."

"Mith wha—?" I mumbled around the breath strip he'd popped into my mouth.

"Your performance. Look up." He used a corner of the damp towel Elaine had been using on my face to gently wipe beneath each eye. "Open again."

"Her performance?"

Oh, *gracias,* Elaine. Even mumbling was restricted now, since Andre was busy applying a coat of lipstick.

"Yeah, they're running the show on a monitor in the greenroom on a half-hour delay. That way, you lovely talented darlings can catch your performances and decide whether to celebrate or commit hara-kiri." He reached over to where I'd kicked off my silver stilettos and slipped them back on, then adjusted my neckline and did a quick fluff of my hair.

"There. That'll do for a quick fix, although you'll have to let Bianca have at you before you go back onstage for the vote announcement."

Which was going to come an hour after the show's conclusion, live, over the end credits of *Noches en Paraíso,* which, in a miraculous twist of fate and programming genius, happened to be the very same *telenovela* that Chianna and Frodo—*damn*—Fredo, our hot, hot, *hot* hosts happened to star on as a hot, hot, *hot* couple.

Convenient and taking shameless advantage in a way that only Latin television can. But at least the live audience didn't have to suffer through the *novela.* They got to dance to tunes spun by a supercool DJ or have a cocktail . . . basically got to party as someone's dreams were about to get shot to hell based on the whims of grannies who liked pretty boys and teenagers with unlimited minutes on their cellphones or high-speed Internet connections.

Moi? Cynical? Or maybe it was just the whole hurling my entire lower intestine thing making me cranky.

"Come on." Andre hauled me off the sofa and Elaine handed me my guitar, which had been resting on the other sofa. Before he opened the door, he leveled a stare at me. "It's no secret what you came in here to do, girl. There was some buzz. Trick is to act like it don't matter one bit, because trust me, you won't be the last it happens to."

Couldn't have timed it any better. No sooner did Andre open

the door than Guillermo, the shy, quiet guy from Argentina who was an absolute animal onstage, went running past us, flushed and sweaty, hand over his mouth in the universal gesture.

I was probably a horrible person for poor Guillermo's agony making me feel so much better.

"Save some breath strips for him too, okay, Andre?"

"Absolutely, *mi muñeca*. He's a sweet boy."

We made our way back to the greenroom where a crowd was already beginning to gather around the big, flat-screen monitor that a couple techs were hooking up. As it flickered to life and images began flashing across the screen, I staked out a spot against the wall. Good spot for viewing, and maybe more important, a clear path to the door if my performance blew chunks and I had to make a quickie exit.

"You didn't suck, so quit looking like that."

I accepted the bottle of ginger ale Elaine held out along with the handful of *galletas Maria* she must've snagged from the buffet on our way into the room. Had to say this about our production company—in true Latin fashion, they believed in making food available everywhere, at all times, and in mondo quantities.

"Easy for you to say." I took a bite from one of the bland cookies and chased it down with a sip of soda. "*You've* seen it. Whereas my mind is still conjuring hideous images." And probably would until I saw the carnage for myself. I nibbled my way through the rest of the cookie like a nervous rabbit as I watched the opening credits roll with our pictures flashing by while Gloria's *Oye Mi Canto* played. At least my headshot was good. Photoshop is a godsend.

Fredo and Chianna were all sparkly capped teeth and charm—in other words, boring as shit. Part of me wanted them to quit babbling and get *on* with it already. Of course, the other part of me wanted them to go on forever, 'cause if they went on forever, then they wouldn't get to me. I had the brief reprieve of the ten-minute clip of "behind the scenes" footage taken with the camera crews who'd been following us around. Lots of shots of us in meetings with Esperanza, modeling different looks in wardrobe, and snippets of our rehearsals with Gabriel and the house band, all set to this custom reggaeton chart with a really groiny beat.

"Here you go, Ali." Elaine's voice floated toward me, soft and reassuring. "You were fantastic, *mija*."

Uh-huh. Whatever she said.

Hail Mary, full of grace . . . And felt the rest dribble straight out of my head as I saw myself . . . not the *me* myself I was used to seeing every day, but the one I'd seen for the first time that day in wardrobe, the one Andre had called a "star." Because that self-assured chick who crossed the stage in the flowing silver-blue satin trousers and sapphire blue tunic with tiny rhinestones sprinkled all over it? Who calmly settled herself on the stool and propped her guitar on her lap? Wasn't me. No way. Just couldn't be.

The lights dimmed, leaving a lone spot illuminating me/her on the stool.

"You looked like a moonbeam out there, Ali."

I tore my gaze away from the screen and gawked at Jaime, who'd somehow just appeared beside me. That was just . . . the most poetic, sweetest— I took another gulp of ginger ale to ease the tickling in my throat and desperately hoped I wasn't carrying the scent of eau de barf.

"Moonbeam?" Was this guy for real?

"*Shhh.* Just watch. You were amazing."

Dazed, I watched myself count off the funky, intricate intro to "Bamboleo," a José Feliciano chart by way of the Gipsy Kings via a Venezuelan folk song. How about *that* for covering the Latin bases, huh? A little on the vintage side, but that's what suited me and, more importantly, was aimed right at the audience the producers thought I'd appeal to. Besides, our music director and I had worked up this totally fresh arrangement, keeping it jazzy but with the *most* raucous flamenco-style guitar breaks that kicked total ass. In fact, didn't waste any time getting into one of those breaks, just four measures in. My stomach got all knotty and tense as the camera zoomed in for a close-up on my hands and—

My *God.*

Jaime was right. Elaine was right. I was . . . amazing. I'd never before seen myself playing like this. Grainy footage from a home video or a couple shots from a distance as I performed at a *quinces* or a family party, sure, but *this*—this was high-quality, supersharp definition. Those were *my* hands, moving with incredible precision, each tone clear and vibrant, even at the juiced-up tempo.

Then a pan back as I began singing, my alto throaty and almost seductive. Holy cow, Papi probably had a conniption when he heard me. *I* was almost having a conniption. Honest to God, I *never* sounded quite like that during rehearsals. Then all of a sudden, in a whirl of lights, the horns jumped in, the guys in the band moving in a blaze of color and sound, with their open-collared red-and-black shirts, and their hot, syncopated riffs, the flute carrying high and sweet over the bright, rich sounds of the brass section. And there I was, throwing my head back, laughing, before lowering it for another one of those crazy solo runs along the strings of my Bernabé, which had never looked more beautiful, glowing under the stage lights.

"Look, Ali—*look* how you had them all."

My gaze darted to Elaine and back to the screen where the cameras were panning over the audience, showing people swaying and clapping in their seats, couples dancing in the areas that had been left clear between every few tables. One of the reasons the producers had opted for a nightclub rather than a theater. They wanted to have the room for dancing, if people felt the spirit move them. Right—*if.* There was a laugh. There was just no way you could put a bunch of Latinos in a room with music and *not* expect dancing. Sort of like serving *arroz* without the benefit of *frijoles.* Just didn't happen.

Judging by the way those couples were dancing, they were feeling a metric buttload of spirit, too. And I'd done that. *I* had done that.

Then the camera zoomed in on Sosi and Papi at their table. Sosi bobbing her head and grinning like a fool—a blessedly familiar expression. She'd always looked like that when I played—my biggest champion and fan outside of Papi.

Papi. He looked floored. Utterly and completely like he'd been slapped upside the head repeatedly with something very heavy. Oh boy. Guess I'd done that, too.

I held that last note out for what seemed like forever, until the final scorching run by the horns and it was over—my head thrown back, my right arm straight up, in that showy, blow-'em-out sort of finale that I'd never imagined being able to pull off.

I watched as that stranger who looked like me bowed, a confident, "I know I've just kicked your ass" smile on her face; who was self-possessed enough to turn and acknowledge the band because hey, they'd kicked ass, too, and gracefully accepted a kiss on the cheek from Gabriel, our insanely talented band leader and musical director before walking off, waving to the still-applauding crowd.

And then proceeded to go hurl my lungs out.

You know what, though? It's not like I was even the best one. One of the best, sure, but the preliminary judges had done their job right. It was way safe to say we had a hellaciously talented group, on the whole. Sweet, sexy Guillermo had most of the girls saying, "Juanes *who*?" while Tonio sang this ballad, half in English, half in Spanish, that was like the essence of Frankie J, Chayanne, and Marvin Gaye all wrapped up together. Ha—I even caught Elaine fanning herself a little.

Even Fabiana, much as it pained me to admit it, bounded out there to "La Copa de la Vida" and pulled a total Ricky Martin, driving the crowd crazy as she shimmied in her black leather pants and encouraged them to rush the stage and sing along with her during the chorus.

But at the end of the night . . . after the votes had been phoned in or done via the Web and tallied up, and we were all herded back onstage for the announcement, I wasn't surprised to be accepting applause as part of the group that was going on to the next round.

The real surprise would've been if I didn't make it.

It was really gratifying, too, how happy most everyone was to see me move on.

Emphasis, of course, on "most."

13

Oh no. No, no, *noooo.* It was just way too early for the Black Eyed Peas' "Let's Get it Started." Even if it was noon. Which it wasn't. A bleary squint at my digital clock revealed it to be . . . 6:30? In the *morning*? Was she *insane*?

I shoved my head under the pillow and waited for the Peas to stop. Which they did. Then started. Again. It was hopeless. Reaching one arm out from beneath my nice, warm covers, I grabbed my cell, cutting off the customized ringtone.

"Sosi, is Orlando Bloom on your front step?"

"No, but—"

"Then is he sitting at the end of your bed, feeding you peeled grapes and telling you you're the most delectable thing in the world, more exquisite than even Liv Tyler with elf ears?"

"No, but—"

"Then why are you calling me at—" A quick glance at the digital clock again, making sure the hideous truth was still as hideous as I remembered. "Six thirty-four A.M. on the first morning I've had to sleep in, in nearly three *weeks*?"

"Because it's the only chance I'll have to talk to you before I have to go be a peppy youth counselor at Camp Hell on Earth, and you get back to working on that Latin Superstar thing."

"Shut up." Rolling over, I shoved my hair out of my face and rubbed sleep from my eyes. "Come on, Sos, it's an arts camp, not juvenile detention. How bad can it really be?"

"Oh yeah?" I jerked the phone away from my ear as her voice went up to outraged yelping levels. "You try taking an hour-long bus ride, with thirty-seven screeching monsters for a field trip to an art museum where they'll giggle over the naked people pictures, then suffer through another hour-long trip back, *then* we'll talk."

"Trade you Fabiana."

"Never mind." Ha. I could almost see her shuddering at the prospect. "I'll take the monsters."

"Thought so," I laughed. "All right. So what's so important you had to wake my ass up?"

"Go turn on your computer."

"What?"

"Come on, Ali, I don't have a lot of time. Just turn it on."

"Okay, okay . . . jeez." Kicking off my tangled sheets and bed-spread, I stumbled across the room and jabbed a finger at the power button, getting it on the second try. "What is it?"

"You'll see."

Okay, I knew Sosi *way* too well. And she sounded *way* too cheerful for six-whatever-it-was in the morning. Almost like she was trying not to laugh hysterically. "Sosi . . ."

"You running yet?"

The blue start-up screen gave way to my desktop wallpaper of Sting's *Nothing Like the Sun* album cover. "Yeah."

"Open your browser and go to salsafresca-dot-com."

"What?"

"Just *do* it."

Muttering really nasty things under my breath, I fumbled for the earpiece for my phone at the same time I one-handed typed the address Sosi had given me. And proceeded to drop phone, earpiece, and my jaw as this huge picture of me—from last night?—began building onscreen. But how could that even be possible? It was only last *night*. But no . . . there it was . . . on my screen . . . me, in the spotlight, clearly at the end of the performance with my head thrown back as a big, ginormous "Es Picante. Es Fresca. Es . . . Ali Montero" arced across the top of the screen in a fancy-pants silver script that . . . oh, God help me, *sparkled.* Entirely too gaudy for this early in the morning. Entirely too gaudy, period.

"Ali? Ali? Do you see it? Are you there? *Ali!*"

My horrified stare never leaving the screen, I groped around on the floor for my phone. Finally grabbing hold of it, I tossed the earpiece aside as a lost cause. "Sosi Cabrera, if this is your idea of a joke, I swear, I'm going to kill you. This is so not funny."

"*Te lo juro, mija.* Not me. Check it out—looks like it's a couple kids from Mexico who are crushing on you big time."

"Oh, come *on.*" Crushing on *me*? Please. But she was right about it being two kids. There was an "About Us" link that, when I clicked on it, revealed two boys, fourteen, fifteen maybe, from Cabo San Lucas. Life must be mighty slow out there if they had nothing better to do than *this.*

"Just look around the site, girl. It's like the 'I Love Ali' homage. In English *and* Spanish."

As I started clicking on the other links, the true depth of the horror dawned. Oh man, she wasn't kidding. There was a whole series of screen caps from last night's performance and the behind-the-scenes video montage. Biographical info they had to have gakked from the show's site and—

"Sosi, they've got my ninth grade yearbook picture!" Complete with braces and the gigantic zit on my chin that all the concealer in the world hadn't been able to hide.

Just kill me *now.*

"Yeah, actually, I was hoping you wouldn't find *that.*" Her voice was sympathetic. "But the caption they wrote for it is really nice, Ali."

"Before she became the beautiful performer we all met on *Oye Mi Canto,* Ali Montero was another student just like the rest of us," I read out loud. "I still *am* a student just like the rest of us!"

"Not anymore you're not, Ali. Not to people like those two kids." Man . . . Sosi's voice was so serious, so not like her . . . I almost dropped the phone again.

"I'm not gonna change, Sos. I swear."

"Like I'd let you," she snorted. "You know I'd slap you into next week if you went all Brunhilda."

But you know, I could hear something that sounded like relief in her voice. Prompted me to repeat, "I swear," with what I hoped was a nice dose of conviction. Because I wasn't going to change. Not as far as Sos or Papi or Elaine or anyone important to me was concerned. I mean, come on—they *knew* me. Could call me on the carpet on everything. And slap me into next week. Besides, outside of two boys with clearly eccentric tastes from Resortville, Mexico, who was going to care who *I* was?

"How'd you find this anyway?"

"Google, natch." Her voice was back to its normal, cheerful self. "Wanted to see if there were any newspaper reviews of the show, actually, and this site came up near the top of the search."

I kept clicking through the site, careful to avoid the Ninth Grade Terror. The pictures I was seeing still didn't look much like me, but that *was* the outfit I'd worn last night. All silver and blue, which probably had something to do with Jaime saying I looked like a moonbeam. The memory of which, along with that of the whispered "break a leg," made me go a little warm and shivery.

"All right. Gotta jet." Sosi's voice came over the phone again. "Have to get coffee in me before I can face the monsters."

"Okay, Sosi. I'd say thanks for calling and telling me about this, but I'm not sure you deserve anything approaching gratitude for doing this to me so early in the morning." I shook my head at the tacky, sparkly Salsa Fresca banner that, the more I looked at it, almost seemed to be fluttering from my upraised hand, and sighed. "At least they didn't use alimontero-dot-com."

"They couldn't."

Her voice was way too matter-of-fact. "They couldn't?"

"Nope. I reserved it."

"What? You did? When?"

"Same day you auditioned and Jaime said you'd made it. Went home and reserved alimontero-dot-com and alegriamontero-dot-com and ali-dot-com. Didn't know which one you'd want to use, so I figured I should snag them all. One-year subscriptions for the time being. Happy early birthday."

"Use? Subscriptions?" It was like the chick was speaking a foreign language.

"Yeah, for your official website."

"Wait, wait, *wait!* Aren't we getting just a little ahead of ourselves here, Sos?"

"Nope." She was totally calm and sure of herself. "You win this sucker and that's going to be one of the first things your fans are going to demand from you, I guarantee it. I'm planning on heading up your street team already, so don't let anyone else snag that gig, okay?"

She was crazy. She was insane. And it was one of the reasons I loved her as much as any real-life sister I could have had.

"Go," I said, laughing. "Get your coffee and tend to your monsters. I'll call you later."

"Promise?"

"Absolutely. I'll be figuring out what chart to do for next week—may need input."

"Ooh, can't wait. Okay, I'm outtie. Monsters await."

"Have fun." Setting the phone aside, I browsed through the site one more time, before taking a deep breath and typing "Ali Montero" in the Google search engine.

I am such a goob. Hadn't even occurred to me to look for myself online. But, of course, it would occur to Sosi. She'd probably been checking since she reserved those domain names, the sneaky *chica.*

After a couple seconds, the list came up. The official site for *Oye Mi Canto* was first, no big surprise there, with Salsa Fresca right after, and then a list of newspapers, beginning with the *Miami Herald.* That was the link I clicked first.

> MIAMI—Last night's premiere of new Latin American talent show 'Oye Mi Canto' came loaded with the expected Jennifer Lopez and Ricky Martin imitators, pretty and reasonably talented, but possessing little to set them apart from the thousands of other pretty and reasonably talented singers out there in search of that elusive prize: stardom. There were, however, a few pleasant surprises in the two-hour telecast, beginning with the first performer of the evening, Miami native, Alegría Montero. Only seventeen, young Ali, as she's known, nearly blew the roof off trendy nightclub Venezia, with her skilled, rousing rendition of "Bamboleo," setting the bar to a near-impossible high, challenging the other performers who had to follow.
>
> A few came close, especially Argentine heartthrob-in-the-making Guillermo Correas, with his hard-driving

rock appeal, and New York-bred Tonio de la Cruz, a natural balladeer with a smoky, sexy stage presence. Joaquin Arzeno came from the Dominican Republic armed with Justin Timberlake moves and a Daddy Yankee attitude that lit up the audience and the dance floor, while other local product, Fabiana, will likely go far with her high energy and made-for-video appeal . . .

14

The next couple weeks settled into something of a normal pattern, that is, if normal was fifteen- and sixteen-hour days spent rehearsing and interviewing and rehearsing and trying on clothes and rehearsing and going into the recording studio to lay down tracks. Did I mention the rehearsing? To think, the first week I'd bitched about not playing or singing at all. Now there were days I wondered if my fingers were going to stay attached.

Of course, amidst the rehearsing and other stuff, there was that little thing called the competition.

Week two said good-bye to Riann, from Nicaragua, and Natalia, the Venezuelan beauty queen who was way up on the More Style than Substance scale. Which is probably what ultimately did her in—her style, or lack thereof, in the form of one seriously fugly yellow-orange, beaded-and-sequined catsuit. First, *not* a good color on anyone—and all those beads and sequins on a butt that rivals Beyoncé's? Couldn't even remember what she'd sung, but I could remember *that.* Tragic.

Poor Andre. We had to run for the smelling salts to revive him when he saw her on the monitor, because that wasn't at *all* what he'd sent her out of wardrobe wearing. Actually, I would've *killed* for the outfit the bimbo ditched—a sexy-as-all-get-out, fitted black tuxedo worn with nothing underneath except a burgundy bra with rhinestone trim that caught the lights just right.

Super, super hot, but Andre had slapped my wrist just like a cranky nun when I reached for it on the rack during one of our try-on sessions.

"No, precious. Not for you. At least, not for another five or six years. I definitely do not want your Papi coming after me for letting you go out onstage in that, seeing as I'm very fond of my boy bits."

So the wannabe beauty queen had gotten it and had ditched it for a getup that made her look like a tacky drag queen—Andre's words, not mine, I swear.

Then, week three saw a big "see ya" to Jorge, the cute SoCal Chicano and Mirta, our lone Peruvian contestant. Guess the native music-gone-dancehall approach didn't do it for the viewers—a shame, since I thought it was a pretty happening chart, but honestly, when it was all said and done? Better her than me.

So here we were, beginning of week four, down to ten of us, five girls, five guys, and having a big group meeting for the first time in ages. We'd been so "go your own way" the first few weeks, I had little more than a passing acquaintance with the other competitors, especially with my going home every night. Which came as more of a relief than I would've ever imagined. Even if it was past midnight, which it was a lot, Papi would always be waiting up, and he'd make me some tea with honey and lemon for my throat and give me a hand massage with the good Ahava hand cream to keep my hands supple and relax them after the hours of practice.

Really, the biggest constants in my day-to-day life at the McMansion were Bianca, Andre, and Gabriel, the music director; Elaine, of course—and Jaime.

Somehow, no matter how nuts the day was, we always managed to catch up with each other, usually at lunch or dinner. It was . . . nice. He was nice. Okay, more than nice.

"Okay, *mis angelitos,* we're starting to cook with some serious gas now." Esperanza was on her step stool so she could look over us, but with the hordes considerably thinner for this meeting, didn't use a microphone. "First things first, our ratings are going through the roof and our U.S. network affiliate has decided it's time to start adding us to more markets. More markets means more audience, more audience means more revenue—and votes, of course," she finished with a laugh.

Waiting a minute for that to sink in, she went on. "Now, since the last thing anyone can call the entertainment industry is static, we're going to be shaking things up from here on out, keeping you lovelies on your toes. A lot of it is going to be musical in nature and on that, I'm going to let Gabriel give you the goods, but I do have one little surprise for you."

She shot us this genuinely evil grin that had me feeling a little sick. Why did I have a feeling this wasn't going to be as great as *she* thought it was?

"Starting this week, we're going to have a pair of celebrity commentators. They're going to rotate every week, and while they don't take part in the voting process, it's possible what they say may have an impact on the voting. They could love you, they could hate you—just think of them like Forrest Gump's box of chocolates: you never know what you're gonna get."

"¿Qué?" Guillermo whispered next to me.

"Luego," I whispered back. It would take more than just a few quick words on the sly to explain Forrest's particular brand of wisdom.

Tonio piped up from his place in the corner of the big sofa. "*Oye, chica,* you gonna tell us who the first pair's gonna be?"

"Nope." Her grin got bigger—my nausea did, too. "That's part of the fun. Surprise for the audience, surprise for you. Surprises all around."

Oh, now that wasn't nice at *all.*

"So that's my big news—I'll let Gabriel take over from here." Stepping down from the stool, she moved aside as our music director, short, round, and one of the most kick-ass musicians I'd ever met, moved the step stool, preferring to lean against a table.

"*Bueno,* here's the deal." He looked at each of us in turn as he spoke. "As professionals there are any number of things to which you must become accustomed. One thing you should expect, and should *want* to do, is to stretch your boundaries—expand your musical horizons. So this is something we're going to begin working on this week—mixing up styles, trying new things. Then as we continue on, we're going to ultimately come full circle, examining your unique identities, what sets you apart from the pack and makes you stand out as potential stars."

The crack of popping gum echoed like a shot. Fabiana, sprawled in a big chair and staring at her latest nasty manicure. Could she look any more bored with the whole thing? But Gabriel didn't even bat an eyelash—just ignored her as much as she seemed to be ignoring him.

"Another aspect of the profession is collaboration. You've been learning what it's like to work with the band—"

Crossing his arms, he smiled, showing two deep dimples that made him look like one of Santa's swarthier elves. "Now you have to learn to work with each other."

Say *what*? Oh, please, please, *por favor,* don't let that mean what I think it meant. Again, Tonio to the rescue.

"Yo, man, what's that mean exactly?"

"What it means is that this week, we're pairing you up and your performance will consist of a duet—in a musical style you haven't tried yet, of course."

Oh yeah. It was true.

"It also means you live and die as a pair."

Dang, but Esperanza looked happy, in a really evil sort of way, sitting on the table behind Gabriel, one leg propped up. I was kind of surprised she wasn't cackling and rubbing her hands together.

"Meaning we're going to get voted off as a pair?"

My voice. I wasn't even aware of having said anything, but it was definitely my voice. So I must've asked the question. And Esperanza was nodding.

"You got it, Ali. It was the best way we could come up with to keep things totally fair. Ensure there wouldn't be any potential sabotage of a partner, not that we're saying any of you would do such a thing."

Yeah . . . *riiiight.* I know *I* wasn't the only one who snuck a look toward Fabiana, who was still ignoring the proceedings. Or at least pretending to, because really, how interesting could blood-red nails be? Even with tiny gold dragon appliqués.

"I want Guillermo."

She wasn't ignoring anything—and she wasn't completely stupid. Guillermo had been superpopular every week, every performance kicking ass, girls waiting for him outside the club, passing him their phone numbers and giving him stuffed animals and huge bars of the imported Spanish chocolate that he'd mentioned was his favorite during some interview. Wouldn't have surprised me one bit if he was the top overall vote-getter. Being paired up with him? Great way to guarantee moving on.

"You seem to think you have some say in the matter, *mija.*"

Gabriel wasn't a screamer. Even when rehearsals went until nearly midnight and we were hoarse and ready to drop, he kept this even, mellow tone that reminded me so much of Papi when he was in teaching mode, it brought out this automatic respect and desire to do my best for him. So even now, he didn't raise his voice, but the look on his face . . . *mira,* that was a different thing. He looked like he wanted to smack Fabiana straight upside her peroxided head.

"Guillermo's going to be paired with Ali; Fabiana, you're with Tonio—I've got a Tejano chart in mind for you two."

"What?" Her jaw dropped as her head swiveled around to glare at me. "Why does the *nenesita* get Guillermo?"

Oh, this *nenesita* shit was getting real old. I was so not a baby girl. At least, not hers. "Bite me, Fabiana."

Momentary silence as everyone in the room turned to stare at me. *I'd* have turned to stare at me if I could. And here I'd been trying so hard to ignore her ass—not lower myself to her level—but man, there was only so much high road a girl could take.

But because Brunhilda couldn't stand to have the spotlight on anyone other than herself she immediately grabbed the attention back, whining, "And Tejano? No way."

"What's your problem, you gotta bitch about every damn thing and have it all your way?" Tonio shoved a scuffed Adidas sneaker into Fabiana's chair, hard enough to move it a couple inches and make her shoot him a nasty look.

"This Queen Bitch act of yours is getting real old, yo. Nobody's won yet."

"Key word is 'yet,' *boricua.*" Fabiana's bright green (and way fake) gaze met Tonio's dark brown as they stared each other down. "I don't know why you doubt it, but I *am* going to win and I'm not going to do it singing that Texican polka crap."

"Kiss my ass, bitch." All of a sudden, Monica was on her feet, her hands balled into fists. Couldn't blame her for being pissed—seeing as she was from Texas. And loved Tejano. "It was good enough to make Selena a multiplatinum star."

"Getting shot and killed was what made her a multiplatinum

star. At least here in the real world outside of Texas and Mexico, and this is where it counts, baby."

Pins dropping would have sounded like the "Anvil Chorus." That's how quiet it got.

I was folding myself into my corner of the sofa, trying to stay the hell out of the way of anything that might come flying. Next to me, Guillermo actually edged forward, like he was looking to get in the middle of things—was he *high?* But then, he leaned in front of me a bit, blocking my body with his.

Even scared as I was, I took the time to send a little prayer of thanksgiving. Look, I could stand up for myself okay, but in the living room equivalent of a street fight? Not my natural habitat and right now, I was big with the love for chivalrous Latin guys.

Finally, after it seemed like the silence was going to explode and take us all with it, Esperanza spoke. "Fabiana, it never ceases to amaze me how your ego is superceded in magnitude only by your ignorance."

"What?"

Guess the words—especially in the Spanish that we'd found out over the last few weeks she was really only barely fluent in—were too big for her.

"Never mind." Hopping off the table, Esperanza came to stand in the middle of the floor, nodding at Monica that she should sit down. Which she did, but her hands stayed clenched, and she looked like she still wanted to take a swing at something. Next to me, Guillermo relaxed, but down at the other end of the sofa, Tonio was still shaking his head and muttering under his breath—at least until Esperanza shot him a look that shut him up in a hurry.

"All of you listen to me and listen well." Esperanza's voice was soft, but her stare was hard and cold as she looked over all ten of us. "First rule of showbiz? Nothing—and no one—is a sure thing." Now her stare shifted right to Fabiana and she switched to English, her voice going even softer. "You've got issues with how the show's being run? The door's right there, and much as I hate clichés, don't let it hit you on the ass on the way out. Are we clear?"

Crystal, baby. At least to me.

But Espie and Fabiana just kept staring at each other. No surprise, Fabiana broke first, although she tried to mask it, tossing her hair and muttering, "Whatever."

After all that drama, it was a major relief to get up to the rehearsal studio, since Guillermo and I were first up. You know, besides the fact that he was so talented and well, let's face it, *hot,* I was really happy to be paired up with Guille for a couple other reasons. For one thing, he was the closest to me in age, twenty-one, and while his scorching rock god stage presence might've made people think he was always that Sex On a Stick, in real life, he was actually almost as reserved as I was. Made him sort of soothing to be around.

"*Oye,* Ali, there you are."

True to his habit, Gabriel rose from the piano and came to give me a kiss hello. Guillermo was already here, but no kiss from him, just a shy nod and quiet, "*Hola,* Ali."

"*Hola,* Guille." I added a wave to my greeting as I returned Gabriel's kiss. "So what've you got cooked up for us?"

He laughed and flicked a finger across my nose as he turned and led the way back to the piano.

"You sure you're up for it, *chiquita*?"

"When have I failed to live up to one of your challenges?" I shot back, lifting the strap of my gig bag over my head and beginning to unzip it.

"You're not going to need it, Ali."

I paused, midzip. "Expanding boundaries?"

"Such a smart *nenesita,*" he teased.

"Urgh." Shuddering, I rezipped my bag and set it carefully in the corner. "Don't call me that. How can something that's supposed to be an endearment sound so totally gross?"

"You don't need to worry about her, Ali. She's completely useless."

Both Gabriel and I stared at Guille. To say he wasn't given to outbursts would be understating it. I mean, that may've been the most words I'd heard him say all at once in the entire time we'd been here. And the tone of voice, while not loud, was scathing and dripping with a nice dose of dislike, so yeah, it qualified as an outburst.

Guille shrugged and hooked a thumb through one of the belt loops on his baggy jeans shorts. "I'd have performed with her if that's what Gabriel wanted, but I'm glad it's you," he added in that lilting Spanish that was so unique to Argentina and was also part of what made him so darned irresistible to the girlies.

Gabriel pointed an approving finger at him. "Whether or not you win this dog-and-pony show, *that's* why you're going to succeed, *mijo.*"

Well, that—and the talent and stage presence and rock-hard bod that his loose U2 concert T-shirt couldn't quite hide. Not to mention the long, streaky blond hair and blue eyes—like a lot of Argentines, there was more than a little German lurking in the boy's DNA.

I know it sounds like I was crushing on him big time, but not really. It would've been easy, don't get me wrong—did have a pulse and all—but these days my tastes were more about lanky and green-eyed.

"Well?" I demanded, reaching for the sheet music on the piano, my eyes widening.

"You recognize it, I take it."

My gaze met Gabriel's, which was . . . oh yeah, he was laughing at me, even if he wasn't laughing out loud. "You have *got* to be kidding. Me? Do this?"

"Pushing out of your comfort zone, Ali," Gabriel reminded me. "Of all the contestants, you're probably the most well-rounded, musically. But I haven't heard you try anything like this."

"There's a lot I haven't tried, Gabriel," I protested. "Dancehall, reggae, hip-hop . . . hell, I'll even give heavy metal a go. Is there such a thing as Heavy Metal *en Español*?" And could I sound any more pathetic?

"Come on, Ali, you can do it. *We* can do it." Guille's hand was on my shoulder, friendly and encouraging. "It will be fantastic."

"I don't know . . ."

So not convinced. And could you blame me? "La Tortura." Shakira and Alejandro Sanz. In a duet that was so wicked hot, it was a miracle the speaker cones didn't melt every time it played.

"Órale." Slapping his palm on the piano to get us to focus, Gabriel slid a disc into the stereo. "Let's just try running through the vocals a time or two. Let you two get a feel for each other."

An hour and three run-throughs later and I was ready to scream, with Gabriel and Guille looking worried. Oh God, I was going to screw this up. For me and for Guille, and he so didn't deserve it. But this wasn't going to work, and it was going to be all my fault.

It wasn't the music—not really. There was no denying it was a great chart and our voices were so good together—Guillermo's warm, slightly raspy tenor blending with my alto like caramel and chocolate. Totally natural combo.

But I just couldn't let myself relax into it, and you could hear it. I sounded shy and hesitant and like the lily-livered virgin I was. Not at *all* what this chart demanded. This song needed verve and energy and sexual heat. I was coming off as bland as *natilla.* I knew what it was—at least part of it. I kept seeing that damn video in my mind's eye, Shakira covered in black goo, dancing—if you could call it that—writhing and sliding across a table toward Alejandro in moves that were probably illegal in several states. I mean, you just *knew* the word "virgin" had left girlfriend's vocabulary a long time ago. More importantly, Alejandro knew it. The way he stared at her . . . touched her—

I mean, even *I* knew what lust was, even if it was just being acted out for the camera.

However.

That said, it was one thing when it was just me and my guitar onstage, me envisioning some imaginary lover—so what if he did take on a familiar form on occasion? Still only existed in my tiny little mind's eye.

It was another thing completely to be expected to perform a song like this with a living, breathing person. I mean, this was all about selling the product, baby. This was one smokin' song and when it came to selling it, Guille was Neiman Marcus with a red-hot salesman; I was 7-Eleven with a disinterested clerk.

"*Ay,* stop, stop . . ." What hair Gabriel had left was standing on end as he ran his hands through it *again* and jabbed the pause button on the remote, stopping us midway through the fourth attempt at a run-through. "*Parece* que . . . we're going to have to find another chart, *niños.*"

And he looked so disappointed, I felt a few tears stinging my lids. God, I was pissed at myself. I'd never once been so completely kicked in the ass by a piece of music in my life. And I wasn't even *playing.*

"No—" Guillermo stared down into my face, his hands on my shoulders. "You can do this, Ali. I know you can. What can we do to make it work?"

"If there was just some way for me to get the images out of my head, Guille."

I'd already explained my little video hang-up after the first attempt at a run-through. Then it was worth a laugh. Now, not so much.

"You don't have to be Shakira, Ali."

"I know that, but I can't help seeing her. It's . . . unsettling. And you just *know* everyone else, in the audience, on TV, will be seeing it, too. And I just can't . . . um, perform, like that."

Behind us, Gabriel muttered something uncomplimentary about videos and sullying music.

I shrugged Guille's hands off and went to the fridge in the corner, with its endless supply of bottled water, ideal for those rehearsal-strained, parched throats. How about for those throats that were tight and scratchy because you were about to cry? Would the water work as well then?

Such a loser. Snagging a trio of bottles, I nearly dropped them as a breathy moan and a throbbing insistent beat began echoing through the huge rehearsal space. I looked over at Guille, who was watching me, one of his sandy brown eyebrows raised.

"What—"

Now a smile crossed his face as the vocals kicked in, but slower, with a different vibe. No less sexy and seductive—just different. Less frantic, somehow. Not at all like the version the video was set to.

"It's a sort of reggaeton remix." His smile got way big and I tell you, if I wasn't all about big, green eyes, my heart rate would've been up in seriously dangerous territory.

"You want to give it a try? Just sing over the vocals for now?"

I felt my own grin beginning to spread over my face. "Yeah."

And an hour and a half later, I was ready to scream again—but for a world of different reasons.

15

"You're pissed."

Silence. Not the comforting kind, either, but big, resounding, echo-y silence. I slouched into my car seat, with that nasty, uneasy feeling hiking up and down my spine. But I was just too tired to deal.

It wasn't until we were finally home and I was about to head upstairs that Papi finally said something.

"You're whoring yourself out for this show, Alegría. You do understand that, right?"

Maybe the real shock wasn't so much the words, but how they came out sounding. Conversational . . . casual . . . hateful, but in a pleasant sort of way. Like it was no big deal.

I spun around, my hand grabbing onto the banister. "One. It was one performance, Papi."

"That's where it starts, Ali." Even in the low light coming from the small lamp we left burning at night, I could see how dark his eyes were. How upset he really was, no matter how calm his voice stayed. "Compromising yourself just once. Makes the second time and all the times after so much easier."

Honestly, I was ready to spit nails. Palms sweating, fingers curling hard around the handrail, but somehow, through some force of will or something, my voice came out as calm as his. "Was it that the song is so different from my usual style, Papi? Or was it that I was good? That Guillermo and I made it work?"

"Is that what you think?"

"We're alive to fight another day, so yeah, I'd say we made it work."

"But that wasn't you, Ali."

"It could be," I retorted, which a little nasty corner of my brain was happy to see actually shocked his self-righteous ass.

Oh, I was just way, way too exhausted for this. How stupid *did* everyone think I was?

Dropping onto the bottom step I looked up at him. "Do you really think I could do that all the time? That it could really be me?"

"It sure seemed as if you enjoyed it."

Which had apparently come as a big surprise to everyone—not just Papi. Sosi had stared at me afterward as if I'd grown a second head—or in her words, "Damn, *chica* . . . you were . . . you and Guille . . . and you . . . Oh my *God.*"

Even now, I could still feel the adrenaline—a juiced-up sensation that had begun even before the lights went on. Knowing that something—everything—was going to be different tonight. Beginning with how we'd started out, already onstage, rather than coming on from the wings as we'd done every other week, the club mostly dark except for the eerie red glow of the EXIT signs and the small lamps at the sound board. The stage was almost completely bare, the few band members we needed situated just off to one side; just as we'd rehearsed, the first spot came on, timed perfectly with my first breathy moan, illuminating me standing on the top step of a set of risers.

Slowly, following the path the spotlight paved for me, I prowled down the steps, singing the unbearably sensual and tough lyrics about a woman confronting the lover who's been screwing around on her and she knows it and it hurts like hell, but she's trying to decide if she'll take him back anyway. And he's trying to beg her forgiveness and that's when a second spot came on, illuminating Guille, slumped in a big leather chair, wearing tuxedo slacks and an ivory dress shirt left untucked and mostly unbuttoned, looking very morning after and wicked sexy, with his stubble and messy hair.

There was no stage, no audience, no cameras—there was just me and Guillermo, locking eyes and attitude as I walked up to him and pulled him from the chair, making him face me, face up to his infidelities, because clearly, this guy was a player and liked it, but he still loved the woman who waited at home. I wasn't buying any of his crap anymore, though, and told him so, every time he went through his litany of excuses in the chorus, but he just wouldn't give up, pulling me in and holding me close until I almost gave in, before somehow finding the strength to push him away and we wound up facing each other, breathing hard, a huge gulf between us—the affair finally over.

All I saw were Guille's eyes, narrow in his shocked face; all I heard was the blood rushing through my ears. Then a sudden flood of light, the gulf between us reduced to the width of the stage, breaking the fantasy and revealing the audience going completely insane. A slow smile broke across Guille's face, prompting an answering grin from me as we walked toward each other, back to being just Guille and Ali. Meeting in the middle of the stage, we clasped hands and took our bows as the audience continued to clap, shrieks and whistles piercing the air.

Backstage, though—that was a different story. Even all the people who'd seen us during dress rehearsal, who should've known what was coming, should've expected it, looked, I don't know . . . shell-shocked or something, as Guille and I came offstage, sweaty and hanging onto each other for support.

When I saw the replay, I got it. I understood. It was weird—

here I thought I'd finally gotten used to seeing the person onstage and up on that screen and thinking of her as really being me—but that chick up there tonight? *That* had gone to another new level altogether. Brown leather pants ("Because black's overdone and red's just so obvious, *mi vida,*" according to Andre) and a pale blue rhinestone-studded T-shirt, my hair a little wilder than usual, looking like the kind of woman who would only take so much from her man. And Guille in his ladies' man evening clothes, a perfect, elegant contrast.

Chills had run across my entire body watching the replay—we'd been so in tune with each other on that stage, just played off each other perfectly, and you could tell we'd known it from the expressions on our faces as we performed, the extra bite we gave the lyrics. It had worked, man. Totally and completely worked.

Those chills turned to big goose bumps when I heard that audience reaction again. They bought it and loved it and wanted more. A lot more. And standing there . . . God, I wanted nothing more than to give them more of what they'd wanted. It was *so* intoxicating. So cool to know that I could do that—have it in my repertoire, even if it wasn't an everyday thing for me.

Beat the shit out of me why I was the only one who saw it that way, though.

"Okay, yeah, I enjoyed it, Papi. You're sitting there acting like I committed a cardinal sin—what's next? Confession?"

"Just about looked like it might be necessary," he snapped.

"It was *fun*—I had a great time performing. And it was even more rewarding, considering how hard a time I had with that chart."

Now he was rolling his eyes and making some sort of "yeah, right" snorting noises. Which really hurt my feelings, even as it pissed me off even more.

"I did, you know. Have a hard time with that song."

"It's a simple song, Ali."

True. The lyrics were a little tough, but overall, nothing I couldn't handle. That had never been the issue, though. "Not the music, Papi—the delivery. That's what took the practice and I didn't think I was going to be able to pull it off because it is so different for me. And I did it and the audience loved it, and I loved that they loved it. *They* got it."

"They got a young girl rubbing up against a good-looking man and growling out some sexy lyrics. That's what they got."

"Rubbing up?" Oh, that was totally unfair. There had been little to none of the rubbing-up action. Didn't need to be, really. The lyrics and how they were delivered said it all. Plus we had to work around that pesky Latin American-audiences-and-me-being-underage crap. Trust me, Esperanza and the rest of the show runners hadn't forgotten that *at all.*

"That's really all you saw?" Him. Of all people, who knew music and maybe more importantly, knew *me.* Or should.

After a long stare, he shrugged and admitted, "Your voices did sound good together. I would love to hear them on something different."

Okay, then. But then he had to go and spoil it by adding, "Maybe without some of the body contact as a distraction."

I could *not* believe him.

"Thanks, Papi. I'll make sure to pass on the glowing compliments." I hauled myself up and turned to head up the stairs, tossing over my shoulder, "You know, Papi, I seriously think you need to get laid. Maybe then you'd be able to put your issues aside enough to really appreciate my performance."

I half expected him to follow me and maybe turn me over his knee and spank me. Never mind I hadn't had a spanking since that whole trying to build a pool in Sosi's backyard stunt when I was eight. That was a pretty mouthy, smart-ass comment for *any* daughter, but a nice Catholic girl who didn't generally talk back? I can only attribute his restraint to pure shock.

And the fact that he wound up venting his spleen elsewhere.

16

"Do you have *any* idea how close you came to being locked in the house for time immemorial?"

I stowed my gig bag and backpack in the backseat of the Mustang and dropped into the passenger seat, yawning. This talking-back stuff made for a total lack of sleep.

"Ali, what the hell did you say to the man?"

"He didn't tell you?" I mumbled through another jaw-breaking yawn. God, today was going to suck. All I wanted to do was go back to bed.

"No." Glancing up at Papi's window, with its closed blinds, she shook her head and shifted into reverse, pulling out of the driveway. "Amazing, really, when you consider he bitched at me on the phone until past two in the morning."

"If he didn't tell you what I said, then what on earth did he bitch about?" I reached around the seat and rummaged in my backpack for my shades—too freakin' bright out here.

Concentrating on navigating through morning traffic, Elaine didn't say anything until we were at a stoplight, where she could turn and look at me. "Mostly he was going on about how you were wasting your talent on the show and why couldn't you understand that?"

"Yeah, well, can't he understand that it's my talent to waste and that just because *he* doesn't get it doesn't mean I'm wasting it," I muttered as the light turned green and she turned her attention back to the road. "Elaine, that wasn't worth more than two hours of bitching. What else did he say?"

She sighed and curled her hands around the steering wheel—sort of like she wished it was someone's neck. "Jesus . . . *mija,* I think you two really need to talk—"

Oh, this did not sound good. "Elaine, we talked last night—you can see how far *that* got us. Just tell me."

Taking a deep breath she finally said, "He was complaining about how far you'd gone in the show."

"Yeah, so?" Of course I'd gone far in the show . . . what'd he think, that I was . . . was going to—"Oh my God. He totally thought I was going to get booted off before this, didn't he?"

Elaine got *reaaaal* interested in traffic right about then, paying superclose attention to the big-ass Caddy weaving in front of us with what appeared to be a giant beehive hairdo steering it. Once we were clear of the scary lady, I turned to Elaine.

"That's what he thought, right? Let Ali have her little bit of fun, because she won't be able to hack it? Then I'd crawl back home with my little tail between my little legs and be ready to go back to high school and do college and become a teacher just like him. *God!*"

"No, no . . . you've got it all wrong, Ali. It's not you. He knows you're more than talented enough to take this whole thing." She was patting my hand, her voice all soothing and trying to calm me down. And trying to keep me from clawing the center console of her car to shreds because I had my nails digging into it.

"It's just your style is so different from the others. He didn't think the demographics you'd appeal to would be strong enough to carry you quite this far, that's all. And I think seeing you last night . . . the way you were able to perform more like the others—in leather, no less—really freaked him out."

Probably because it meant I'd be getting more votes. Holy crap.

"So he really thought I'd be voted off before now. He was counting on it." And now I was crying, even though I was trying like crazy not to, biting my lip so hard it hurt and staring out the window as I swiped away tears and sniffled and probably looked horrible. "He so needs to get a life and butt out of mine. I swear, he really *does* need to get laid."

Thank God we were already on the highway and morning traffic was its usual parking lot state, the way Elaine was staring at me. "Is *that* what you said to him?" She looked half-horrified, half like she was about to crack up. "*Ay, madre santísima,* his little girl telling him he needs to get laid. No wonder he lost his mind."

"I don't know why. Not like it's not true."

"Is that what you really think?"

"Oh, please," I scoffed. "When was the last time the man actually went out on a date?"

Elaine sighed. "Girl, what you don't know about your father—" She stopped, this look on her face like she thought she'd said too much.

"What?"

She looked away from me, pressing her lips together.

"What is it, Elaine?"

Turning back to me, her eyes narrowed, she snapped, "Come on, Ali, grow up and think. Just because he hasn't dated in the conventional sense doesn't mean he hasn't had a life, *entiendes*?"

No . . . I didn't understand. But Elaine kept staring at me, one eyebrow raised and slowly, I started to get it. "But- but . . . who? *How?*"

Okay, not *that* how. Duh, even in Catholic school we had Life

Management, aka, the Sex Class with a nice touch of Fear of God thrown in for good measure. It was just—he was always home if he wasn't at school or at a Los Gitanos gig. If he went out at all, it was with me and Elaine.

She shrugged trying to look casual, but I could still read the flash of pain in her dark brown eyes. "Visiting professors . . . older grad students, never his, of course. Anyone he can see during daytime hours and most importantly, who's guaranteed to leave, and *God,* he'd absolutely kill me for talking to you about this."

"Why?"

Not why would he kill her but why would he . . . *be* that way? Someone better kick me if I asked where, though. Just wasn't ready to go there. I mean, what if it had been at home, like on the sofa or something? Or the kitchen table? Look, I'd seen enough movies to know it wasn't just about a bed. But what was naughty and exciting on the big screen was totally Skeeve Factor Twelve when it came to imagining my father doing it—especially if it was on the kitchen table I ate at every single day.

Elaine understood the nature of the "why," though.

"Because of you, *mija.* Or at least, that's how it started."

"*Me*? I've never been against him dating."

"No, not because of that." Reaching out, she ran her hand over my still-damp hair. "But when you were little, he was so worried about raising your expectations if he brought them around. Then it became more about setting a bad example for you, bringing women home that he had no intention of staying with in any kind of permanent way. After a while, I think it just got to be habit. An excuse for him *not* to think about permanent relationships."

And the way she sounded so sad just made me want to cry all over again. "Why don't you hate me?"

Her hand moved from my hair to my cheek. "Oh, Ali, how

could I hate you? You're such a big part of him, and it's how much he loves you, his devotion to you that's—"

"Why you love him," I finished when her voice cracked and faded.

"Yeah, well, a big part of it anyway." She laughed softly. "Not to mention, the dating idiocy aside, he's one of the brightest men I know. Don't ever discount the brains when it comes to guys—it can count for a lot." With traffic moving a little faster she was only able to spare me a quick glance and a small grin as she added, "And at the risk of grossing you out completely, I also happen to think he's pretty hot."

From anyone else, yeah, it would've been squickworthy, but from Elaine? "Yeah, I guess for a dad, he's okay." Guess she liked that tall, lanky thing, too.

We crawled along with traffic, waiting to merge onto 395 to head toward the island.

"Elaine?"

"Yeah?"

Probably wasn't any of my business, but . . . "Why haven't you ever, you know, said anything to him? Done anything?"

It was one thing for me to think he was a pinhead for not going after her when I thought he might like her as more than his best friend, but to know that she was in love with him and had been for God knows how long and hadn't done anything? Why?

"Because."

I sighed and stared out the window at the jagged edges of the Miami skyline, shiny and beautiful and distinctive against the bright morning sky. Me again. But Elaine surprised me by reading my mind.

"Not because of you, *mi vida*. Because of him. He hasn't been ready."

Hasn't been ready? "It's been fifteen years since Mamá died. When's he going to be ready? When *he's* dead?"

"He's a man, *mija.* Even when they're as smart as your father, they can be a little slow sometimes."

No kidding. Look how long it was taking him to understand what performing meant to me. Or, judging by what I'd found out this morning, *not* understand. Still.

All right, then. Obviously, there was only one way to prove it to him. What had been my goal all along now became a moral imperative.

Now I *had* to win.

17

I listened close to the music flowing through the earbuds, rewinding a few seconds on the iPod and playing it again. Pulling one of the tiny buds free, I noodled another couple measures' worth of chords on the Steinway, changing a couple notes, getting them right, then scribbling the final result on the staff paper in front of me.

"Hey, where's Gabriel?"

"Ahhh!" I spun around on the bench, with an added, "Oh *shit,*" as my iPod, connected by the wire to the earbuds, followed my spin and slid off the piano, landing at Jaime's feet.

"Oh man, I'm sorry, Ali. I waited until you looked like you were done. I don't think it's screwed up—" He had his head bent, pushing buttons and scrolling through the menus on my music player.

"Gabriel's daughter is stuck at the beach—locked the keys in their rental car." I rubbed at my sore ear. "He had to call someone from the company and go rescue her. He should be back soon if traffic's not bad."

Without lifting his head, he muttered, "Oh, okay. Wasn't that important. I'll catch him later. Where's Elaine?"

"She had to double-check on a point for the abstract she's working on—but she gets better wireless reception over at the big house than up here." Considering that the whole "chaperone" thing was getting more fluid as time wore on, she didn't feel any real need to be Velcroed to my side 24/7. We were to the point where it was only important if the camera crews were around or any show bigwigs popped by.

"Right."

I just sat there, watching him messing around with the iPod, wondering what else to say, if anything. This was the first time I'd been alone with him in a couple days—since the duet. He'd been another one of the avoiders. Which was weird. The other people who'd steered clear had been the remaining competitors, outside of Guille, of course, and Tonio, who wasn't fazed by *anything,* much less me. But for the others, it was like that performance had all of a sudden made them look at me in a different light.

The other contestants I could really give less of a shit about—but at least them, I understood. They thought they'd had me pegged and *whammo,* with one song and Guillermo's help, I'd gone and busted all the cute little preconceived notions. Even Monica had looked at me the next day like I was a completely different person. I wasn't the known quantity anymore and it made them way nervous. But Jaime—no idea what was going on there.

Couldn't let it affect me, though. Another week, another performance, another round of eliminations to survive. This week's challenge was to perform in a more intimate setting, with just one or two of the band members. So much more my speed.

Of course, I was putting my own twist on it, performing a flamenco-style reworking of Kelly Clarkson's "Hear Me." Yeah, so on the surface, Kelly Clarkson and flamenco went together like pineapple on pizza, but you know, I *liked* pineapple on my pizza. And this was going to work so fantastically. Besides, I thought it would be a kind of fun inside joke, performing a song by the first American Idol, seeing as every English-language magazine and newspaper article about *Oye Mi Canto* insisted on referring to us as "Latin American Idol."

Now while the small, acoustic-setting gig was liable to be

harder for some of the others, for me, it was like breathing again. Even mastering difficult runs was more welcome relief than a real challenge.

Which actually left me time to wonder about why Jaime was avoiding me and why all of a sudden my father and I couldn't seem to communicate. I had apologized for the bitchy, uncalled-for "needed to get laid" comment, and shock of shocks, he'd actually apologized for his bitchy, uncalled-for "whoring" comment, so things were sort of better at home. But knowing that he'd expected me to lose before now? That hurt more than anything I could remember hurting and I *just* couldn't bring it up with him. Not without feeling like I was going to bawl like a baby and blow the adult approach all to hell. So I'd been burying my misery in another project—on piano, which required more concentration for me and kind of fit the melancholy mood better anyway—which was what I'd been in the middle of when Jaime showed.

"Here—"

I took the iPod from Jaime. "Thanks."

"You've got some collection of music there, Ali." He leaned on the piano. "A little bit of everything. Except for Sting and the Police. I think you've got *all* of everything there."

He was smiling. At me. And talking to me. How pathetic was I that it made me feel a little better? Even if I was still confused about the silent treatment. I was supposed to be mad about that, right? No, not mad—hurt. Which eased a little with the smile and the way the green eyes did their irresistible crinkling thing at the corners.

"Yeah, well, Sting's sort of my hero." I rolled the pencil I'd been using back and forth on the piano, following its distorted reflection in the glossy, ebony surface. "No fear, you know? He's taken a little of everything, jazz, pop, samba, new wave, reggae, Middle Eastern, and molded it all with his own vision. Plays multiple instruments. Surrounds himself with stellar musicians from all over the world. Continues evolving. Makes it all work."

I kept rolling the pencil, zeroing in on the rhythmic clicking sounds it made, back and forth, back and forth . . . could hear the music inherent in the sounds, hear the threads of songs.

"You know, I once read this interview with him, and he was talking about his process and evolution as an artist—what made a real impression was how he said he'd sculpted this singular career, no role model, just making it up as he went along. Just went with what really excited him."

Still had that clipping in an old music journal. Had it printed out and taped to my computer's monitor, even. That's how deeply it had affected me. "Pretty powerful stuff. It's not like he's a performer of any one style, he's just . . . Sting, and that's what's cool."

"Like you."

I shrugged, still staring down at the pencil. "It's what I aspire to, at any rate."

"No." All of a sudden his hand was there, over mine, stopping my pencil fidgets. "I mean, you're just Ali. Unique. But you can also do everything. It's why everyone's so freaked, you know. Everyone already knew you were unique, but that you can go mainstream and do it so well? They didn't bargain for that."

Yeah, I *knew* that already. Didn't explain about *him,* though. "Did it freak you, too?"

"No—I was freaked, all right, but not because of that." And then he was sitting close beside me on the small, padded bench, his thigh warm against mine. Lacing our fingers together, he brought them down to the keyboard, a few dissonant notes echoing through the room.

"Ali, you're only seventeen."

Yeah. Knew that only too well. And Jaime was holding my hand. I was clear on that, right?

"Getting to know you has been amazing; you're funny and smart and so outrageously talented—"

Uh-huh. His thumb was tracing these patterns across my knuckles, so light I could barely feel them, but at the same time, I could *really* feel them, sort of everywhere, especially in the pit of my stomach. "And I work for the show."

Sure, whatever. Thigh, pressed up against mine and since we were both wearing shorts, well . . . actual skin-to-skin action going on, the hair on his rubbing against mine that, thank *God,* I'd remembered to shave this morning.

"It was hard enough before to keep reminding myself that I work for the show and you *are* only seventeen, but after the other night—*damn,* Ali. It's why I've stayed away. I can't just think of you as only seventeen anymore and I don't care that I work for the show and I probably, really, shouldn't be thinking about doing this."

Somehow, don't ask me how, our heads had turned toward each other, foreheads touching, and his hand that wasn't holding mine was brushing my hair back and tracing more of those crazy-light patterns along my cheek.

I swallowed hard. "You know, I turn eighteen in October."

"Oh?"

"Yeah."

I swallowed again and suddenly, desperately tried to remember what I'd had for lunch and had it had onions in it? "I'm one of those weirdos who was born too late to start school with other kids my age, so I had to wait a year. I'm almost always the oldest in my class."

"Okay."

I so wanted to look into his eyes, try to see what he was thinking, but I couldn't. Mostly because if I tried, close as we were, I'd go cross-eyed—probably not a good look for the moment. So I focused more on what I *could* see . . . the skin of his cheek, smooth along his cheekbones, rougher lower down with stubble that was darker than the hair on his head. His mouth, which was just how a guy's mouth should be, narrow and defined with an adorable little dip right in the center of his upper lip.

I could also just make out the corners of that mouth turning up.

"So it, um, means I'm really closer to eighteen than seventeen," which came out sounding sort of warped and garbled because I was nervous and I really, really wanted him to do what he was so close to doing, and what would he think if I did it first?

Forget what he might think. I *had* to.

Closing the last couple inches of distance between us, I lifted my hand to his neck and *oh,* his lips were this unholy combination of firm and soft and had me feeling all . . . *melty.* Last guy I'd kissed was David Santiago, my date for the Winter Ball. He'd kissed okay, I guess, real smooth and clearly knew what he was doing to the point that he'd popped a breath strip right before he leaned in and kissed me right at the big fortissimo climax of "My Heart Will Go On." Sosi thought it was romantic. I thought it was cheesy.

No breath strip kisses from Jaime. He'd obviously had a slice of the chocolate cheesecake for dessert at lunch. Much, much nicer than breath strip kisses. And whether or not I'd had onions was obviously not an issue, since Jaime was leaning closer, his mouth opening as the hand on my cheek moved to curve around my neck and the other squeezed my hand . . . and squeezed . . . and squeezed *really* hard.

"Ow." I jerked away, shaking my hand.

"Jeez, I'm sorry, I'm such an ass."

"No, no . . . it's okay." But couldn't stop shaking the hand and flexing the fingers—*de verdad,* the boy had some kind of grip. Then Jaime shocked the life out of me by taking my hand in his again, in a much gentler grasp, and lowering his head, kissing first the back, then turning it over and kissing the palm and wow . . . could the guy be any more romantic?

He looked up at me and now I could look into those streaky green eyes all I wanted. "Better?"

"Oh yeah." Probably should've been way embarrassed by how breathy that came out sounding, but he seemed to like it, his eyes lighting up and a smile curving his mouth that I couldn't help but smile back at. But the longer we stared at each other, the less it was about smiling and more about . . . well, chocolate cheese-cake.

Straightening, he shifted so he was straddling the bench and leaned in again, both arms sliding around me while one of mine went around his waist, the other up into that thick red-brown hair. *Oye,* my mind was going places it had *never* gone with the David Santiagos of the world, images of beds and sofas and kitchen tables as we kept kissing, for I don't know how long.

Oh man, oh *man*. Seriously vivid images but, *no* . . . He understood that, too, even better than I did, since he was the one who pulled away when I might've tempted fate for just one more kiss. Just one more—

"God, Ali . . ."

No, not the place or time. Breathing hard, we were back to foreheads touching, my hands digging into Jaime's biceps while his rested on my waist, just beneath the hem of my T-shirt. I couldn't help but shiver; his fingers trembled, then tightened.

Darned moral barometer. Especially when it came in the form of Papi's voice saying, "Wait until you're really in love and absolutely sure, *mija*. Then it's magic."

Yeah, I know. The man couldn't deal with seeing me in leather pants and singing Shakira, yet he'd still given me the most honest sex talk I'd ever heard.

"Jaime, it's just . . . I can't . . . not here and . . . I— I've—" Couldn't quite bring myself to say the rest, but not like he didn't know—or couldn't guess. "I— I hope it's okay."

"Of *course* it's okay." He pulled back, but his hands stayed on my waist, warm and secure. "What kind of guy do you think I am?"

I blinked. He was glaring at me, his eyes all narrow, and even through his tan I could see bright red splotches on his cheekbones.

"I, um . . . well—that you're older and in college, and you *are* from New York and—" And could I sound like any more of a humongous dweeb? I hadn't sounded this lame since the day we met.

"Gee, I'm flattered, I think."

Well, at least the volume had ratcheted down a notch on the annoyed look. He took my hands in his and looked down at them. "Yeah, I'm more experienced than you," he admitted in a quiet voice. Looking up at me with this crooked half smile, he added, "Not as much as I'm guessing you think, but enough."

Ouch. Was this what feeling jealous was like? Because in the second after the words left his mouth, I wanted to totally stomp on any other girl who'd ever gotten near him and don't tell me it wasn't rational. Rational sucks.

"Hey."

"What?"

"I don't just *like* you, Ali." Again, he lifted my hands and kissed the back of each one and there I went with feeling all melty again. "I respect you, too—" Looking away, he laughed, this short, embarrassed sound. "*Por tu madre,* you must think this sounds so totally bogus and like some cheap line."

He took a deep breath and looked right into my eyes, his hands tightening on mine. "Look, what I'm trying to say is . . . I'm good with you calling the shots, okay? Whatever you want."

Dude. Was he really for real? Because this was seriously too good to not be a dream.

"Can we maybe work on that calling shots thing together?" I heard myself asking. Yes, strong moral barometer. But sudden, major onset of screaming hormones, too. Not sure how well they could coexist.

Boy, did that make him look happy. Like he was really pleased I trusted him that much. Well, of *course* I trusted him that much. Wouldn't have done as much as I did if I didn't trust him.

"Sure." His smile got even bigger. "Just be kind to me and don't wear any more leather pants, please?" We sat there and laughed, and now that things between us had calmed down some, kissed some more—lighter, sweeter, just . . . nice—until the sound of footsteps tromping up the stairs brought the fun to an end.

After a quick glance over his shoulder, he ducked his head for one last kiss, his tongue teasing mine. "I'll see you later," he whispered. By the time the door opened, he was on his feet and over by the door, saying hi to Elaine and asking Gabriel whatever it was that had brought him up here in the first place. Man, I had to remember to thank Gabriel—maybe buy him a present—even though he wouldn't have a clue why.

"Alegría Montero . . . what've you been up to?" Elaine's voice was barely above a whisper, but her face was absolutely screaming curious.

"What?"

"*Oye mija,* I've been around the block a time or twelve." She cocked her head toward Jaime, then back at me. "Certainly enough to recognize beard burn," her fingertips brushed the tingly, sensitive skin by my mouth, "not to mention, the classic hand-in-the-pocket pose."

The *what*? I glanced over at Jaime, who yeah, had a hand

crammed pretty deep in his pocket and was sort of shifting around on his feet. Talking to Gabriel, he still managed a look in my direction and smiled. Just a little one, but it was enough. Heat lurched all the way from my stomach clear up to my scalp.

"Uh-*huh* . . . wondered how much longer it was going to take him."

I shifted my attention to Elaine, who was smirking at me. All Miss Know-It-All. "Oh, please. How could you be so sure?"

"The boy's been making eyes at you since day one, Ali. Miracle is that he held out this long."

I grinned down at the keyboard, running my fingers along a few of the keys. "Apparently, it was the leather pants."

"It always is," she said with a wicked grin. A pause, then, "You're being careful, right?"

More heat. Most of it right in my face. At the very tip of my nose. Pure Rudolph syndrome. "Nothing to be careful about," I muttered.

"But if there is, you will be. Right? You promise?" she insisted.

My "yeah" came out faint and barely audible, but it was enough for Elaine. With a deep sigh, she leaned on the piano.

"Good, because I'd hate for your father to kill us all."

Yeah, that would definitely suck, what with things getting so interesting.

18

"Okay, *mija* . . . tilt back and open wide."

"Ow." I blinked hard against the sting of the Visine Bianca was applying to each of my swollen, bloodshot eyes. Needed to be done, though. I looked like the walking dead.

"Now close your eyes." Following her instructions, I felt something cool being applied over each eye. "Just sit there for a few minutes with the teabags and then I'll finish your makeup."

"Is the DayQuil kicking in yet, *muñeca?*"

I pressed my fingertips against my sinuses, then tried an experimental sniff out of each side of my nose in response to Andre's question. Not bad. No more impulse to scream and cling to the ceiling just from touching the sinuses, and there was some air moving on each side. Hopefully, it would continue to clear up in the next hour before curtain, and I'd be able to suck enough air down to my diaphragm to make it through the performance. Then I could go home and die.

"Yeah, it's working."

"Okay, shush. Save your voice." I could feel him fluttering around like a nervous *tía.* "There's a cup of tea with honey on the table by your elbow—be careful, it's hot."

"Thanks," I croaked out.

Fingers pressed against my lips. "No more talking. I mean it."

Fine by me. The fire throat had been gone for a couple days, but there was still a little hoarseness that Jaime said sounded really sexy, but wasn't necessarily good for singing. I'd have to gargle with hot salt water before I went on—totally disgusting, Old Country remedy, but couldn't deny it worked. Relaxing back into the chair, I just let Enya's floaty, ethereal vocals wash over me and coasted on the slight buzz from the cold medicine. Was I a lightweight or what? Even the stuff that was supposed to keep you functioning turned me into a drooling idiot, so I could only take half doses.

"Ali, I'm taking off the teabags now."

Huh? What? Must've dozed off a bit, since it seemed like Bianca had just put them on not two seconds ago. I blinked up at her, trying to bring her into focus.

Elaine, who, as always, was sitting next to me, touched my arm. "You okay, *mija*?"

"Yeah. Just a little spacey is all." I blinked some more. "How do they look?" I asked Bianca.

She was dabbing concealer around my eyes and blending it with the foundation she'd already done. "A lot better. But I'm going to take it relatively easy on the eyes tonight—no point in irritating them again."

I sat there and sipped my tea, which had cooled to comfortably warm.

"There. That'll do and you'll look just gorgeous." Bianca ran the big poofy brush over my face, setting the makeup with a dusting of powder. "Thank God for this more intimate setting thing they've got going tonight. The softer lighting is going to really work to our benefit."

Our benefit. I couldn't help but feel a real wave of gratitude for her and for Andre and everyone around me. They were really going out of their way to make me feel better and help me make it through tonight's performance.

"I'm keeping your hair simple, too, just a wide headband holding it back—don't want to aggravate any headaches." As Bianca moved around to the back of the chair, I blinked some more. Holy cow. I must be more stoned on DayQuil than I thought. Because in the mirror, staring at me, was none other than . . . Cap'n Jack Sparrow? Naaah . . . aside from the fact that it was mostly in Sosi's dreams that Johnny Depp had a habit of making cameos, Cap'n Jack wasn't . . . *blonde*.

"You're done, Fabiana." Bianca's voice was calm as she brushed my hair. "Why are you back in here?"

To give me horrible visions that would haunt me for years to come? How else to explain the lowrider black leather pants and thigh-high silver boots? Or the silver-and-black zebra-striped rib-tickler and big, billowy white shirt, tied up high under her boobs? The dangly rhinestone navel jewelry? The hair that was back to that huge, spiral-permed look with the addition of random braids, a la Jack Sparrow, and what was *with* the ginormous earrings? Those suckers would've looked better wired for electricity and hanging from the ceiling.

Because it was all just so right for an intimate setting.

What had the chick been thinking? Or more accurately, what had Bianca and Andre been thinking? Then again, she was doing Madonna's "La Isla Bonita," so maybe island, pirates . . . who knows?

"I need more eye makeup."

More? She already looked like a raccoon. But Bianca's face was totally calm and pleasant as she called out, "Teresa, Fabiana needs a touch-up—you about done?"

A black-and-purple–streaked head poked around the opposite side of the vanity. Teresa's eyes widened as she took in Fabiana. "Uh, yeah. I'm just finishing up." Shaking her head, she ducked back to her side.

"Let the junior trainee finish with her."

Bianca's voice remained calm. "Teresa's got a couple minutes. I don't. Either she works with you or you go out as you are. Your choice."

"Fine. Guess some people need all the help they can get."

Oh, I was so over her these days. I might've even laughed at her pissy attempt at a put-down, except for the look she leveled at me in the mirror as she passed wasn't either pissy or laughworthy. It was . . . I don't know. Creepy and mean and sent a genuinely nervous shiver down my back. Or maybe it was just the cold meds making me twitchy and hypersensitive.

"Pot, meet kettle, yo."

My eyes watered as tea went down my throat and up my nose at the same time and I struggled not to choke. Tonio rounded the vanity and grinned at me. *"¿Cómo te sientes?"*

"Better, thanks," I managed around a choking giggle.

"Good. Because if I'm movin' on, I want it to be straight up, right?"

"Right." Tonio and I—we understood each other. And both rolled our eyes at the not-so sotto voce "as if" that floated from the other side of the vanity.

Holding out his fist, Tonio said, "Break a leg, Ali."

I tapped mine against his, saying, "Ditto," and nodding as he left the room.

Oh yeah, he was gonna move on tonight. No doubt. With his thing for scorching ballads he was a natural for the intimate setting. Tonight he was going to be crooning a Spanish version of Los Lonely Boys' "More Than Love," with arch top jazz guitar, upright bass, and drummer backing him up. If what I'd heard during dress rehearsal was any indicator, he was going to have the little old ladies panting over the song and the little young girls panting over how totally hot he looked in his fitted navy suit and cream-colored shirt, his small gold cross just showing at the open neck.

"All right, *mija,* go get dressed."

"Thanks, Bianca." I blew a kiss, not wanting to spread my germs any more than necessary, and made my way with Elaine toward the adjoining dressing room. Once inside, we closed the door firmly and stared at Andre.

"What?"

"What on earth have you put Fabiana in?" Elaine demanded.

"Doesn't it just look *fab*ulous?" For a second—just a second—I thought he was serious. Then I saw the raised eyebrow and pursed lips and dang, I was really slow on the uptake with these cold meds.

"Andre, I can't believe you. She looks like Johnny Depp in drag."

Throwing up his hands and shrugging, he turned toward the garment rack with my name taped to it. "I got tired of arguing with the little twit over her outfits every week. *Mira,* she thinks she looks great like that, good for her. I tell her she looks great—she's out of my face, I'm spared a headache and ensuing wrinkles."

"And the fact that she actually looks like a cheap hooker?" Elaine asked.

Talk about your nasty, evil smiles. "Well, that's just a little added bonus, as far as I'm concerned."

Goes to prove . . . don't piss off the hair and makeup people. Good thing she had talent if not range. Not being catty—just honest. She was a total devotee of Latin pop and did that stuff very, very well.

But enough about her. Time for me to get dressed and I was so ready to get into this outfit, had been looking forward to it since Andre showed it to me a few days ago. To go with the flamenco nature of the song, he had me going Gypsy tonight, with a tiered lace-and-tulle skirt in graduated shades of reds and a simple, black three-quarter-sleeve top. Black flats and huge sliver hoop earrings to complete the look. Taking the hangers from him I went into the screened-off changing area; ten minutes later and I was set.

"Where's my guitar?" I looked around the dressing room, my heart rate ramping up—gig bag wasn't anywhere, not leaning up against the wall or resting across one of the chairs. Where was it?

"You didn't bring it in?" Andre's eyes were wide. He knew how I was—remembered nearly getting his hand bit when he'd tried to take the Bernabé from me that first day.

"I—I don't remember—" Stupid medicine. I *never* just left it lying around anywhere. I always, *always* knew where it was.

Opening the door and poking her head out, Elaine said, "Relax, *mija,* it's right here in makeup. Must've just left it when we came back here."

I was feeling dizzy and lightheaded again, but that was just from the sheer relief. "Oh, *gracias a Dios.*" I rushed over and picked it up.

"Breathe, Ali. It's fine. It's right where you put it when we came in."

"I know. I just feel . . . weird, Elaine. I'm sorry. I know I'm being a real dweeb."

"No, you're fine—it's okay." She rubbed my back as we went out into the hallway. "Look, go find your quiet place and relax—I need to run to the restroom and then find your father."

"Okay."

I was still holding onto my gig bag like a baby holds onto its favorite doll, but the breathing and dizziness were settling down as I made my way to the out-of-the way corner I'd staked out that first week.

I'd just settled into my chair and lifted the Bernabé to my lap when I heard, "How's that cold you gave me?" followed by a light sniff.

Smiling, I didn't bother looking up from playing a light, soft run, then adjusting the tuners. "You have to quit saying that, Jaime Lozano. You know darned well it was *you* who gave me this nasty-ass cold." From the first day we'd kissed . . . or the day after . . . or maybe the day after that . . . who knew? Who cared?

"Semantics." His breath was warm against my ear as he whispered, "Regrets?"

Still didn't look up, but my smile got bigger. "No."

"Good."

As he moved around to stand in front of me, I looked up. "Do you want me to leave you alone?"

What a sweet guy. He knew how I was about my head space.

"If you can keep from whispering in my ear, which, don't get me wrong, is very nice, but very distracting, I think you're okay." It *was* nice to have Jaime nearby—his presence was comforting in the same way Elaine's tended to be. Another run . . . something felt odd, but I couldn't quite figure out what.

"Don't you have stuff you need to be doing, though?" What was wrong? Or was it just me, with these stupid cold meds? Everything had felt so majorly out-of-whack for the last hour or so.

"We've settled into such a good groove and with fewer contestants, it's not so frantic. I've got a few minutes."

"Uh-huh . . ." Only half heard him. Good groove . . . not as much to do . . . "Oh, *shit,* ouch!"

"Ali? What is it, what'd you do?" Dropping to a knee, Jaime had my hand in his. "Damn, you're bleeding. What happened?"

Rhetorical question as we could both see the broken string hanging from the neck of my guitar. The string that had snapped across my index finger and cut near the cuticle and was stinging like an absolute mother.

"Dammit, dammit, dammit. *Move,* Jaime." Sorry to be so

rude, but now was not the time for niceties. He knew it, too, just standing and moving aside as I laid my guitar on top of a nearby table. "I knew something was wrong. I *knew* it."

But how could this be happening? These strings were less than six months old and nylon strings, if you took care of them, had a long shelf life. The only way—

Oh.

Oh, *God. Idiota.* Sucking on my bleeding finger, I ran the tips of the fingers of my other hand along the remaining two tenor strings.

"*Shit,*" I muttered. I felt them again. Just to make sure. Yeah . . . there they were—tiny nicks sawed through each of the two remaining tenor strings. Guaranteed to snap if I'd been playing full out.

Like onstage.

During a performance.

"Ali, what is it? What happened?"

"Someone cut into the strings, Jaime. Someone tried to sabotage me." I was so unbelievably pissed I could feel tears gathering in the corners of my eyes as I rapidly unwound the tuners and loosened the strings. Pulling them free, I moved to untie them down by the bridge.

Reaching into the outside pocket of my gig bag, I groaned. "Oh no—" I felt around again, just to make sure—checked the inside of the bag—checked the outside pocket again. "Oh, this is totally not for real."

"Now what?" Jaime's voice was calm, thank God. I grabbed onto the sound of it and hung on like crazy, because I was about two seconds away from completely freaking out.

"All my extra strings are gone." Right out of Sabotage 101. "Go get my father, Jaime. Tell him I need a set of tenor strings."

"What about one of the other guitarists? Won't they have strings?"

"Papi uses the same kind I do." Made a huge difference. I didn't have time to see if anyone in the band used the same kind, and I knew he always carried extras in his car. Just like I always carried extras in my gig bag. But they were gone—all of them.

"Bass strings are fine—idiot probably thought she needed wire cutters for those," I said, more to myself than to him. "Just get him, *please*."

Didn't ask twice, didn't badger for any more explanations, just took off to do as I'd requested. Somewhere, in some rational corner of my brain, I knew I'd really appreciate that later, after this stupid nightmare was over.

While I waited, I checked over every inch of the instrument, headstock, neck, frets, double-checking the bass strings just in case, even shaking it lightly to make sure she hadn't shoved anything in the body. Taking my chamois, I rubbed it down, top to bottom, and so help me, if I found so much as a scratch that hadn't been there before, I was going to take great joy in yanking every bleached hair from the bitch's head. Because there was absolutely no doubt in my mind who'd done this.

Clear as a bell, I could see that mean, angry look she'd shot me back in makeup. She hated me? Five-by-five. I pretty much hated her, too, and if that meant a bunch of extra turns on the rosary for penance, well, that was an acceptable tradeoff.

"¿Qué pasó?"

"Strings got cut, Papi. And my replacements are gone."

"Anything else?"

"No. It's fine. I've just checked it over, top to bottom."

Setting the restringing supplies on the table, he muttered

really vile stuff under his breath in Spanish until Elaine's sharp, "Not *now,* Roberto," made him stop, midunmentionable.

"How much time until you go on?"

"She's got a little over thirty minutes." All of a sudden, Esperanza was at my side, answering for me. "What's going on, Ali?"

"What do you *think,* Espie? Fabiana. She's got some nerve, messing with my axe." With a vicious yank, I ripped open the new package of strings, tearing the bag nearly completely apart.

Papi looked at me. "You want me to do this?"

"I can do it." My hands were shaking as I unwound the strings and the finger that had gotten cut was still stinging like crazy, but I would *not* let her beat me this way.

"No time for heroics, Ali."

I already had the first string through the hole in the bridge and was doing the double over-and-under loop that would lock it in place. "I've got it. But I need you to tune it." With this congestion clogging my ears, there was no way I could tune from scratch.

Everything got real quiet then—or at least, it got quiet in my own head as I watched, sort of detached, my hands moving steadily over the Bernabé, bringing the string up to the peghead, threading it through the roller, looping and winding it into position.

After the last one, I looked up at the clock and took a shaky breath. Ten minutes gone. I still had a little over twenty until I went on. Relief, first. Then shock as I realized the rest of the world *hadn't* come to a complete stop—the show had already started, the backstage area buzzing, people rushing around, just like always. I saw Jaime and Esperanza, talking in the wings and glancing my direction. Hadn't even realized they'd left—that Jaime had left—but I suppose he'd had to. Had to do his job and all. But then as he turned to go do something, he smiled at me—let me know he was still with me, in a way.

I stepped aside, leaving room for Papi. "Can you clip the

ends, too?" Because *now* my hands were shaking again—adrenaline overload, I guess. I wasn't sure I could handle the cutters to trim the ends of the strings. And I still needed to gargle because my throat was back to feeling itchy and my words, as they came out, were edging back toward hoarse.

"Yes, he will." Elaine's voice was firm as she took me by the arm and led me back toward the bathroom. She stayed right beside me as I gargled, as I sat on one of the stupid purple sofas and just shook, when I ducked back in and asked Teresa to do a quick touch-up on my makeup. She was there on one side of me, Papi on the other, as I waited in the wings for my cue.

I could see them there, along with Jaime, as I settled myself on the stool next to Gabriel with his flamenco guitar and Adán on the Steinway grand behind us, as I did a quick final check on the strings, and listened to Adán play the gentle, syncopated intro to "Hear Me." Then they were gone as the world around me faded and it became about me and the music.

It was perfect, the single spotlight bathing the three of us, keeping the rest of the stage and the club in pure dark, making it feel like we were by ourselves, just jamming. Making it easy to fall under the spell of the music, add a few new flourishes, my voice soaring as the song built and crescendoed. It was so familiar and so right and so completely mine.

One thing *was* different, though. Don't think I'd *ever* felt a song so completely before . . . really felt as if the lyrics meant something very personal, but every time I sang the words "hear me," my voice had this ring of authority—of confidence—that only continued to grow. And for the first time, I wasn't shocked by the audience reaction—I expected it, welcomed it, as I stood there and took my bows.

"Well done, *mi vida*." Papi's arm went around me as I came offstage. Even as happy as hearing his words made me, hearing how proud he was, I didn't need them. Didn't need all the "congrats" and "good jobs" that rained around me as we made our way from the wings farther backstage. I only needed one thing.

Rounding a corner, I got it—came face-to-face with Fabiana, walking down the hall by herself, while I was walking with Papi and Elaine and Jaime, pausing to accept a hug of congratulations from Tonio.

Talk about symbolism. There I was, surrounded by not just my people, but one of my fiercest competitors; there she was, all alone. And she'd failed. Why it was me, out of everyone, she had it in for I didn't know and really, didn't much care. She hadn't beat me and, looking at each other, we both knew it.

Pulling the broken strings from my pocket, I dropped them down by her feet. "I'm telling *you* now—stay out of my way and we'll all be fine."

19

"So you're totally sure it was her, *mija*?"

"Sos, I swear to you, if you'd seen that look she shot me—" Jaime's hand tightened on mine as I shuddered again, recalling it. "She totally hates me. I just wish I could figure out why it's only me she seems to try to sabotage."

"Because, Ali, you're a woman."

I stared across the table at Guillermo. "Come again, dude?" I mean, duh, yeah, I was a woman . . . girl . . . woman . . . but what did it have to do with the "Fabiana Hates Ali Show"?

He shrugged like it was something I should understand. "She's one of those types who is naturally threatened by other women—sees them as competition."

"Well, of course, she's competition, Guille," Sosi protested. "It's why you guys are all there. It *is* a contest. And Ali's hardly been the only woman."

"*Sí, seguro,* but Ali's so completely different from Fabiana. She is sweet and genuinely nice and has even her competitors cheering for her even as we want to beat her." He winked at me. "It's contrary to how Fabiana's mind operates. She does not understand it and it makes her very . . . *¿cómo se dice en inglés?* Jealous."

Sosi huffed out an impatient breath. "In other words, she's a psycho-crazed loon from hell with anger issues."

"¿Qué?"

"Loca." Sosi switched to Spanish and simplified.

"Ah." Guille's face cleared and he dug into his bowl of ice cream. *"Bueno, sí, bastante loca también."*

Whatever. It was giving me a headache. And this was supposed to be a relaxing afternoon off, just hanging at the mall with Sosi and Jaime and Guille.

I'd about fallen over when Elaine had told me that, after that performance, Jaime had formally introduced himself to Papi. Not only that, but he asked if it would be okay if he could spend some off-time with me, and if Papi would prefer, it could be at our house, with his supervision.

You can also imagine my reaction when Papi told me later that night that he thought Jaime was a nice young man and that as long as I went with Sosi, we could hang somewhere public, like the mall.

So here we were, a couple days later, at Bayside, on a gorgeous, sunny afternoon. With my morning rehearsal, we'd had Sosi meet us at the McMansion, since it didn't make sense to go all the way back to Coral Gables to pick her up when we wanted to head over to the open-air mall on the bay. As we'd been getting ready to leave, I'd seen Guillermo, sprawled on one of the big family room sofas with a book, and on impulse asked if he wanted to come along. Wasn't at all sure how much he'd gotten out since we'd been here, and didn't want Sosi feeling like a total third wheel. Besides . . . in spite of my "don't get close to the competition" rule, I *liked* Guille. He wanted to win every bit as much as I did, and wanted to do it honestly every bit as much as I did.

He'd seemed really grateful for the invite and so . . . here we were. Perfect hot, bright Miami day, the sky as blue as it could be, making the palm trees and the water of the bay with the cruise ships and pleasure boats on it look like something out of a tourist ad. The sounds of salsa music competing with hip-hop and reggae and no fewer than a half dozen languages. The air humid and salty and thick with the aromas of garlic and *plátanos maduros* and jerk spices, all of them drool-inducing enough to make an anorexic supermodel want to eat.

It was home, you know? All of it. It was Miami in a way that secluded barn could never be, and I was jazzed to be sharing it with these people I genuinely enjoyed spending time with.

But, of course, over lunch, when there could've been a million things we could talk about, what we'd wound up dissecting was the whole guitar sabotage mess. We'd already pretty much figured out when she'd done it—her only chance—my brain meltdown where I left my gig bag in makeup while I went to wardrobe. If no one was paying attention to her, it wouldn't have taken but a few seconds for her to grab a pair of nail scissors or something, just reach into my bag and snip. Difficult, yes, but not totally unlikely.

I was actually really lucky, too, the one had snapped when it did. Still pissed me off beyond redemption when I thought about them potentially breaking during the performance.

Sosi looked up from her waffle bowl of Cherry Garcia. "So is the show doing anything about Brunhilda?"

"What can they do, Sos?" I pushed my own half-finished bowl of Coconut Almond Fudge Chip away, smiling a little as Guille looked at it, then at me, eyebrows raised. Pushing it toward him, I said, "I mean, we all *know* it was her, but there's no substantial proof, no one saw anything, so there's nothing anyone can really do. Except I sure as hell won't be letting my axe out of sight anytime soon."

"Man, that's totally bogus," Sosi groused as she broke a piece of her bowl off and popped it in her mouth, chewing viciously. "They can't even say anything to her?"

"Actually, they can." Surprised, we all turned toward Jaime, who was staring down into his bowl, shoving his spoon into the melting blob, his mouth set in a straight line. "She's been told to watch her step."

After we finished with our ice cream, we began walking around, checking out the different shops and giggling at the sunburned tourists. At least Guille and Sosi were giggling. I was trying to, but with Jaime just sort of smiling and nodding as we walked, hand-in-hand, it gave me a case of the uneasies.

"You're being awfully quiet."

"Sorry."

"No big."

But it was. I could tell. Just wasn't sure how to say anything . . . everything was still so new. Not just us . . . but for me as a whole. I'd dated, on the über–rare occasion, usually to a school dance or a *quinces* with a Papi-approved escort, but hadn't actually had a boyfriend since Justin McCarthy in the second grade, who used to give me half his peanut butter sandwich every day. That is, too, if you could consider Jaime my *boy*friend in a traditional sort of way, which I guess he was, since I wasn't seeing anyone else and I knew he wasn't seeing anyone else and—was this a totally lame idea, coming to the mall? But it was the only way we could—

"*Aguanta,* Ali."

He slowed our pace so that Guille and Sosi got a few steps ahead of us, and look at Sosi, grinning like a fool as Guille put his hand on her back and led her over to one of the freestanding kiosks filled with sunglasses. While they tried on ridiculous-looking shades and laughed at themselves, Jaime and I sat down on a nearby bench.

"We've been busted."

Busted? "Didn't realize there was anything *to* bust."

He sighed and released my hand so he could put his arm across my shoulders. "No, all things considered, not really, but the whole 'you're underage and I work for the show' sitch could make things sticky."

"Oh, come on, Jaime." Without thinking I put my hand on his knee and squeezed. "You're hardly some creepy child-stalker, and I'm not some little kid who doesn't know her head from her ass."

"I know, but I did get a pretty stern talking to from Esperanza before we left."

"Oh no," I groaned. A stern talking to from Esperanza meant he probably still had whip marks on his back.

"Hey, it's cool. She knows me, and I actually had already spoken to her about us."

"You *did*?"

"Well, aside from the fact that she's my boss, she's also my cousin," he admitted with a sheepish grin. "Second, on my father's side. She helped get me the initial interview last spring, although she didn't have anything to do with my being hired. Just a little nepotism." He held his thumb and forefinger a teeny bit apart.

His fingers playing with the ends of my hair, he said, "I figured it was best to be straight up with her about things . . . I don't know, guess I just had a feeling."

"And?" I prompted.

He grinned again, a bigger one this time. "She told me as long as I didn't do anything that would justify your father *or* mine killing me, or otherwise land me in jail, that it was cool. Just play it discreet, especially if there were any camera crews or producers in the immediate vicinity."

Talk about your big sigh of relief. And I could understand why he hadn't said anything about Esperanza being his cousin. He wanted to be taken seriously every bit as much as I did, not as someone's pity hire. But wait—

"So if things are cool with Esperanza, why did you say we've been busted?"

Oh boy . . . I knew that look on his face. The smile had disappeared, his eyes had gone narrow, and on cue, those red spots made an appearance, high up on his cheekbones. "What is it, Jaime?"

He made some sort of sighing, exasperated noise in his throat, like he really didn't want to tell me, but didn't feel like he had a choice. "Someone," his voice leaving no doubt as to who "someone" was, "came to Esperanza and told her I was screwing a minor."

"What?" I hissed out between clenched teeth.

"Relax, Ali." His voice was low and soothing and he was rubbing my neck.

"How could she?" I spluttered. "Of course, you're—we're—you're *not*."

"Of course we're not, and Espie knows that. Espie's also well aware *someone* is carrying on a raging affair with a cameraman." He paused and one of his eyebrows went up. "A very *married* cameraman."

"¡Mentira!" Less clenched teeth, more jaw-dropping shock. And kind of loud, judging by the alarmed looks Guille and Sosi sent our way through matching funky amber lenses.

"No lie, *te lo juro*." He grinned again, this sort of nasty, devious grin. "Brunhilda tried to play the 'you can't prove anything' card, but Esperanza made it real clear she has no qualms about hiring a private investigator who could. Fabiana's nuts, but even she's smart enough to know that the kind of info Espie could dig up would get her booted off the show so fast, she'd be leaving vapor trails. So trust me, she's been told, in no uncertain terms, to watch her step."

"Maybe I am too naïve for prime-time TV, Jaime, but I just don't understand why she thinks something like that would even come close to working. I mean, at the very least, she has to know Esperanza doesn't like her."

"Yeah, but she also knows Espie's fair and all about the show. If she even *thought* for a New York minute that you and I were doing what Fabiana said we were doing, I'd be on a plane headed for JFK as we speak."

He took my hand in his again. "She's doing this because she's getting desperate, Ali. Every week that goes by and you both survive . . . I just—" His fingers tightened around mine and he shifted on the bench to face me better.

"Please promise you'll be careful? You know I've got your back, not to mention a bunch of other people do, as well, but she just makes me nervous as hell, so just . . . be careful, okay?"

It was kind of hard to swallow and not because of any sore throats, you know? If this was what having a boyfriend was like, I could get very, very used to it.

"I promise."

I brushed my fingers across his cheek and leaned in to give him a kiss—just a little one. That turned into another one and just one more until we heard, "Okay, okay, enough with the PDAs already. You're making me jealous."

I glared at Sosi, who was standing there with this totally unrepentant grin and a pair of wicked-cute pink-lensed sunglasses. "You're making me weep purple Kool-Aid, girl."

She shoved the glasses up on her head and pretended to glare back. "Your concern for my emotional well-being is overwhelming, *chica,* it really is."

"Oh, but you have nothing to be jealous about, Sosi," Guille broke in. *"Es una dulzura."*

Jaime and I just sat there and shook with the struggle of not laughing at the look on her face as Guille took her hand in his and kissed the back of it, a move he managed to make look elegant, even in his ratty board shorts. Green Day tee, and flip-flops.

"Ali?" I turned my head from side-to-side, not recognizing the voice, not seeing anyone I knew. Then I heard "Guillermo?" in the same breathless voice.

"Ohmi*gawd.* It *is* you guys. *Oye,* girls, look . . . *look!* It really is Ali and Guillermo, I told you so, I told you. Can I have your autographs, *por favor,* ohmigawd, no one's going to believe this! It's them, it's really them!"

20

Holy Blessed Mother of—

Next thing I knew, Guille and I were standing there, surrounded by four young teenage girls, more or less the same ages as my little fanboys from Mexico. Only two or three years younger than me, not that much different, but at the same time they seemed *so* young. And they wanted *my* autograph? Looking at me like I was some sort of hero or something? I mean, it was one thing when I saw a website done by some fanboys three thousand miles away, but when it was literally staring you right in the face? Totally and completely alien.

Had to admit it was also kind of cool and they *were* cute, especially the one who seemed younger and more shy than the others, kind of hanging back, but looking at Guille as he signed scraps of paper for her friends, like he was the yummiest thing since a scoop of Ben & Jerry's.

"Do you want his autograph?"

Big brown eyes lit up and she nodded, like I was Santa asking if she wanted a pony.

"Easy, girl, you don't want it to snap off." I laughed, patting her on the shoulder. Getting Guille's attention, I whispered in his ear that he should do something special because she seemed so shy, so after he signed her piece of paper, he took her hand in his and kissed it, just like he had Sosi's, leaving that poor girl looking like she'd just been run over by a truck. Feeling proud of my good deed for the day, I started to turn to sign for one of her friends, but stopped when I felt a touch on my arm. Same girl.

"Yours, too, *si puedes,* Ali." She held her paper out, still looking a little dazed. "Please?"

Then as they kept squealing and had us posing for pictures for the camera phone one of them had, more people started gathering around, trying to figure out what the fuss was, and Guille and I kept signing and posing and—

"Jaime?" I tried to look over the growing number of heads and finally I spotted him and Sosi, standing just to one side, where they could sort of keep an eye on things. But with the way this scene was growing, he couldn't hear me unless I yelled really loud.

"So are you and Guille going out?"

"Is that why you're out together?"

"I'll bet you're going out."

The English was too fast for Guille to follow—not like it mattered because he was fielding his own version of the same questions in Spanish; I think I may've even heard someone asking in Portuguese, as well. But before either of us could say no, totally *not* going out, all of a sudden I heard, "Oh, how cute, look how he's staying close to her, they *must* be going out and wouldn't it be sweet if they ended up the two finalists?"

"So how long have you guys been going out?"

"Was it since the duet?"

"Everyone's been talking about it on the message boards, how hot you guys were."

"You so looked like a couple. See? Told you they totally had something going on."

And they were pressing closer and closer and I was trying to sign and smile and be gracious and Guille *was* trying to stay close, but the more people showed up and recognized us, the more people got between us until all I could see of him was the top of his head and then I was spun around so I couldn't see him at all. Then people were grabbing at me, at my shirt and my arms, making sure I would sign for *them* next, turning me one way, then the next, to pose for one more picture, Ali, and look over here, Ali, and it was getting so hot . . . and I was having trouble breathing and all these people, my God—

"Jaime!" But there was no way he could hear me . . . not over all these people, no way.

All of a sudden, I felt myself grabbed by the wrist and yanked from the group. As I tasted fresh air, I could vaguely hear Guille's voice calling out, "Ciao, good-bye . . . we'll see you soon. *Muchos besos,* ciao."

Without looking up, I knew it was Jaime who had one hand, Sosi the other, as we took off running, then took a sharp turn. Finally glancing up, I could see we were in the parking garage and heading, at a slightly slower pace, for Sosi's car. When we got there, I dove into the backseat and huddled against Jaime, his arms around me as one hand stroked my hair.

"Ali, are you okay?"

Taking a deep, shaky breath, I glanced up at Sosi, who was looking pretty much as stunned as I felt. "Yeah, I'm okay. It was just . . . *man,* Sos, it was so scary. It got so out of control."

"It really wasn't that bad." Jaime's voice was quiet as he kept stroking my hair. "I don't want to scare you, but I've seen it get much worse."

"I—I know, Jaime. But, like, on *ET* or *Access Hollywood,* to people like Nicole Kidman or Marc Anthony or something. Not to people like me. This was happening to *me,* you know? I never imagined anything like that." My breathing was getting shaky all over again, as I could feel all those bodies jostling me, touching me, feeling like they were trying to get a piece of me.

My glance met Guille's, who was riding shotgun, but was currently turned around and facing me. "Didn't it freak you out?"

"Bueno . . ." I could see him struggling—like he wanted to be supportive, but it was all over his face. His eyes were bright and even as he looked a little embarrassed, his smile got bigger and bigger. He'd really dug the experience. As shy as he tended to be one on one, he'd really enjoyed that minor-league crush of humanity.

"No, Ali, it didn't bother me," he finally admitted. "It was fun."

Man alive, he could have that kind of fun. Wrapped in shiny paper and tied with a freakin' bow. As Sosi started the car and headed toward the exit, I relaxed back against Jaime, who continued stroking my arm.

"It's not going to get any easier, you know." His voice was pitched soft, so only I could hear him below the Antigone Rising disc Sosi had slipped into the player.

"You don't think it was just a fluke? Since we were with Guille?" Which was what I'd already started convincing myself of before Sosi even hit daylight and turned onto Biscayne Boulevard.

"They saw you first, Ali. Maybe it was a little crazier because the two of you were together, but—"

"Right," I sighed.

"You know—" His voice dropped even further, to barely above a whisper. "You've already made enough of an impression that someone's going to snap you up for a recording contract. Like they did with Monica." Who'd gotten voted off this week, which sucked. But at the same time, less than forty-eight hours after she'd left, we'd heard she signed a contract—with Selena's old label, no less—which definitely did not suck.

"With this shit with Brunhilda . . ."

Leaning back a little, I tried to look into his eyes. However, he seemed *real* interested in studying my hand, his gaze cast down as his thumb brushed over my knuckles, so all I could see were short, thick lashes curving beneath his eyes. "What are you saying, Jaime?"

He looked up then, his gaze dark and intense. "You can bail, Ali. You've got nothing left to prove."

You'd think that kind of high-handed crap would totally piss me off. Be a little too much like Papi. However, his heart was in the right place—I knew where he was coming from.

"I have to finish this."

He sighed and a corner of his mouth twitched up in a half smile. "I kind of knew you'd say that." Oh man—he *did* understand. And his soft, gentle kiss reassured me that yeah, he'd have my back.

Sosi and I parted ways with the guys at the big house, Jaime and I hanging onto each other like mad as we kissed good-bye. Even with the Brunhilda discussion and the fan craziness, both of us were definitely sorry to see the afternoon end. I was happy enough to stay quiet on the drive home, so immersed in reliving that last good-bye kiss and all the warm tingly feelings it had evoked, that I wasn't even clueing into the fact that Sosi was seriously not acting like herself. For one thing, she wasn't talking my ears off about how hot Guille was or teasing me to death about Jaime and PDAs. In fact, it wasn't until we were sitting in my driveway that I realized she hadn't said a single word the entire drive home.

"Everything okay, Sos?"

"Yeah."

But it sure didn't look like it, the way she was turned in her seat, one arm propped along the steering wheel, chewing on her lip as she studied me.

"What? Do I have something on my face?" I started touching my cheeks, my hair. "Oh man, tell me I didn't just kiss Jaime good-bye with Coconut Almond Fudge Chip streaked across my nose or something."

That brought a smile to her face.

"Oh man, I do, don't I?" Digging in my pocket for a napkin, I started rubbing above my lip and at the end of my nose. "Oh shit, why didn't you say something?"

Now she was laughing, the evil bitch. "Relax, Ali, you don't have anything on your face—not that Jaime would've noticed. Or if he had, he would've just licked it off or something."

"Ew," I laughed. But not really *ew.* I mean, the thought of Jaime licking ice cream off . . . could lead to some hot kitchen table fantasies, but now was not the time. "Seriously, then, Sosi. What's up?"

"Come on." Taking the key from the ignition, she got out of the car. Grabbing my stuff from the Civic's trunk, I met her at the door and followed her upstairs to my room. Nothing we hadn't done a thousand times before, but there was definitely something weird going on here. Setting my gig bag in the corner and tossing my backpack beside it, I watched as she sat down at my computer and began tapping away at the keyboard.

"I haven't said anything—"

"About what?" Pulling another chair close to her, I sat down and glanced at the screen. "Oh . . . boy."

It was a Google search listing—for me. The first and only time I'd done it, there hadn't even been enough entries to merit a full page of listings. And I hadn't bothered looking again, because . . . well, it just didn't occur to me that anyone would care. Now I was feeling genuinely stupid as I grabbed the mouse and scrolled down to the bottom of the screen to see how many pages of entries there were. The numbers stopped at ten, which meant there were at least one hundred listings with my name in them somewhere. Just like before, the *Oye Mi Canto* official website was at the top, with salsafresca.com right after it; a bunch of newspaper and magazine websites, no big surprise there, I guess, since we'd been getting more and more press every week. The big surprise was all the other sites. Sites with names like I Love Oye Mi Canto and Joyful Noise, and oh jeez, Darling Ali and OMC Hotties.

"You knew about all this and you didn't say anything?" I kept scrolling and clicking and, oh man, now we were getting to some seriously squicky stuff, like Caliente Latina Singers and South of the Border Booty. "Holy shit, my father would totally lose his mind if he saw any of this."

"Yeah, I know." Sosi sighed, propping her chin on her hand. "Thank God the man doesn't know much exists on the 'Net beyond Jazz Connection and ESPN-dot-com. Elaine knows, though."

My jaw dropped. "She *does?*" Suddenly I felt completely stupid. "Of *course* she does. She spends half her time on the 'Net, doing research. She'd think to look, wouldn't she?" Unlike oblivious old me—I was as bad as Papi.

Sosi nodded, busy again at the keyboard, clicking through screens so fast I couldn't even tell what she was doing. "Yeah. She was actually the one who told me not to say anything to you. She didn't want you freaking."

Closing my eyes, I shook my head. "Then why are you saying something now?"

"Because of what happened today at the mall, Ali. I mean, I knew about all this stuff, how popular you're getting, and watching what happened and how fast it happened *still* freaked me out. I can't even begin to imagine what it must have been like for you, in the middle of all those people."

And once again, I could feel all those bodies jostling, touching, feeling like they were trying to get a piece of me.

"It was . . . weird, Sos. Just not my thing at all."

"I'm thinking maybe you better get used to it, *mija*."

Part of me really, really wanted to believe this had been a one-time gig, but there was something in Sosi's expression, in how dark and serious her brown eyes were, that wouldn't let me hang on to that fantasy. We'd been friends for way too long for bullshit and she wasn't about to start now.

"Most of the sites are crap, of course, but you should at least check this out." Sliding from the chair, she picked up her keys. "Jaime's right, you know."

Sliding into her abandoned chair, I glanced up from the official *Oye Mi Canto* message board, which showed that there were currently two hundred eighteen people online and where the first topic post read,

WE MET GUILLE AND ALI!!!!!!

"About?"

"You can bail now and no one's going to hold it against you. You've been amazing, Ali. That's not going to go away. People aren't going to forget." She took a deep breath. "But if you keep going, this is only going to get bigger." She leaned down and kissed my cheek. "I'll call you later, okay?"

"Okay, 'bye," I replied absently as something new occurred to me. Rummaging through my desk drawer I finally found a sheet I'd tossed in there weeks ago. Typing in my name and the password printed on the sheet, I accessed the e-mail account that each of us had received for fan mail.

Mailbox full.

"Oh boy."

21

"Our ratings have been totally through the roof, *mis angelitos,* so our English-language parent network has decided to bag syndication and do full-out, prime-time national broadcasts for the last three weeks of the run."

We were in our usual gathering spot in the McMansion's family room, which seemed ever more spacious and airy as we were whittled away and which pretty much rendered Esperanza's step stool unnecessary. She was lounging at chair level along with the rest of us, trying to look relaxed, but her foot was twitching like a mad thing.

From his spot perched on the back of the sofa, Tonio said, "But this is good, right, Espie?"

She nodded with a grin that was a little tense around the edges. "Good for more ratings, good for higher-end advertising revenue, good for more exposure for you guys, good on a lot of levels."

"But?"

She shrugged as her gaze traveled from Tonio over the rest of us: Fabiana, slouched in another chair, studying her nails, of course. Joaquin and Chelo, both sprawled on the floor, Guille and me, sharing the sofa with Tonio.

"But it means some changes," she said. "Actually," she amended, "a lot of changes." Taking a deep breath, she looked down at her always handy clipboard, although dollars to donuts, she had everything on there memorized. "We're staying at Venezia, but adding more tables and chairs—less room for dancing, more room for the suits and their guests, including, no doubt, a well-placed celebrity or two. There are going to be more cameras and probably some upgraded lighting. We'll have a second set of guest commentators, for the English-language audience, and a new pair of hosts, as well."

"Wait a minute, what about Chianna and Fro—damn—*Fredo*?" I asked. Yeah, they were cheesy hosts, but they were *our* cheesy hosts, you know? I was used to their brand of cheddar.

"Don't worry, Ali, we get to keep them." Esperanza's smile was reassuring—and relieved. Looked like she was happy something was staying the same, too. "They stay the onstage hosts—the English-audience hosts are going to be backstage in a setup like you see on E!'s red carpet coverage, little director's chairs, watching the show on a monitor. That way they can snag you guys on the fly for postperformance interviews."

Jeez—look how Fabiana perked up at the word "interviews." "Poser" seriously took on a whole new meaning with that chick, I swear.

"I understand at least one of the new hosts is being plucked right from the current crop of hot, young bilingual actors so that we keep the 'exotic' touch—" We all laughed at the face she pulled on "exotic." Even I could recognize that as utter network suit language. Exotic, which to them probably meant brown eyes, a slightly darker skin tone than average, and a last name like García.

"*Oye,* I can give them some good exotic right here, Espie," Chelo said, his hand casually resting on the crotch of his baggy jeans as he flexed his other arm, making his Virgin Mary tattoo ripple in a menacing way totally alien to *la virgen.*

"Down, boy." Espie laughed as she tossed a balled-up piece

of paper at him. "We don't want to scare them—*much.*" We all laughed then—mostly at the idea of Chelo scaring anyone. I mean, yeah, he was scary-*looking,* with the burly, tattooed bod and shaved head, but otherwise he was totally one of the sweetest guys, calling his girlfriend and their little girl every day and always talking about how he was going to use the money he'd already earned from the show to get them out of Tijuana and to somewhere better.

"*Con permiso,* Esperanza—"

"Of course, Guille."

"You're still going to be our stage director, *sí?*" He was asking the same thing I'd been wondering. I mean, all these changes and everything, the parent network swooping in, like some colossus and shifting things at their whim. Not that I was against the increased exposure or anything—but like Chianna and Fredo, Esperanza had been with us since the beginning. She was like our general and to go into battle without her . . .

"It took a little strong-arming by our exec director, Guille, but yeah, you get to keep me, too, and I get to boss around the gringo network boys."

I breathed a sigh of relief at her familiar evil pixie grin. Those gringo network boys were gonna be in for a nasty surprise if they thought they could push around Esperanza.

"Before we go over for dress rehearsals, I need to tell you about one last change and it's a monster."

Monsters were rarely good.

"Because we're going prime time for U.S. television, we're not going to be able to announce the results postshow like we have been."

She paused and waited—however, no one asked. We just waited for the inevitable bomb. "The network has decided that we're going to have a special half-hour recap show the night after the regular show broadcast to announce the winners."

Boom.

She was even kind enough to add the handy explanation.

"Our systems have been starting to get jammed as our viewership increases. A couple of times it's been a close call, getting the final votes tallied and now, with the three-hour delay for the U.S. Pacific broadcast and to allow those viewers the opportunity to vote, it just makes more sense to wait until the next night."

"Man, this is gonna suck," Tonio grumbled. "Having to wait until the next night?"

"*Entiendo, mi vida,* but the recap's at least going to be just filmed stuff from the night before, so no extra work for you guys needed, other than to show up at the club." She stood and gathered her stuff. "Be grateful, guys. The other option was doing it on the morning show. Imagine Katie Couric in your face at seven in the morning?"

Okay, that would most certainly rot. But Tonio was right, too. In all, this was gonna suck. Not just because it meant waiting an extra twenty-four hours, but more because we'd gotten so used to the day after being really low-key; those of us who remained sort of breathing a collective sigh of relief just out of the shared experience of survival. This had the potential to eighty-six the sigh of relief and, in its place, add a whole new load of tension. Imagine, wandering around this barn, not knowing who was going to still be there at the end of the day and who was going to be packing their bags? Worse still, since it was usually the day we started work on the charts for the next week, it would blow royal chunks to spend an entire day rehearsing something that you might never get the opportunity to perform.

But what could we do? The parent network was going to be picking up the tab for the rest of this ride. We were just the talent, theirs to do with what they wanted. So we just gathered ourselves up, piled into the various cars and vans, and made the short trek from the island over to the nightclub.

Where we met all the changes, up close and personal.

Backstage at Venezia was always about hustle and bustle and barely restrained chaos on dress rehearsal days, but this went beyond barely restrained chaos and straight on to sheer insanity. It was like the intensity, which had increased every week, had all of a sudden been kicked up to about Warp Eight, so that it was this tangible thing everyone was feeling and feeding off of. Seemed like there were twice as many bodies crammed backstage and the minute we got there, Espie and all of her assistants began rushing around, looking even more crazed than what passed for normal for them.

"Esperanza!"

"Yo sé, Gabriel, yo sé."

Oh. My. God. It was nothing short of Armageddon, I swear, our stage set in pieces and littering backstage like big bits of acrylic shrapnel. The band members were wandering around, trying to find places where they or their instruments weren't in danger of getting flattened, and there were tons of people rushing around with hunks of metal and microphones and lights, looking like they weren't paying a damn bit of attention to where they were going, just yelling and expecting that the rest of us would automatically get out of their way.

Gabriel, his hair on end, eyes blazing, and practically breathing fire, charged toward us, nearly wiping out over an acrylic set piece that blended into the surroundings. "What in God's name do they think they're doing?" he growled, ducking as a workman swung a piece of riser that barely missed braining him.

Craning her neck and looking around, Esperanza sighed and reached for her cellphone. "What the hell are you doing?" she barked into it as she began picking her way through the rubble. "This was supposed to have been finished two hours ago—I even *gave* you the two-hour cushion for any potential screwups."

In pure pixie-in-charge mode now, she snapped, "*Oye, cabrón,* I'm fluent in no fewer than three languages and I was reasonably sure you had the ability to understand at least one of them when I told you this had to be done by one, no exceptions."

She skidded to a halt so fast, we all very nearly ran into one another, trying to avoid running into her. "*Excuse* me? No. Absolutely not. One hour. One. You hear me? Or else I pack up my kids and you have to fly blind tomorrow night with your fancy-ass lighting system and new set. They're pros, they'll know what to do. Prove to me you do, as well."

Snapping the phone shut and clipping it to her belt, she took a deep breath, muttering, "Zen . . . I will be Zen if it kills me." Spinning on her heel, she plowed right into Joaquin's chest. "*Ay, por tu madre*—you guys just scared the shit out of me."

Stepping back, she closed her eyes for a second, like she was trying to visualize something peaceful—like Shalim's butt—then opened them and smiled at us. "*Bueno,* as you can see, they're upgrading the set along with the lighting and I'm told it's going to look fantastic. While it looks like the gringos are working on Cuban Standard Time, they're assuring me they'll actually have this done within the hour."

Can you say collective "shyeah, right" expressions? To which she responded with, "Hey, happy thoughts. I'm trying to be Zen here, okay, people?"

Waving her hands, she shooed us back toward a fairly clear area. "Best bet for you guys is to maybe go outside and grab a *cafecito* or a soda from the *lonchero* wagon or maybe try to find somewhere quiet—" She took another look at the chaos. "Okay, well, relatively quiet and out of the way. Regardless, I don't want y'all taking off too far because we're going to need to get on it once we get the go-ahead from the set and lighting twerps. It's going to be a long day if they have any adjustments to make—and you *know* they're going to have adjustments to make."

As if on cue, her phone started beeping. Flipping it open she listened for a second, then with her eyebrows headed for her hairline broke in, "No, I said one hour and if you don't think I meant it, you just try me." Waving at us again and mouthing "one hour" she took off, probably in search of a weapon capable of incurring major blunt-force trauma. With all this crap around, she wouldn't have far to look.

"She's out of her mind if she thinks I'm hanging around here. They want me bad enough, they'll come find me."

We watched Fabiana pick her way through the set pieces and head toward the exit.

"Probably in a closet with her cameraman," I muttered under my breath.

"¿Qué?"

I glanced up at Guille. *"Nada."* Could be Jaime and I weren't the only ones who knew, but I wasn't about to get busted for telling tales out of school.

"Yo, so who wants to go hit up the shiny Meals on Wheels?" Tonio asked, referring to the aluminum-sided food service truck parked just outside. "I could use some jet fuel." As Joaquin and Chelo took off with Tonio, Guille looked at me.

"Are you coming?"

"Nah." I shook my head. *Café cubano,* aka jet fuel, would make me way too twitchy to play, and I already had a bottle of water. "You go ahead, though. I'm just going to try to find somewhere to park it."

And maybe, if I was really lucky, catch a minute or two with Jaime. Hadn't seen him at all today and now, knowing about all this insanity, I understood why. Poor guy was probably losing his mind.

"Can I bring you anything, then?"

"*No, gracias,* Guille, I'm good," I said, holding up my water bottle. With a nod, he took off after the others, while I scoped out where I could park myself. I didn't need much—just a chair and enough room for me, my gig bag, and my backpack. After ducking past some workmen, I spotted the perfect place: an almost-cave created by the piles of percussion equipment that I seriously hoped the music techs had taken care of and not these yahoos who were massacring the set.

Settling down onto the percussionist's stool, I pulled out the staff paper I kept in my backpack, along with my iPod, so I could work on my current transcription project. Unfortunately, too much ambient noise was bleeding through my earphones—couldn't really concentrate. And without the piano to noodle around on, even harder.

Sighing, I shoved the iPod and staff paper back into my backpack as my gaze landed on my gig bag. If there was anything this show and the constant rehearsing had done for me was to increase the need . . . I found myself having to play, more and more. Even after days where I'd rehearsed so much my fingers felt like they were about to fall off, first thing I found myself wanting to do every morning was pick up the Bernabé and just play a little, even before I'd brushed my teeth.

Why not? Not like it was going to bother anyone, right? And even just the ritual of getting ready to play soothed something in me; rubbing it down, playing a few notes, adjusting the tuning, playing the beginnings of a Bach partita as a warm-up. Each step, every little ritual, and I felt this hard knot of tension deep inside easing. It was fun, too, just sitting back and playing random bits of whatever floated through my mind—bits of "Regresa a Mí," since this week we had a "how we got here" theme going and were performing our original audition pieces. Naturally segueing into a little bit of "Bella Luna," a guitar break from "Spain," then I found myself playing the intro to one of my new favorite songs, "Lonely No More."

I laughed a little as I played the intro, remembering how brokenhearted Sosi had been that Matchbox Twenty was taking a break, because she *loooooved* them, but I'd been psyched to see what Rob Thomas would do solo. Come on, after his success with Santana, I'd had a feeling the boy wouldn't disappoint, and he *so* hadn't. I loved this song like nothing else outside of maybe Sting's stuff. After I discovered this acoustic, Latin-jazz version Rob had recorded, I fell in love even more.

Automatically, I began singing. Not loud, really—but I couldn't seem to play this song and *not* sing it. So what if it was a "guy" song? Story of my life, as low-pitched as my voice was, and this one was right in my range—change a few lyrics and, perfect.

Halfway through the first verse, a soft, syncopated beat joined in, surprising me. Glancing down, I found one of the band's percussionists sitting on the floor, tassa drum propped between his knees, while next to him a couple of the other percussionists were using handheld instruments, the *shekere* and guiro providing sweet, tropical flavors. More people who were just wandering by paused, began gathering around, including more of the band members. Tito eased his upright bass off the floor, picking up the chord changes and joining in; by the bridge, Stefan had his flute out and he and I did some nice solo trade-offs, nothing especially technical or flashy, just—pure.

Then when I returned to the chorus, voices, in the form of Tonio, Guille, Chelo, and Joaquin, joined in, these gorgeous, tight harmonies that underscored my alto and left me all goosebumpy. The first time we'd ever all sung together—not that you'd know it to hear us. As the song continued to grow in intensity, you could just sense how it was totally working its spell on us—players and listeners alike. And after the last note died away, we simply sat there, looking at one another, grinning like total fools.

Say what you will about music—call it the universal language or maybe more the Universal Home for Wayward Geeks Who Don't Fit Anywhere Else, but there's no denying you put a bunch of musicians in the same vicinity, you were almost always guaranteed to get something beautiful.

And just now, we'd done what all musicians loved best—tapped into our mutual touchstone and had it affect us in the best way possible.

Cool.

22

Guille.

Tonio.

Fabiana.

And me.

I suppose there was a sort of synchronicity that it was the four of us—a delicious inevitability, if you will. I mean, Guille and Tonio had been no-brainers almost from the beginning and just because God likes to play cruel jokes, I couldn't have made it this far without having Brunhilda right there, dogging my ass, every step of the way.

So there we were, the Final Four.

"It's kind of like March Madness, you know? Sweet Sixteen, surviving to the Elite Eight and now, the Final Four."

Jaime just stared at me as we walked down the hall backstage.

"College basketball," I clarified.

"I know what March Madness is, Ali." But he was still staring. I was starting to feel like I had a big, ginormous zit on my nose or something. And no handy mirrors or even reflective windows in which to discreetly check. Damn.

"What?"

"You're a basketball fan."

"Yeah, I'm a fan. Why? Is that weird?" Really. Just because

music's such a huge chunk of me doesn't mean that's all there was. I have layers, dammit.

"Not weird." We paused outside the door to makeup. "You are so unbelievably cool, Ali."

He thought I was cool. Didn't matter that I was the one on TV every week or that I was getting fan mail or being interviewed by magazines or slick television hosts. That someone like Jaime, Mr. New York Supersmart College Guy, thought *I* was cool was one of those things I just could *not* get over, no matter how many times he told me. No matter how many different ways he had of showing me.

His mouth brushed against mine, once, then again, not so much brushing but more lingering, making me lean into him, curve my hand around his neck, and hold on as my knees got weak.

Not so much cool as seriously hot.

Pulling back slightly, he whispered against my mouth, "I'll catch you later before you go on."

Uh-huh. Go on. Stage . . . *yeah* . . . perform. Perform.

Taking a deep breath, I stepped through the door and tried to push Jaime out of my mind so I could concentrate on the gig, but damn, pushing him away was getting harder and harder to do. I don't know . . . did I *have* to push him completely out? I mean, how bad could it be to let Jaime linger in my thoughts a little? Maybe letting him be with me in that way could even add something to my performance. Something to ponder.

"Ooh, look at the dreamy expression. Someone's been playing and not her guitar."

"Shut up, Andre." But I could feel myself smiling and blushing and probably looking, just like Andre had said, dreamy.

"I'm just teasing, precious—just a little. He's a sweet boy and I approve." Wow. Andre approved—and actually looked serious.

Well, as serious as a guy could look in a pink paisley silk button-down.

"Thanks." I set my gig bag in a safe, out-of-the-way corner. As I did, the door opened again and Elaine blew in. "Hey, how's Papi doing?"

"Getting more nervous by the minute, it seems," she replied, flopping down into a chair.

"Why? Because I might lose—or might not?"

"Let it go, Ali." The glare she shot me made me feel about two inches tall.

"It's tough," I muttered, feeling my face flame up.

"Win or lose, he is very proud of you, *mija*. Especially after the string fiasco. I think you really proved a lot to him that night."

"I know."

Down to feeling about one inch tall—and kind of like *Tía* Bernice in the process, who was known as the family mule, holding grudges over weird, imagined insults for years. I kept this up, next thing you knew, I'd be wearing Hawaiian print capris with clashing blouses, my black bra strap hanging halfway down my arm. Spending my days arguing with the guy at the meat counter at Publix because I wanted a pound of *jamón dulce, por favor,* not one-tenth of an ounce over or under and he'd better keep adding or taking away until it was right or else I'd go to the manager and by the way, was that ham fresh? Because if it wasn't . . .

Oh yeah. I *really* needed to let this go. Maybe after this circus was over, Papi and I would be able to sit down and talk everything over. Get it out in the open, because despite the setbacks, despite Fabiana, despite the stress and the disagreements with Papi . . . this was what I wanted. I'd thought it before, now I knew it. Performing was the life I wanted.

Hair and makeup were low-key, with soft music, nice vanilla-

and-orange candles burning, and Teresa and Bianca both working on me at the same time. It was funny, now that we were down to only four, makeup and wardrobe, which had been totally insane the first few weeks, had become all calm oasis, while the rest of the backstage area got nuttier and more crazed. Even the greenroom, normally set aside for the performers and the hosts, was full of people I'd never seen before, milling around and eating and drinking and just chattering like a bunch of hopped-up monkeys.

In here, however, we were guaranteed some peace and quiet, since Bianca and Andre guarded their sanctum like rottweilers. Or maybe in Andre's case, a rabid Italian greyhound. Whatever. It worked and I was completely grateful for it, getting to sit back and relax before hitting the stage.

This week I was going for a real traditional Cuban sound—a kickin' Raul Malo chart called "Ya Tu Verás." Heavier on the vocals than guitar, but that was okay. I was saving the guitar fireworks for next week, if I made it that far. In the meantime, this was fun, upbeat, a total party chart that had also earned me about a million kisses from Stefan, our flautist, because he totally got to go to town on this one.

Extra tables on the floor or not, I'd eat my gig bag if I didn't see people dancing by the halfway point. One of my favorite things about this show and what truly set us apart from all the other talent-type shows out there. We were about the whole experience, baby, involving the band, the audience, the viewers, anyone who wanted to join in and be part of *Oye Mi Canto.* Now, some took it a little further than others, of course. Last week, poor Joaquin had had to deal with a chick lifting her shirt and showing off the "These are all natural and all yours, Joaquin," scrawled across her enormous boobs. Poor guy, he'd made it through his chart pretty decently, all things considered, but since the television audience had no idea what had happened, all they knew was that something was off. They figured it was him and just like that, he was gone.

Thing is, you had to deal with those little distractions without cracking. Part of the biz.

"All right, *mi vida.* You look beautiful. Break a leg, okay? We'll be watching."

"*Gracias,* Andre." With a final round of good luck kisses from the crew, Elaine and I headed out toward the backstage area.

"Listen, *mija,* we've got a few minutes still and while I have the chance, I want to go check on your father one more time. He seemed really twitchy tonight."

"Hm, okay." Only half hearing her, I looked around, trying to scope out a place where I could sit and do my final warm-ups in relative quiet. Probably should've just stayed in makeup, since I was going on last anyway. Truth was, too, even a couple weeks removed from the Bayside incident, I was still a little spooked by the thought of large crowds.

"*Ay,* Ali, *mi vida,* there you are, we were looking for you."

'Scuse me, who are you? I wanted to say, because I had no freakin' clue who the lady with the scary, face-lift-tight red ponytail was, but clearly, she knew who I was; judging by the tag clipped to her collar, she appeared to be one of the many recent Super Importants who'd descended on us in the last week.

"Um, yes?"

"*Sí,* Ali, this is Gloria Marquez and her *abuelita*—you know, they won the contest to come backstage and meet the competitors—"

Contest? There had been a contest? First I'd heard of it. And they wanted me to meet these people *now*?

I swallowed down "leave me the hell alone, don't you see I have to get ready?" and instead, held my hand out and smiled, exchanging greetings and accepting the *abuelita*'s gushing compliments and accompanying kiss, hoping it wasn't leaving a big geranium-colored imprint on my cheek. Mental note to self: Have Espie check before going onstage.

"We need to get rid of the guitar, it's taking up too much of the picture."

What? I glared at the bossy photographer and tightened my grip as he rolled his eyes. "Come on, sweetheart. I don't have time for this. Just set the guitar down, let's get these pictures and be done with it."

He could "sweetheart" my ass until the cows came home—I wasn't setting my Bernabé down, especially not in this madhouse.

"It's okay, Ali, I'll hold it for you—nothing will happen, I promise." Face-lift ponytail lady reached for my guitar. "Really, *mija.* It's just for a second. Let's make the fans happy, hm?" she added quietly, as she bared her fangs . . . um, smiled.

Okay, fine, but I really wished Elaine was here. Even Andre or Bianca. But sooner I got this over with, sooner I could get ready to perform. I handed the lady my guitar, swearing to myself I'd keep an eye on her at all times, even if it meant the pictures would show me staring over my shoulder like a paranoid fugitive.

Easier said than done.

Somewhere between "All right, big smiles, the three of you, let's think fame and fortune," and "Okay, yes, *Abuelita,* smile for us, you were a model when you were younger, weren't you?" I lost sight of her as she turned to talk to some other VIPs, making my heart rate ramp up in a hurry. A few more inane-photographer phrases and no sign of Scary Ponytail later, and my heart was pounding even harder, leaving me sweating and short of breath.

"Where *is* she?"

There. *There* she was. Talking to some other suit person and not . . . holding . . . my . . . guitar. Oh God. Oh *God.*

"Where's my guitar?" I demanded. She looked blank for a second, like she didn't even recognize me. Didn't recognize that she'd promised nothing would happen to my axe.

"My guitar, dammit, where is it? You said you'd hold it. You promised." My voice was getting loud and we were starting to attract attention, which she didn't seem to much like. Tough shit.

"¡Cálmate, niña!" she hissed, grabbing me by the arm and leading us through the knots of people crowding backstage toward the wall. "It was so bulky, I just set it down for a second . . . I didn't think it was that big a deal. It's right here." She looked around, all casual and taking her own sweet time, while I tried not to grab her stupid ponytail and snap her neck. "*Oye,* I know I set it here somewhere."

"You stupid bitch." I was beyond niceties at this point. "It's not a clipboard or a set of keys that you just put down and forget where. It's an eight-thousand-dollar-instrument—it's . . . it's my life!" And I was starting to feel sick as I shrieked at this idiotic woman who had the nerve to look pissed. There was no way anything good was going on here.

"Ali, what's going on?"

I fell into Esperanza's arms as she reached for me. "Oh God, Esperanza, my guitar is missing, she had to have taken it, she had to, they wanted some stupid pictures and I didn't want to give this stupid woman my guitar, but Elaine went to go see Papi and no one else was around and she promised nothing would happen to it and now it's gone, Espie, it's *gone!*"

As I cried in Esperanza's arms, I could hear her growling, "Didn't I tell you to leave her alone until afterward? No pictures, *nada,* until she was done? Derrick, make sure she's escorted to the VIP area out front and not allowed backstage again. Carry her if you need to."

"Sure thing, boss."

"You can't do that."

"The hell I can't, lady—backstage is mine and these are my kids you're screwing with." She pushed me away from her. "Okay, you need to calm down, Ali, and let's think. She's probably just hiding it, trying to throw you off your game."

In that moment, I loved Esperanza as much as I'd ever loved anyone in my life. Loved how she didn't doubt that what I was thinking was probably what had happened. Looking around at the assembled crowd, she asked, "Did anyone see Ali's guitar? Maybe pick it up off the floor and get it out of the way for her?" No accusations, no threats—not yet.

There was a lot of murmuring and confused looking around. In the meantime, Esperanza was barking into her headset, "Get the band to play a couple charts as filler—we've got a situation back here. Ali's guitar is AWOL. No, one of these goddamn VIPs who are wandering around, wreaking havoc. I told you it was a mistake to let so many of them have backstage passes. Yeah, thanks."

She started to shove the mouthpiece out of the way, but stopped when something else came through the headset. "*¿Qué?* I can't—*ay, Santa María* . . . no . . ."

My heart thudded to a stop. I know it did. And I know I didn't breathe. Because I knew whatever she was hearing wasn't good. Especially the way that she took off running toward the back exit, me right behind her.

"Ali, *no!*"

Esperanza's voice was a tinny echo in my ear as I pushed past her.

No, no . . . *no!*

All I could see was a flash of leather . . . a small bit of black hanging over the edge of the metal garbage drum just outside the back door to the club, flames licking at the edges, eating away the deep burgundy "Ali" that Papi had had custom carved into the strap. But it was enough—I fought off the hands grabbing at me, feeling fabric tear as I tried . . . so hard . . . was desperate to get to it. To save what was attached to that strap. What was making the flames glow with an eerie blue light as they ate away spruce and rosewood and top-line French polish. Getting close enough to feel the heat . . . just close enough to where it went from pleasant to painful, then, gone—as I was yanked away.

"Ali, no . . . you'll hurt yourself. Please, Ali—it's gone."

It's gone.

"Jaime—" The fight left me and I sagged back against him, staring at the flames and seeing in them the outline of my beautiful instrument. Seeing how proud Papi had been when he gave it to me for my fifteenth birthday. Hadn't wanted a tacky party with an ugly dress and nasty cake. Hadn't wanted a car or a trip to Europe like the other girls. Just wanted a Bernabé. One of the finest instruments in the world and this one had been mine. Been . . . me.

"My guitar . . . she destroyed it . . . my guitar."

"I know . . ." His hands were warm as they rubbed my chilled arms. How could I be so cold when there was so much heat so close by?

"I'm sorry. I'm so sorry—I know how unbelievably inadequate that is."

"No . . . no. It's okay." I stared some more at the fire that was already beginning to die down to a smolder. "It's okay," I repeated as I straightened and pushed through the crowd that had gathered, past Bianca and Teresa and Andre and Esperanza, looking stunned. Past faceless strangers who were crowding around looking curious. Past Guille and Tonio, who looked upset and angry.

But not her. She wasn't out here. Why would she be? She'd had the best seat, front and center when it went up.

"Ali?"

I could barely hear Jaime through the insistent whine in my ears . . . obliterating everything but the need to find her. Find her right now and put an end to this shit. And I found her, all right, on my first try. Right where I expected—in makeup, staring at herself in the mirror, putting on more lipstick, a small smile curving her mean, red mouth.

"You fucking bitch."

God, but her head made a satisfying sound as it hit the wall.

23

"Ali, stop—don't do it."

Oh, but it was tempting. So, *so* tempting to take her and pound her stupid, mean face into the wall. Had size on her, we were about the same height, but I outweighed her by a good twenty-five pounds; had surprise, too, since all she was doing was staring, total shock in the fake green eyes, not moving except to rub the back of her head.

"Why not?" Breathing hard, I continued staring at Fabiana, just *daring* her to say anything. Give me *any* excuse to tear into her. "Why the hell not, Espie? She can screw with me, spread lies about me and Jaime, sabotage me, and get away with it, but I can't do a thing to her? *Why?*"

But I wasn't talking to Esperanza anymore. I watched Fabiana's eyes get wider as I took a step toward her. "What the hell did I ever do to you?"

Another step, then Espie's hand on my arm, holding tight, keeping me from reaching out for Fabiana.

"*Mija,* you *can't*—it's an immediate disqualification."

"I don't give a shit."

"Alegría—is this really how you want it to end?"

I blinked at Papi's quiet words—the fog around me clearing. I shivered as I felt something drop over my shoulders—Elaine, draping her jacket around me since the beautiful black chiffon top Andre had chosen for me tonight was shredded, hanging open, exposing the thin black camisole I wore beneath.

Esperanza's hand returned to my arm, gentle now as she gazed into my face. "*Mi vida,* I have to know what you want to do—if you go on, it has to be in the next five minutes."

"Can't she bail, Esperanza? Get a pass or something, considering the sitch?" Tonio asked, staring at Fabiana. He and Guille had edged into the room, putting themselves between me and her. Just behind me, I could sense Papi and Elaine—and Jaime.

Esperanza glanced over her shoulder at Fabiana. "Given the circumstances, they're letting her move to next week, T. But she can't bail—she has to perform. If she doesn't, she forfeits outright—show rules."

"Dammit, Espie—" All of a sudden, Jaime was beside me, his arm around my shoulders. "Ali's the one who's been wronged here, who got her instrument destroyed, yet she's the one who stands to get punished? That's bullshit and you know it!"

"I understand, Jaime, believe me, I do, but my hands are tied here. Look, we all know what her guitar means to her, but to everyone else, it's just an instrument and there are plenty around here she can use." Espie rubbed the back of her neck, looking from him to me. "It's in the contract *she* signed. If there's nothing physically restricting her from performing, she *has* to perform or forfeit her place."

I turned away and found my father's gaze with mine. "Papi?"

Tell me what to do . . . please . . . I can't think anymore . . .

But even as the silent questions crowded my mind, he was shaking his head. "No. Since the moment I said you could do this, it's been yours, Ali. There's no shame in walking away right now—but the choice has to be yours."

I looked from face to face, seeing in each the same thing . . . no shame at all in bailing right now, no one would blame me one bit. And it was so tempting . . . I was so tired, just wanted to go home, to my room, to my bed, curl up in a ball and pretend this whole stupid thing didn't exist; that I didn't have stupid websites or autograph seekers. That I could wake up, talk to Sosi, go downstairs and find my Bernabé propped in its stand, gleaming and beautiful and perfect. That none of this had ever happened.

Out of the corner of my eye, I caught a self-satisfied smirk.

"Andre, I need a new shirt."

"Let's go, precious. We'll get you show ready."

Before I turned to go into wardrobe, I locked gazes with Fabiana whose smirk had dissolved to a pissy frown. "I already am."

"Ali, Gabriel has one of his guitars ready for you to use," Esperanza said.

"Okay, thanks." Grabbing the sheer silver top Andre held out, I headed into the changing area, then poked my head out between two of the screens. "Espie?"

She stopped short, already halfway out the door. "Yeah?"

"Tell the higher-ups no free pass. Whatever votes I get—that's what I'll go with. I want to earn it." More than I'd wanted anything else before in my life.

Collective jaw drop. "Ali, are you sure?" Elaine asked in a hushed voice.

"Absolutely. I've come this far on my own gas. I live or die this way."

Esperanza smiled and shook her head as she pulled the mic for her headset around to her mouth. "Girl, you got more guts than any twelve guys I know." With a thumbs-up, she took off.

I tore off the remains of my black shirt and slipped the silver one on over the camisole. The rest of my outfit was fine, so Bianca next, standing still while she and Teresa did the speed dial version of makeup repair and we took off running toward the wings, Teresa still brushing loose powder over my face.

Just before I hit the wings, I felt a hand grab my arm—Jaime pulling me close. "Kick total ass out there, babe," he whispered in my ear right before he kissed me—right there, in front of God and everyone. Not a little kiss, either, but this hard, open-mouthed number that sent heat flaring from the pit of my stomach straight out the ends of my hair. *Whoa—*

"Ali, come *on,*" Esperanza was hissing as Jaime let me go and I stumbled toward her. "Okay, you're going on in five, four, three, two, one, go, go, go . . . break a leg."

It all happened so fast, didn't have time to freak—to panic or think—until I was out onstage. Until I saw Chianna and Fredo, their smiles toned down from the usual perky and dazzling to sympathetic as they led the applause. Until I saw Gabriel, holding out . . . *ay, no,* his prized Rodriguez, an instrument every bit the equal of mine. Offering it to me with a sad expression so totally foreign to his round face. And the tears started to clog my throat . . . cutting off my air and blurring my vision, but with a deep breath, I fought them back.

Not now.

Not the time.

I could cry later.

And I knew from his expression that he was completely aware it couldn't possibly be the same. For a guitarist, their instrument is so unbelievably individual, such an extension of themselves. He knew . . . the way only a fellow musician—fellow guitarist—could know. How I'd lost a piece of me.

I walked to him, ran my hand over the rich, smooth cedar top, and kissed his cheek.

"No thanks, Gabriel."

He cocked his head, curious, but didn't say anything, simply replaced the guitar in its stand, watching as I walked to the big

Steinway grand, silently asking Adán if I could. As he slid off the bench, I waved at the rest of the band to sit.

Wasn't going to need them for this.

Settling myself in front of the keys, I could hear murmurs and whispers, but they faded almost immediately as I went into my zone where everything fell away but the music. I was going to need that faith in the music right now—big time—because I was flying genuinely blind. I mean, sure, I'd been playing the piano almost as long as I had the guitar, but last time I'd performed in public, I'd been wearing pigtails, my feet barely reaching the pedals. But there was something compelling me to play this—my project that I'd been working on during my off-time, the first few chords so familiar, I could feel the wave of recognition from the audience, even through the zone.

Not like that came as any big shock. I'd yet to meet anyone who hadn't heard "Imagine" at least once in their lives. But most of these folks had probably never heard it in Spanish, the words every bit as poignant and poetic in that language as they were in English.

Or maybe it was just the feeling I was putting into it, every bit of hurt and pain I couldn't let out any other way, because really, I just couldn't understand what had gone so terribly wrong. Why what had started out as nothing more than me wanting to prove myself, prove that I wanted to perform, prove my ability to survive in the world of professional music, had turned into this . . . vendetta. I didn't understand *why* this one woman had decided I was such a threat to her that she had to attack and take away the most integral part of my musical being. Except—

She hadn't.

I loved my guitar. I would always mourn the loss of my instrument. But as I played and sang John Lennon's beautiful words of peace and hope for a better world, I felt a sense of calm begin to wash over me, steadying my hands, which had fumbled a bit at the outset.

Because I hadn't quite finished the transcription, I switched to English, the words as written fitting me like a glove. I *was* a dreamer. No matter what, music would always be my world, my dream, and I hoped that anyone listening could hear that. I performed for them.

I performed for me.

The last, sustained note died away into complete and utter silence. Such a *loud* silence, man, that it snapped me out of my trance, awareness returning that I really wasn't alone.

Behind me, I heard one lone pair of hands clapping. Twisting on the bench, I saw Gabriel, standing there, clapping slowly, rhythmically, and one by one, the rest of the guys in the band joined in, adding in the age-old musician's tribute of pounding their feet against the floor.

Then, with a sound like a crack of thunder, the place absolutely exploded. Clapping and cheering and whistling and foot stamping that went on and on and on as I sat there at the piano, stunned. And when I finally got my brains back and actually stood and bowed, it got *louder,* if you can believe that noise.

I stumbled into the wings, my ears ringing so hard . . . it was like the applause wasn't fading at all.

"*Vamos,* Ali."

I glanced over my shoulder, staring at the arm Gabriel offered. "Huh?"

"They want you again, *chiquita.* Don't deny your fans." He was smiling, that Santa's elf grin, as he flicked his finger across my nose. Dazed, I put my hand in the crook of his elbow and let him lead me back out onstage where the place was going completely nuts. They'd partially raised the house lights and—

Oh . . .

There, at his usual table near the front, was Papi and he was clapping like crazy and pounding his foot on the floor and even from the stage, I could see the tears on his face and he looked . . . oh God, *so* proud. Then he looked up at me and mouthed, *Te amo, Alegría.*

Hand to my mouth, I ran off the stage and into his arms, hugging him tight. "I love you, too, Papi."

24

So you'd think after all that, everything would be peachy keen, right?

I'd slayed the big, bad Brunhilda, beat her at her own game, discovered an even deeper well of inner strength, yada, yada, yada. Now everything would be fluffy kittens and My Little Ponies and all that fairy-tale stuff with a side of flan. I'd be one happy Cuban girl.

Think again.

As Tonio would say, "It just don't work that way, yo."

Truer words were never spoken, dude.

Spent the night well enough, so totally drained, I was just this side of dead. Waking up, though? Numb. That's all. Just . . . numb.

Okay, not totally. Started out numb, but as the sleep woozies fell away, I felt a sharp, hot flare of pain as my blurry gaze registered my gig bag, in the corner of my room, half-unzipped and sagging, because there wasn't anything in there to give it shape. Remembering the reason it was empty *wasn't* because my guitar was downstairs in its stand. And for a second, I couldn't breathe and I regretted, *so* much, not slamming her head against the wall again and again. My fists twisted in the sheets, I could *feel* the reverberations shooting through my arms as I slammed her against the wall the one time and wanted nothing more than to feel that sensation again—feel those vibrations as her head made contact with the wall.

Boy, did that scare me. Fast as I could, I got that pain in a head lock and wrestled it way, *way* to the back of my brain, relieved that once I did, I went right back to feeling numb. Welcomed numb like a long-lost wealthy relative.

When Elaine and I talked about it, much later, when I was finally able *to* talk about it, she said it was a defense mechanism. My mind's way of protecting itself because I'd suffered such an emotional trauma.

Only thing that made sense out of that whole screwed-up period.

After Papi led me backstage, we were met by Esperanza and a few of Miami Beach's Finest. For a wild, exhausted second, I thought they were coming to take me away because I'd shoved Brunhilda into the wall. Don't think she didn't try, too—complaining to anyone who would listen that I was crazy and had attacked her and she had witnesses.

You notice I said anyone who would listen? Not too many people paying attention to *her.*

No, the cops were there because there'd been a fire and reports would have to be filed for the insurance companies and God knows why else. All I knew was it sucked beyond the telling that I had to repeat everything that had happened, the whole sequence of events, from the stupid photographer, to handing my guitar to the ponytail lady, to her "misplacing it." Then trying not to lose my mind when they turned their questions to Ponytail, hearing her say, no, she really didn't understand why I'd reacted the way I had—just put it down to my playing the baby diva.

She went a sort of interesting ashy gray when Papi and Gabriel both swore as to the guitar's value. Dunno why—that pair of *Sex and the City* pumps she was wearing had to have cost at least eight hundred bucks. Amazing. She could drop that kind of change on a pair of butt-ugly shoes and still not grok that a handcrafted guitar that was as much work of art as instrument could cost close to ten grand.

Words like "third-degree" and "felony" got mentioned, making her twitch as she repeated to the cops that yes, she'd insisted I entrust her with the guitar for the sake of a couple of stupid pictures and she'd sworn nothing would happen to it, but she honestly didn't know what had happened after she set it down.

A brief moment of happy came from finding out Fabiana also spent a nice chunk of time being questioned by the cops because when they asked around as to motive, pretty much anyone in the know, including me, pointed a finger right at her. She'd been stupid—not hiding all that hostility. Thing was, though, she'd been hostile to most everyone and much as I might wish it, you couldn't arrest someone for being a total bitch. Not without the evidence to support they were also psychotic criminals.

In the end, though, none of it really mattered a damn. They couldn't prove anything because no one had actually *seen* anything, and there wasn't enough left of my guitar to provide any viable evidence. And for the Miami Beach Police? Come on—we're talking a city where celebrities engage in high-profile acts of public stupidity on a regular basis, in addition to your garden variety crimes. A torched guitar fell seriously far down the low end of the interest scale. No one had been killed or even hurt and the show's insurance company could replace even a Bernabé without so much as blinking at the expense.

Just really didn't matter. At least not enough to keep the next day from dawning—from my having to return to the McMansion and try to go about my regular day's business. But it was useless. I knew it and Gabriel knew it, which is why he shooed me out of the rehearsal studio after less than a half hour and down to the beach.

"Hey, I've been looking for you."

"Couldn't rehearse." I didn't look away from the wake curling away from the big horkin' yacht that no doubt belonged to one of the other big horkin' estates.

"Gabriel told me to go find something relaxing to do." He wasn't stupid, either, ordering me down to the beach and away from the house. Yeah, I was numb now—major possibility that could change in a hurry if I ran into Brunhilda.

"You couldn't have put on sunscreen to do it?" Jaime eased down onto the chaise lounge next to mine and rummaged through the tote I'd dragged down with me. A second later, he began spreading something cool over my nose and cheeks. "You're turning awfully red. Bianca's going to have a hell of a time covering it up later."

I shrugged. But didn't stop him, either. Actually, his touch, fingers slippery with the sunscreen, smoothing it across my skin, was the first thing I'd actually felt since I woke up and saw my gig bag. Reaching up, I trapped his hand against my cheek.

"Hi."

"Hi yourself." His eyes creased up a little at the corners as his thumb continued massaging in the lotion. Freeing his hand, he swiped it against his shorts and tossed the tube of lotion back into the bag.

"What's up?"

"Aside from the fact that I was worried about you?" He smiled at me, making more good feelings break through the layer of numb. "Espie wanted me to find you. Tell you that you're going to have to go over to the club earlier than usual."

The good feelings melted away. "Why?"

"Press conference."

"Oh no." Pulling my knees up, I dropped my forehead down.

"It'll be okay, Ali." His hand stroked my hair.

"I *really* don't want to rehash this over and over."

"You won't have to. At least not much." He was on his knees beside the chaise, his voice soft in my ear, soothing. "They're going to have a PR flack with you helping to field questions. They're going to answer anything about motive and who might've done it with the old 'ongoing investigation, so we really can't say anything' line."

I lifted my head, looking into his eyes. "Then why do I even need to be there?"

"Because," he said, moving his hand to cup my cheek. "The press wants to talk to *you* about the performance you gave last night. It's tremendous press, Ali. It's made headlines all over the United States and Latin America."

"Great." I shoved a hand through my hair. "Straight-up talent gets acknowledged with a couple inches of column space. Get your instrument maliciously destroyed, you get headlines."

"That's showbiz, baby."

"It's shitty."

"Yeah, it is." Taking off his shoes and socks, he held a hand out. "Come on, let's go for a walk."

Why not? Let's face it, trying to relax was as hopeless as rehearsing had been, although I'd at least made a pretense of relaxing, sprawling in the cushy chaise in my sleek, black one-piece, a stack of trashy magazines on the table beside me.

Holding hands, we walked down to the water's edge and let the waves wash over our feet as we turned and strolled along the shore. "Tell me about New York, Jaime."

We stopped, facing the mainland, the skyline sharp against the superblue sky I'd never seen anywhere but South Florida. I wanted something different—wanted nothing more than to be anywhere but here.

His voice was soft and thoughtful as he said, "In some ways it's really similar, in some ways, it's the complete antithesis." One side of his mouth crooked up as he studied the skyline. "Went into downtown the first week we were here and it was almost like being at home, you know? All the hustle and the bad drivers, you could barely see daylight for all the buildings and people in suits power walking past the winos. The sounds of a dozen different languages and tourists taking pictures of the weirdest shit you can imagine."

"Like what?"

"The winos."

Laughing together, we started walking again while Jaime continued telling me about his city. "It's dirty and loud and brash—no bullshit about New Yorkers, that's for sure. But there are times it's just the most beautiful place in the world, like during fall, when the leaves are changing in Central Park and it's this one enormous blaze of color in the middle of all that concrete."

His eyes narrowed like he was seeing those flaming leaves instead of blue water and palm trees. "Or at Christmas, Rockefeller Center at twilight, little kids skating on the rink, watching the tree light up, then going for Italian at some little mom-and-pop joint that only the locals know. There's so much you can do there—any time of day or night. It's really a city of dreams and endless possibilities."

Turning away from the skyline, we headed back the way we came. "Who knows where my career might take me, but New York's always gonna be home, *tú sabes*?"

Stopping beneath one of the huge palms, he leaned against the trunk and put his arms around my waist. "So how big a dork am I?"

"Not a dork at all." I smiled, taking off his baseball cap and brushing my fingers through the hat hair. "Actually, I'm thinking you maybe missed your calling."

His eyebrows went up. "Yeah?"

"Yeah." I traced my fingers over those eyebrows and his cheekbones and his jaw and mouth, just studying him. "Forget film and TV production. I think you've got the soul of a poet—or a songwriter, maybe."

"Nah," he laughed, blushing a little and looking so adorable, my heart skipped a few beats. "Considering what my dad's paid for my education, the least I should be able to do is articulate what I like."

"Tell your dad the money's been well-spent." For just those couple minutes, he'd transported me, taken me away from heat and humidity and the hell this had all become. I'd felt the crowded New York streets, the sharp, cool air of a fall afternoon brushing over my skin.

Reaching up, I kissed him, loving how his arms tightened around my waist, losing myself in how good he felt.

"Woo-hooo, *aproveche, hermano!*"

My head whipped around at the cheers and wild honking coming from the power boat cruising past.

"¡Oye, mamita, qué almohadas tan suaves!"

Oh my *God.* My face felt like it was on fire as the commentary on my ass echoed across the water and probably all the way down to Papi at the university. For as private as this stupid house was, in some ways there was no privacy at all, between passing boats and random camera crews.

All I wanted was some quiet—to share some time with Jaime that wasn't completely tainted by this whole stupid experience. Was that really all that much to ask?

"Come on."

Pulling me past our abandoned chaise lounges, Jaime led me into one of the little yellow-and-white–striped cabanas that I'd discovered the first week weren't simply tents, but these wood-framed numbers with real floors and wired for electricity even. Maybe money couldn't buy everything, but it could sure buy the impractical, complete with ceiling fan and minifridge.

Urging me down onto the double chaise, Jaime reached into the fridge and pulled out a bottle of water, handing it to me. I held it against my cheek, enjoying the cold, wet feel before untwisting the cap and taking a drink, my throat closing as I suddenly remembered the day of the auditions, the cute, sweet guy offering me the water bottle, assuring me it was okay, it was unopened.

He smiled as I gave him back the bottle. Just before he took a drink, he reached out and touched my cheek. "Never thought it would turn out like this back then, did you?"

Wouldn't even ask how he knew. Was just enough that he was remembering, too. I watched as he took a long drink, then set the bottle on the table next to the chaise.

"Come on, Ali, just relax a little." He lay back and pulled me down next to him.

With Jaime, I'd been feeling for the first time all day—feeling nothing but good things and I wanted to keep that. Didn't want to risk it going away, because if it did, and I could still feel . . .

No, didn't want to feel anything bad. Not anymore. I was kind of tired of the bad.

"Ali, what are you doing?"

Duh. Wasn't that hard to figure out. And Jaime wasn't stupid. Pretty soon, we were back to kissing the way we had been by the tree and then some. As he pulled me closer, one of his legs slid between mine, and I realized this was the first time we'd ever kissed lying down. Closest we'd come was sneaking some time on the sofa in the rehearsal studio. But we'd been too freakin' afraid to do anything more than some heavy leaning against the sofa's arm, knowing that at any moment, someone could walk in on us. Scary, but exciting.

This was exciting, too, but in a different way because I *knew* no one was going to come barging in on us any time soon. Gave me the courage to do some of the things I'd been wanting to, so bad; that my mind had been torturing me with at night. And being with Jaime right now just felt so good.

"*Ay,* Ali," he groaned against my neck.

My heartbeat went into overdrive at the sound of his voice. "Is this okay?" I asked, with his shirt halfway up his chest.

He closed his eyes and bit his lip. "I really should say no, it's not okay." Before I could do or say anything more, he reached back over his head and pulled the shirt off, tossing it aside. Opening his eyes, he took my hands and put them against his chest. Nowhere I hadn't touched before, but always with clothes between us.

God, he felt as nice without a shirt as he did with one, his skin so warm against mine.

"Okay?" he asked, glancing down at himself, then back up, his gaze wide and . . . nervous.

"Oh yeah." He had nothing to be nervous about. But realizing he was gave me another shot of courage, prompting me to lean forward and put a kiss right in the hollow of his throat, then lower, and lower. It was like playing a game of follow the leader with my own kisses, trying not to giggle at the new sensations of skin and hair against my lips, then not wanting to giggle at all as I felt how his heart sped up right below where my palm rested.

It was amazing, too, being able to feel how his muscles clenched and his breathing got faster as I trailed more kisses across his stomach, dipped my tongue into the small indentation of his navel, gently scratched my nails down his chest. Before I could go any farther, though, I was back at his mouth, both of his hands on either side of my head as he kissed me again, something hard and desperate in how he did it and I suddenly realized—all this time, he'd been holding back.

"Alegría."

I pulled back, my hands tight on his shoulders. "That's the first time I've ever heard you use my full name."

"It's such a perfect name for you—Joy," he repeated, his voice going even softer as he pulled me tight against him.

Still holding me close, he rolled us over so he lay over me, one of his thighs sliding and rubbing between mine. As he dropped light kisses along my jaw and neck that made me shiver, his hands skimmed my sides over my bathing suit and curved just under my breasts, his thumbs brushing over them. He was the first boy who'd ever touched me like this. First boy I'd ever really wanted to have touch me like this—

Opening my eyes, I held his gaze with mine as I reached up and eased the straps of my bathing suit down my arms. Watched his eyes widen, his mouth drop open slightly, as I shoved the suit down to my waist before bringing his hands back to where they'd been.

"Okay?" I whispered, shaking from all the new sensations—from what I was allowing myself to do.

Looking from my eyes to his hands, he let out this long, slow breath. "So very okay, baby."

As he lowered his head, I closed my eyes and just . . . felt. And as good as that was, it still wasn't enough. I wanted to be doing more, making him feel as good as he was making me feel. Running my fingers through his hair, I trailed them down his back, to his hips, pulling him more completely against me, arching up—

"God, Ali . . . we can't." He reached down and caught my hands in his, pulling them away from his waistband. Shifting again so we were both on our sides facing each other, he drew our joined hands up between us, holding them tight.

"Not like this, when you're so upset over everything that's happened and just looking to feel better any way you can."

I couldn't look him in the eye. Because he was right and it was just too mortifying. I wouldn't ask. Nope, nope, no— "Don't you want to?" Guess I *could* ask.

"Good God, Ali, don't be crazy," he said, sounding sort of strangled. "Your hands were down there, your legs were around me—you *know* I want to." He put one finger beneath my chin, tilting my head up and forcing me to look into those gorgeous streaky green eyes that were practically glowing in the sunlight coming through the window. "However, when we make love the first time, it's going to be right. Not some sweaty roll on a beach chair—not that that wouldn't be a ton of fun, too." He chuckled then his expression went serious again. "But not for your first time."

I heard everything he said, knew I'd go back and savor every word the way you savored those choice, chocolate-dipped strawberries from Godiva, but one word in particular sort of stuck out.

"When?"

He didn't say anything right away, just lowered his head and pressed his lips against the upper curve of each of my breasts. "Yeah—when," he repeated, his breath warm against my skin. "Don't know when, exactly, but it'll happen." His head jerked up, his gaze finding mine. "I can't see it not happening."

"But the show's over after next week, Jaime."

And could I just kick myself? Really hard? Me *and* my big mouth?

"Did you think we were going to be over just because the show was?"

"I—I . . . don't know." I liked Jaime. So much. Definitely wanted to spend more time with him, get to know him away from this stupid show. Physically, he made me feel . . . amazing. But like in the cartoons, I also had this little devil sitting on my shoulder whispering, "But he's older and more experienced and from New York, and you're just some little lily-livered high-school virgin."

"Ali, it's not going to be over, I promise, okay?" He was looking at me with the oddest expression on his face, his eyebrows drawn together and his mouth set in this tight line. "Not unless you want it to be."

"No, I definitely don't." I curled against him and rested my head on his shoulder, feeling safe about it even though we were both still naked from the waist up, his hand stroking my bare back. Not that I didn't still want him like crazy, not that the hormones weren't still doing some wild merengue through my system, but the urgency, that need I'd had to feel something—*anything*—was gone. Jaime holding me close, his breath ruffling my bangs across my forehead was enough. Made for some really nice dreams as I drifted off to sleep.

25

Oh, *ugh*—I was sweaty, my hair sticking to my cheeks and the back of my neck, but at the same time there was the nicest sensation of something cool stroking up and down my arms and . . . butterflies? Landing on my eyes, my cheeks, brushing across my mouth.

"Come on, sleepyhead. You need to wake up."

"Hm?"

"Ali, *por favor,* it's time to get up."

"Huh? Wha—?" I blinked, trying to bring stuff into focus, not seeing anything familiar except—"Jaime?" I pushed myself up, recognizing as I did the interior of the cabana, but without the streaming sunlight. More dark and shadowy. As I got a little more coherent, I glanced down, running my hand over my bathing suit, which was back up and in position.

"There's only so much I could take, Ali," he said quietly as he ran the damp corner of the beach towel over my forehead.

I knew when I actually woke up I'd appreciate that. Both the gesture and the feelings that had prompted it. "What time is it?" I mumbled, rubbing at my eyes.

"Going on three and about to rain." Thunder rumbled in the distance, like it needed to provide backup. "Espie just buzzed me. You need to go back to the house and get ready."

We sat there, quiet, for a few minutes while I struggled to come completely back to the land of the living. Finally I sighed and said, "I suppose I ought to trot my ass back up there for the fluff cycle." Or on second thought. "Maybe a little more than fluffing needed," I observed, running my hands through my sweat-soaked hair.

Jaime reached out and grabbed my hand before I could run it through my rat's nest hair again. "You look fine." Standing, he pulled me up after him and into his arms. "More than fine." He hadn't put his shirt back on yet, his skin damp and cool beneath my cheek.

"Even though the circumstances that brought it about sucked, I want you to know how grateful I am to have had this afternoon, Ali. I'm glad I could be here for you." Leaning down he whispered in my ear, "And stopping was one of the hardest things I've ever done." Then he pulled back and winked. "Literally and figuratively."

Poet one minute, total guy the next. Both of which made me blush and push at his chest. "*Oye,* put your shirt back on before you make me act like a bad girl again."

His eyebrows went straight up. "Wait a minute—you were the one ripping clothes off—yours and mine—but it's all *my* fault?"

"Absolutely." I grinned and tossed his T-shirt at him. "Isn't assigning blame one of those women's prerogative things?"

"Wouldn't know." Pulling his shirt on, he said, "Never been a woman," in this completely serious, dry voice that made me laugh.

Wouldn't say that the rest of the afternoon was quite that pleasant—I mean, how could it be? But being able to recall bits and pieces of the time I spent with Jaime sure kept me on a more or less even keel. Even dealing with the press went pretty smoothly since I had not one, but two, PR flacks, one from our U.S. network, one from the show's production company. Although I think I sort of surprised them, how smooth I was when the inevitable questions came at me about my guitar, how long I'd had it, what it was like for a musician to lose her primary means of expression. Clearly, the flacks had been prepared for me to choke up and go all weepy, judging by the bottle of water and Kleenex they had at the ready, but I'd be damned if I would break down publicly. Never again.

"So, Ali, was that the first time you've ever played piano?"

I stared at the guy who asked. Wait a minute, was that the creepy reporter from the *Herald*? Oh, please. He knew the answer to this.

"Um, no . . . not the first time at all." I took a sip of water to keep from laughing. "I've been playing piano for years. Not quite as seriously as the guitar, obviously, but I know my way around a keyboard." I shrugged and took another sip of water.

The collective disappointment on their faces was absolutely killing me. It's like they wanted to spin it as this miraculous thing: "Top-notch musician suddenly able to play piano in wake of guitar's destruction." Sorry to bust the immaculate conception myth. Reality's boring, dudes. Even on reality shows. Maybe *especially* on reality shows.

The PR flacks did actually come in handy, making totally and completely sure that Fabiana's path and my path did this nice little parallel thing where they didn't cross. Even down to being led onstage for the announcement—Guille and Fabiana brought on from one side, me and Tonio from the other, keeping her at one end, me at the other, with the guys in between.

"Whatever happens, girl, you kicked ass, you know that, right?"

"Thanks, Tonio. You, too." We touched fists.

"*Que te toque la lotería,* Tonio."

"Gracias, hermano." I watched Tonio and Guille exchange

their "my brother" handshake that had gotten more elaborate every week. The audience had gotten to where they expected it, applauding and egging them on. Couldn't help but laugh as they messed up, then started the whole ritual over again, because they'd developed some crackpot theory about how it had to be perfect or it was *"mala suerte, mija."* They so cracked me up.

"*Tú también,* Ali."

"*Gracias,* Guille." I squeezed the hand he held out before leaning back in my onstage chair, relaxed, just waiting for the commercial break to end so we could get on with it. Had a feeling I wasn't going to need Guille's lottery wish. Not me being arrogant, just a feeling I had. I'd watched the recap on the greenroom monitor and after I got done cringing at my sloppy piano technique and a couple of the minor note clunkers, I got caught up in the performance. Began to understand why I'd gotten the kind of reaction I had last night. There was something . . . indefinable about it, an honesty and emotion that bled from every note—every word.

Not my best technical performance, not by a long shot, but definitely the most heartfelt performance I'd given.

"Yo, we're back on." Tonio's hand gripped mine; out of the corner of my eye, I could see he had Guille's in a tight grasp, as well. Farther down, Fabiana was sitting in her chair, back angled slightly away from us, arms crossed, even as she smiled pleasantly into Camera One.

The two pairs of announcers, Chianna and Fredo and the American TV pair, came out together. They traded off variations on a theme of the same recap in Spanish, then English, asking for applause for each of us in turn, then clustered together, looking down at the huge card with the finalists.

"In fourth place . . ."

"En cuarto lugar . . ."

Then Chianna, in her smooth, telenovela actress voice announced, "Tonio de la Cruz."

Oh no . . . Tonio. Releasing my hand, he turned and gave Guille this huge, back-slapping hug and another round of their handshake, before turning back to me and giving me a kiss and a hug.

"Tonio, I'm so sorry."

"One of us had to go, baby. It's cool, it's been a good ride."

Nothing, but *nothing,* fazed him. He was going to be fine. At Guille's silent urging, I moved over into the now-empty chair between us, holding onto his hand. Poor guy, he was trembling. I tightened my hand around his, making him smile.

"In third place . . ."

"En tercer lugar . . ."

You understand, I was still kind of in that relaxed-zone sort of place. Which was why, when Fredo said, "Ali Montero," and it was met with a split-second of dead silence from the audience, it didn't actually register. It didn't even register when the crowd exploded into a big collective "boo!"

It wasn't until Guille took me in his arms and hugged me, whispering, "*Ay,* Ali, *lo siento, mija.* I really wanted us to be the last two," and I looked past his shoulder and saw Fabiana with this truly stomach-churning, triumphant smile that it hit me.

I was gone. Voted off the island. I'd had immunity and I gave it up and now I was paying the price for being such an arrogant fathead.

Guess heartfelt hadn't mattered for much out in TV World, no matter what the in-house audience thought.

I did manage to whisper, "*Felicidades,* Guille." Managed to make it to the hosts, say my good-byes, and managed to make it off the stage where I waved off Elaine and Jaime and Tonio and everyone else and just found a wall to lean against, trying to breathe. My arms crossed over my stomach, I took these short, gasping breaths, trying to wrap my brain around the fact that it was done. I'd wanted it to be done . . . and it was. Fair and square. It was what I'd wanted, right? But right now, fair and square really sucked.

"*Bueno,* if you hadn't been as attached to that cheap piece of wood as a baby to its *mami*'s tit, maybe you would've actually survived. Was that it, *nenesita*? It was your *mami* substitute?"

Slowly, I opened my eyes and found her standing maybe fifteen feet away. Smirking. Gloating. I didn't move away from the wall, but I did straighten, and in the back of my mind I recognized the look of fear that crossed her face. She didn't know what I'd do. She was taunting me here because she could, there were people around and she was pretty sure I wouldn't do anything to her. But not totally sure.

Good.

"Do not *ever* speak to me again." My voice was low and hard and steady. A voice I'd never heard coming from me before. "You and I both know that last night I outperformed you and outclassed you in every way, no matter what the numbers say, and I didn't have to cheat to do it."

I pushed away from the wall and walked toward her, stopping a couple feet away. "You want to win that bad? Go right ahead—you can have it, and live with the fact of knowing how far you had to sink to get it." Not that it mattered to someone like her; for her, it was a way of life.

She tossed the spiral-permed curls and tried for one of her usual "whatevers," but it came out seriously weak.

"Yeah, whatever—*Hilda.*"

I was through with her. Then I smiled, as I realized—really *was* though with her. As in, done being around her. Maybe I wouldn't get to compete next week, but I also didn't have to stress over what crap she might pull, what stupid comment about my appearance or ability might worm its way into my psyche. Hey, whaddaya know—I was *free.*

Blowing past her, I paused to give Guille a huge hug, because man, my money was on him now. No way Brunhilda could beat my boy. I stopped and hugged Espie and Andre and Bianca and Teresa in turn, each of them looking at me like I was nuts. Saw Elaine and Papi standing together and looking concerned.

"Ali?"

I took Elaine's hands in mine and leaned in, kissing her cheek. "It's okay, Elaine, it really is." Laughing, I turned to Papi and hugged him tight. "I'm so sorry for everything, Papi."

"Está bien, mija." His hand stroked my hair. "But . . . are *you*?"

"I'm so seriously fine, you have no idea." I pulled away, grinning so big, my face was practically hurting. "I swear."

Spying Jaime down by makeup, I ran toward him.

"Hey!" I launched myself into his arms, feeling kind of giddy and dizzy and stupid.

He caught me and hugged me close. "Hey, I'm sorry."

"It's fine." Really, *really* was fine.

"Yeah?"

"Yeah, no more Brunhilda, you know? I mean, I wish it had been the other way around, no Brunhilda, and me and Guille as the finalists. But better than me and her as the finalists—I mean, could you imagine?"

"No way in hell."

I started to lean in to kiss him, but the tone of his voice stopped me cold. "What's up?"

"Nothing." He smiled, but for the first time since I'd met him, it didn't reach his eyes. No lighting up, highlighting the varied streaks of green, no crinkly action at the corners.

"Uh-uh, Jaime Lozano. You can't pull that 'nothing' stuff with me. What's going on?"

His eyes were narrow and those two red spots were there on his cheekbones—another dead giveaway. For sure now, he was upset about something.

Blowing out a deep breath, he opened the door to makeup and pulled me in behind him, all the way through to wardrobe, closing that door behind us. He yanked off his headset and monitor, throwing them across the room. "*Dammit.*"

"Jaime?" Now he was scaring me, because this was clearly beyond upset and on into rage territory.

Turning back to me, he wrapped his hands around my upper arms, stroking down to my elbows then up to my shoulders and back down again. "I was going to tell you earlier today, I swear I was, but this afternoon . . . it was just such a beautiful interlude, Ali. And I couldn't blow that. You finally seemed to have found some peace with everything that's happened."

I stared at him, willing him to meet my gaze, but he wouldn't—couldn't—look at me. "Just tell me, Jaime."

"It really should be you and Guille."

Relief. Big and in those crashing waves you read about in books. "Well, of *course,* it should be me and Guille, but there's no accounting for tastes, Jaime—" I stopped, seeing something really wrong in his face. Something that twisted and churned in my stomach, sort of like when I'd seen that hateful smile on Fabiana's face out onstage. "Wait—when you say it should be me and Guille . . ."

"It was fixed, Ali. They wanted you off."

"How—" *Fixed*? *Off*? "How do you know?"

"VIPs in the greenroom." He pressed his lips tight together. "Last night while you were changing, I went to go in there—grab you some water. But before I got all the way in the room, I overheard some suits bitching about you performing, that it would've been much easier if you didn't and it could be called a straight forfeit."

If I thought I couldn't breathe *before*.

"Ali." Jaime's hands were cupping my elbows, holding me up.

I blinked, trying to make sense of it. "But, they gave me the free pass. I was going to go on . . . next week . . ."

"Then I'm guessing they would've just named you in third place next week." His breathing was coming as fast and harsh as mine as he held tight to my arms.

"But why?" I managed to choke out.

"I don't know, baby, I swear." His hands were back to rubbing my arms . . . they were so warm . . . I was so cold . . . "But from what little I got, it was all about not letting you win. They didn't even want you coming in second place—they really wanted you off this week."

I grabbed his wrists, holding him still. "Why do you say it should be me and Guille?"

"Because that's what *I* want. So bad. It's what should've been, Ali." He looked away again. "The way you performed was so fucking phenomenal. I guess I was hoping your votes would be so overwhelming there'd be no way they could do that to you."

We stood there, staring at each other, while I tried—so hard—to figure out what was going on here.

Let's see . . . no matter how I performed last night, I could've gotten my pass—had one more shot at the whole thing. Instead, I insisted on taking my chances with the votes, went out there minutes after losing my prized Bernabé, performed my guts out . . . lost, fair and square, but maybe not? But I did. They'd said so, right there onstage, *"en tercer lugar."* But Jaime was standing right here—in front of me—telling me that it might not really have been the right result. Because he'd heard last night—*last* night—before I even went on, that I wasn't going to make it.

See, that's what my mind kept coming back to, what it zeroed in on because it kept repeating like an old, broken record. Jaime knew. He knew last night, when he kissed me. He knew today—this afternoon—in the cabana. He knew tonight. He knew at any number of times when he could've told me and kept me from making a complete and total fool of myself. Because if I'd known, if he'd just said something, *anything*. . . .

No way would I have gone out on that stage last night, sat down at that piano, and poured my soul out. No way would I have *ever* gone back to that huge, stupid house on the island. No way would I have been on that stage tonight, watching Fabiana smirking as she got what should've been mine.

No way, no way, no way—

If he'd just said *something.*

"Hijo de puta." Like slow motion—I saw my palm connect with his cheek, watched his head jerk to the side, *then* I heard the crack of my skin hitting his. And the last thing I saw of Jaime Lozano were his eyes, wide and so, so green, above a livid, red handprint.

26

I barreled out of wardrobe and straight into Elaine.

"There you are, *mija*."

"Elaine, I want my father." Grabbing onto her hands, I whispered, "I want to go home." I wanted to get the hell out of this house of horrors.

"*Mija* . . . it's okay." Her hands were so warm against mine, I clung tighter, trying to get some of that warmth into mine. I was beyond numb and on to this ice cold that prickled along my skin like a thousand little painful, sharp needles.

"Your father's out front, waiting for you to do the press conference. Then we can go."

Oh, Jesus, Mary, and Joseph. The post-show press conference. "I can't."

"Ali, what the hell's going on, girl? Did you have a fight with Jaime?"

Closing my eyes, I shook my head. "I can't do it. I can't." My eyes snapped open as Elaine shook my arms, *hard.*

"You need to tell me what's going on, Ali."

"I can't," I repeated. "Not right now."

"Then I can't help you and you need to go out there and deal with your responsibilities." Pure, one-hundred-percent, Dr. Garces "don't screw with me" mode.

And I laughed. Kinda more like a bark, actually. Elaine was

looking at me like I'd lost my mind, which, maybe . . . we were heading that way.

"My responsibilities. That's unbelievable. Totally and completely unbelievable. After all this crap I have to go play nice *again*?"

Clearly, God had a mean streak in that famous sense of humor. "Fine. Let's go."

"Ali?" Dr. Garces was gone and she was back to being Elaine—closest thing to a mother I'd ever had.

"Let's just go, Elaine. And then I want to go home."

"Okay, *mija*."

They'd gotten started without me, but only by a minute or so. I slipped into my seat next to Guille, took a sip from the ever-present bottle of water, and proceeded to field questions through this fantastic protective fog that made a convenient appearance. Most of the questions/comments were of the generic variety—didn't take much brain power to answer and didn't really penetrate the fog in any way. But when Guille's hand reached beneath the tablecloth and pressed down hard on my knee, I realized it'd been twitching and bouncing uncontrollably.

Didn't take long to be done with me and Tonio. We were already old news and the press wanted to look forward to the big showdown next week, where Guille and Fabiana would each be performing their version of what would become the winner's first single. Yeah, real original, right? But it was the kind of thing the public loved and the twist would be that each of them would be doing it in completely different arrangements, which Gabriel was currently explaining as Tonio and I got up to leave.

"Ali, I'll see you next week, okay?"

I hung onto Guille, nearly groaning into his shoulder. God, I was so stupid. How could I have forgotten? Not through with this—not by a long shot. All sixteen original finalists were returning for the final announcement show—get together, sing some high-schmaltz "We Are the World" number, then sit around and pretend we were actually happy it *wasn't* us who was about to get a high-profile recording contract and worldwide tour.

Wonder what the odds were of contracting something incapacitating and highly communicable before next week?

"Yes, well, I've had every confidence since the beginning I would be one of the finalists. Everyone was great, of course, but I really felt I had something unique to offer, something that *Oye Mi Canto* and its viewers were really looking for."

The fog . . . it was lifting. And pain and anger were starting to poke through. I had to get out of here.

"Go. *Cuídate, mi amor.*" Dropping a kiss on my forehead, Guille turned back to the table and smiled at the crowd as I made a beeline for Papi, standing toward the back of the mostly empty club.

"*Sí,* Fabiana's correct that every one of the competitors was wonderful in their own way. I think you saw that in our final group of four. Any of us could have won and how could anyone have argued, *hmm?*"

I glanced over my shoulder at Guille, who winked before turning his attention to another question.

"Elaine's got my car outside and running."

"What about hers?"

"I'll bring her back for it tomorrow."

"Papi, I'm sorry." But it was different from the "I'm sorry" I'd given him just a few minutes ago and he knew it.

"Why?"

"You were right. I should never have done this, it was wrong. I—"

"Shh." He put a finger against my lips. "*Vamos.* Let's go home and you can tell me all about it, *mi niña linda.*"

I was crying before we even hit the backseat of the car. Just sobbing out the whole stupid story that Jaime had told me, leaving the front of Papi's shirt a damp, mascara-streaked, runny-nosed mess. Crying so hard, I didn't even realize we were home until I felt a rush of warm air as Elaine opened the door and Papi took me in his arms like I was a little girl, carrying me in the house and on up to my room.

"I'd do anything to keep you from hurting like this, *mija.* Anything, I swear." He was rocking me back and forth, stroking my hair.

"But why would they want me to lose, Papi? Why?" All the crying, the drama, the hurt, twisting my stomach around in hard, painful knots.

"Jaime was absolutely certain about this? No mistake?"

"Completely. Said if it wasn't this week, it would've happened next week." And I was so unbelievably angry at him for not saying anything. "I made such a jerk out of myself—going out there last night."

Hands on my shoulders, he pushed me far enough away to look into my face. "No, you did *not.* Don't ever say that again, Alegría. Don't ever even think that." Reaching over to my nightstand, he pulled a couple tissues from the box and wiped my face. "You gave one of the most remarkable performances of grace under pressure I have ever seen in my entire life. The music didn't just come from your soul, *mija,* it *was* you—your entire being was the music." He pulled me close against him, his words rumbling through his chest and vibrating against my cheek. His voice cracking, he said, "It was the most beautiful thing I've ever seen."

More crying, a different kind of crying, until I must have drifted off, because next thing I remember was blinking at my ceiling, the room dark and still around me. Still fully dressed, lying on top of my covers, but Papi had put the light blanket I kept folded at the end of my bed over my legs and slipped a pair of socks onto my feet, because he knew how cold they got at night.

Rolling over onto my side, I looked at the clock. Three in the morning. Stripping off my wrinkled clothes, I stumbled into my bathroom and cringed at the swollen raccoon eyes and overall blotchy disaster staring back at me from the mirror. Splashing some cold water on my face, I slapped on some cold cream and wiped it off, just to get the worst of the gunk. Not like I had to look good or be "on" for anyone tomorrow. Not anymore.

A faint whistle came drifting up the stairs as I was slipping on a nightshirt. There was a good idea. Tea. And if Papi couldn't sleep, either—well, misery loves company and all that, although God knows I was feeling beyond guilty about all the misery I'd brought him lately. He sure didn't deserve the spoiled brat routine I'd been pulling. When I thought of some of the things I'd said . . . *ugh.* Slime was higher up on the evolutionary scale.

This stupid contest sure hadn't been worth much in the end—sure hadn't been worth nearly losing my relationship with my father.

In some ways, this growing-up stuff rots.

"Hey, I heard the kettle. Want some com—"

I stopped short as Elaine looked up from stirring her tea. Wearing Papi's robe. And unless I was seriously mistaken, nothing else.

"I couldn't leave him."

Well, what could I say to that? Somehow I got the feeling I wasn't actually expected to say anything, so I just came the rest of the way into the kitchen and reached up into the cabinets, grabbing a mug and a tea bag from the open canister on the counter. Adding honey and a splash of milk to my tea, I joined Elaine at the table, who was still stirring hers, just staring down into the mug.

"He was so upset after you fell asleep, Ali. Just . . . devastated. So angry that he couldn't protect you—keep you from hurting." She glanced up at me and I could see that her eyes weren't quite raccoon stage, but still, pretty red-rimmed and swollen for all that. "And I was angry that I'd been there the whole time and hadn't done a better job of protecting you when he'd put such trust in me."

"Not a whole lot you could do about some of it. Besides, it's what I wanted." I curled my hands around my mug, the warmth seeping through my palms and up through my arms, my shoulders, my neck. "Wanted to be an adult in the big, bad world."

"Most adults go an entire lifetime without experiencing half of what you did these last two months, Ali."

Drawing one foot up and propping it on the edge of the seat, I shrugged. "Maybe." Did it really matter? I'd had my foray into the adult world. I'd kind of stunk at it. We sipped our tea for a while, the clock out in the hallway chiming the half-hour mark, a cat meowing a few townhouses away.

"Is this what you want, Elaine?"

I knew Papi was *who* she wanted, but the how of the circumstance? After my close call with Jaime—No. Wouldn't think of that now.

"I've loved him for a long, long time, Ali. I don't know if what I did was the right thing, but for once, he needed someone to take care of him. *¿Entiendes?*" Her eyes searched my face, looking worried. God, like she had anything to be worried about—at least where I was concerned.

I looked away, back down into my mug. "Yeah, actually, I do understand." A couple degrees higher in magnitude from what Jaime had done for me, but—*damn,* I wasn't going to think about him.

"Ali?"

Maybe it was unspoken, but the rest of her question was right there, hanging between us. "No, we didn't." I added a soft, "Came close," because only to her could I admit that. Then I speedshifted the subject away from me because I wasn't ready to say any more than that about it.

"For what it's worth, Elaine, I'm really happy about this. And I don't think it's a one-shot deal, either. I think he's loved you for a long time, too—he's just been sort of a pinhead about it."

"Nice to know my only child has such a high opinion of me."

Elaine and I both snapped our heads toward the kitchen door. Papi was leaning in the doorway, with that glazed, just-woke-up-and-I'm-not-all-that-jazzed-about-it expression we both possessed. In his shorts and Miami Heat T-shirt, without his glasses and with his hair standing on end, he totally looked more college student than college professor.

"However—" He came up behind me and kissed the top of my head, the backs of his fingers brushing my cheek. "In this case, my only child is right. Why didn't either of you ever say anything?"

"Because you were a pinhead," Elaine and I chorused, then broke into giggles as Papi pretended to frown. Which totally melted as he held his hand out to Elaine and drew her into his arms, looking down at her like he'd never seen her before. Guess in a way, he hadn't.

"I'm probably still a pinhead about a lot of things, but not about this. *Te lo juro,* Elaine, not about this—not anymore."

Well, then. They so didn't need an audience and with the

kitchen table being handy . . . Taking my tea, I eased from my chair and started to slink from the kitchen.

"Ali?"

I glanced over my shoulder "Yeah?"

Papi still had his arms around Elaine, holding her like he wasn't planning on letting go anytime soon. He looked concerned, though, as he asked, "You're really sure—"

"Papi, come on . . . for once, let it be about you being happy. I *want* you to be happy." I grinned at both of them. "And at least you already know I like her."

He closed his eyes and let out the breath I hadn't even realized he was holding while Elaine poked his shoulder. "See? *¿No te lo dije?* You raised a very smart girl."

Smiling, I ducked out of the kitchen as I heard them start with one of their Abbott and Costello routines that went silent in a hurry. So at least one good thing had come from this stupid contest. One really important thing that was almost enough to make the whole, painful exercise worth it.

27

Tonio and I rolled our eyes at each other as we sang the syrupy-sweet lines we'd been assigned in the "We Are the World" wannabe song. Seeing as we were facing each other and supposed to be crooning in some pseudo-romantic way, it wasn't like the camera was going to catch us. And what were they going to do to us if it did? Kick us off?

You see what I mean.

Thankfully, we made it through our lines without cracking up, went through a round of the chorus with the rest of the group, then eased over to our assigned spot, stage left, giving way to Guille and Fabiana. Final verse, their big showcase, trading off lines in Spanish and English with Tonio and me standing there practically quivering as we watched that vein on Guille's forehead throb. Fabiana was in rare form, man, cutting in front of him, playing to the camera rather than the crowd, and singing louder in a case of genuinely tacky upstaging.

"Votes are in and done, but she just don't give up, does she?" Tonio whispered in my ear.

"She's gonna work it till the bitter end, dude."

But never let it be said that musicians don't have their own forms of revenge. Gabriel, his own eyebrow twitching as he watched the shenanigans, discreetly sped up the tempo on Fabiana's next Spanish lyric, making her trip over the words a little and as she went to hit a note that was *just* a touch out of her range, he signaled a crescendo that effectively drowned her out.

Then smiled that innocent yet completely sly, Santa's elf's grin when she glared over her shoulder at him. Man, was it hard to make it through the final chorus without wetting my pants laughing.

Yeah. Laugh. I was actually having a pretty good time tonight. Imagine that.

Primary reason was because Fabiana played the diva (like this was a surprise?), holding court in the greenroom during a good chunk of dress rehearsal, only coming out for one final run-through. Which was perfectly fine with Gabriel. Rumor had it he'd just about strangled her on more than one occasion this past week. Guille, on the other hand, rehearsed the entire time, with Chelo and Tonio taking turns singing Fabiana's parts in falsettos that had us all howling, including Gabriel, even as he scolded us to pay attention.

The only bummer was that I hadn't seen Jaime all afternoon. I could only assume he'd been held up back at the house, but hadn't worked up the nerve to ask Esperanza. Besides, she was crazy busy, as usual, and, well . . . this was between me and Jaime. I needed to apologize to him. Big time. I'd picked the phone up a thousand times this last week to do it, and put it down every single time because a) I'd lose my nerve, b) was afraid he wouldn't bother answering if he saw my number on his cell, c) this was something that was just better done in person, and d) all of the above.

Because really, basically accuse a guy of lying and slap him in the process, at the very least, he deserved some face time.

"Girl, at least *call* and leave a message you want to see him," had been Sosi's refrain all week. "How's he gonna know otherwise?" She even called me one morning when I was still asleep to tell me that. Loudly. Shoved the phone under my pillow and could *still* hear her yelling at me.

Couldn't blame her. It was pretty appalling, with a heavy dose of shame thrown in for good measure. The whole mess so hadn't been his fault. He'd been trying to protect me, best way he knew how. And I'd rewarded that loyalty by behaving like a spoiled, self-absorbed bitch. He didn't have to forgive me—but I needed to apologize. 'Course, it went without saying I wouldn't be at all opposed to a little forgiveness.

I wandered over to the craft services table they had set up backstage and grabbed a bottle of water and a few pretzels. Once again, the greenroom had been taken over by the VIPs and with the fourteen of us back here, it was just too much. But it was cool—somehow Esperanza had managed to squeeze a flat-panel monitor and a bunch of chairs into the most distant corner of the backstage area, near craft services, so we could hang and watch the onstage action with convenient access to the munchies. Right now, they had Guille and Fabiana out there, rehashing their final performances from the night before.

Fabiana, predictably, had taken her version of the chart high-powered and up-tempo. Like I said before, limited in what she could do, but girl knew what worked, even if it was fake street cred. She'd probably wind up a poor man's Madonna, without the songwriting chops.

Guillermo, though . . . oh, man. I'd watched him on TV last night and gone goose-bumpy; seeing it again, it was every bit as . . . *wow.* You would've thought he'd go with his strength, the hard-driving rock with a touch of salsa, but no . . . he took the chart that Fabiana had dance clubbed and turned it into the most heart-wrenching, aching ballad that left you searching for the Kleenex. And once more with feeling—*wow.* No doubt, the way he looked out into the audience, looked into the camera, that every woman between five and ninety-five thought he was singing that Just For Her.

Heck, even *I* bought it.

"You taught him that, didn't you?" I whispered into Tonio's ear as we watched the replay.

"Me?" Brown eyes stared over gray-tinted sunglasses. "You out of your mind, baby? I am so gonna have to kick his ass for stealing my moves, yo."

Grinning, I leaned back in my chair and crunched into another pretzel. Kind of fun watching Fabiana go that nice shade of green as she was forced to watch Guille's performance.

"Hey, Ali, your dad wants you."

Oye, now why were they interrupting my fun? I looked over to where Tonio was pointing, at Papi gesturing that I should come over as Elaine stood and chatted with some tall, familiar-looking dude. *Really* familiar looking, but I couldn't quite place him.

"Man, and with Fabiana looking like she's about to hurl." I sighed, handing my water and pretzels to Tonio. "Be right back."

Only response I got was a crunch as Tonio started chowing my pretzels. Hoover.

"Yeah, Papi, what's up?"

"Ali, this gentleman wants to speak to you," he said, indicating the familiar-looking dude. "Señor Braga, my daughter, Alegría."

"Call me Pancho, *por favor.*"

I probably looked all rude, staring, but damn, he was familiar. About Papi's same height, but built more like a football player, with a neat, black-and-silver goatee and rectangular, black wire-rim glasses; sharp suit that Andre would be drooling over if he caught sight of it, and loafers you could practically use for touching up your lipstick. This guy oozed class and confidence—not to mention a hefty wardrobe budget. Who *was* he? Never mind.

Could figure it out later—time to pull out the polite Catholic schoolgirl manners. I held out my hand.

"*Mucho gusto,* Señor Braga."

"Pleasure's all mine, Ali." Taking my hand in a nice, firm grip that suggested he actually meant it, he shook it and smiled. "You don't remember me, do you?"

So we *had* met. But where? When? "I do . . . but I—" And as I stared at him, it all of a sudden came clicking into place. Jackie Gleason Theater. A pool of light in the center of the auditorium. The judges conferring and asking if I could sing anything else. And one silent guy, sitting there with his arms crossed, just watching. Except he'd been wearing a knit shirt and the glasses had been different. And, of course, I hadn't heard him speak a word, so no voice recognition. No name recognition, either, because at the time, I hadn't gotten any of the judge's names, but right now, my mind was clicking like a trail of tumbling dominoes. Pancho Braga.

Pancho freakin' Braga. Holy *cow.*

Only the man who'd done for Latin music what Phil Spector and his "wall of sound" had done for pop music or Russell Simmons for hip-hop. Not only that, but his contributions as an arranger read like a monster Who's Who of artists, across the musical spectrum, in Spanish *and* English. I'd lay my entire *Oye Mi Canto* wardrobe that you could skim almost anyone's CD collection and find *something* with his name in the credits, especially since he'd started his own label a few years back.

"Ali."

I snapped my mouth shut and sent a thank-you glance to Elaine. *Such* a dweeb. Other girls my age went nuts at the mere mention of Juanes. I went googly over a middle-aged producer who's only a revolutionary in the field.

"I'm guessing you do recognize me then?" He was smiling at

me, but more kind, not, "you mock-worthy rube," which was reassuring even as I blushed like a fool.

"*Perdóneme,* Señor Braga, I'm so sorry."

"It's okay, Ali," he said with a laugh. "Really. Come on, let's go find somewhere quiet to talk." Putting a hand to my back and gesturing to Papi and Elaine, he led us down the hall to the greenroom. And he was expecting to find quiet in here? Clearly, he hadn't been hanging around these parts the last few weeks.

Never underestimate the power of, well, *power.* With a glance and a couple quiet words, he had the room cleared out inside of a minute. Way impressive. After the door closed, leaving the four of us alone, he went to the craft services table, checking the offerings, like he had all the time in the world.

"Can I get you a beer or some wine, Señor Montero, Dr. Garces?"

I was offered my choice of water or soda after Papi and Elaine were given their beers and after accepting a Diet Coke and waiting for him to get his own beer, we all settled in on the sofas and chairs.

"So you remember me as one of the judges then?"

"Among other things." Pancho freakin' Braga. Jeez.

"I'm guessing from that response that you're also familiar with my work?"

"Oh, just a little." Couldn't help rolling my eyes at *that* one. Familiar, indeed.

Luckily, the guy seemed to have a sense of humor, just laughing and shaking his head. "Forgive me, Ali. Should have known someone so musically well-versed would be familiar, but it's an odd sensation. We producers and arrangers are far more accustomed to plying our trade in relative obscurity, known primarily to those within the industry."

The guy was my equivalent of a rock god. Only meeting

Sting would be higher up on the "slap me 'cause I'm dreaming" scale.

"I'm sure you're curious as to why I brought you and your family back here."

I exchanged a smile with Elaine at the family comment, but didn't say anything, figuring the question was pretty much rhetorical.

"I was responsible for your being taken off last week."

The warm fuzzies and hero worship took a nosedive. *"What?"* I barely noticed Elaine reaching out and rescuing my soda just before it slipped from my hands. "You *what*?"

"Wait." He held a hand up. "Let's start from the beginning."

"Yeah, let's," I muttered, leaning in close to Papi, who put an arm around my shoulders.

"*Bueno,* let's start with what you don't know. I'm a silent partner in the show's primary production company."

"Okay." Explained maybe why he'd been at the auditions.

"Once I saw you, I wanted you on the show, no questions asked. As a silent partner with a lot of money, I'm happy to say I have that kind of pull. And I was fairly certain regardless of how many competitors we auditioned, we wouldn't encounter too many with your level of talent, so I felt safe in making the demand."

Don't you get it? You're in. The memory of Jaime's voice, echoing, months down the line.

"However, as much as I wanted you on the show, both for your talent and your appeal, I didn't want you winning. Didn't actually think you'd come as close to winning as you did. You gave me a hell of a scare, *mi vida,* surviving so long—"

What *was* it with people thinking I was going to get booted off the show early? I glanced at Elaine; she shrugged and rolled her eyes pretty much like I was doing.

"I guess, in a way, I underestimated your ability to rise to the show's particular demands. I won't make that mistake again."

Leaning back in his chair and crossing his legs, he studied me through his glasses. Fine by me. Gave me a chance to study him back. Kind of a Mexican standoff moment, each of us trying to figure the other out. And as we stared at each other, a really horrible, awful, please-don't-let-it-be-true thought occurred to me.

"You didn't have anything to do with my guitar, did you?"

"Ali!"

"No, Señor Montero." He waved his hand at Papi, but his gaze never left my face. "Given the nature of what I've just told her, it's a perfectly valid question. However, while I openly admit to being a devious, self-serving bastard, my methods are not that crude. Such wanton destruction is, frankly, offensive to me."

"And for the record," he added, "count me among the believers that it was Fabiana. Only person who probably wanted you off the show more than I did." He smiled and quirked an eyebrow. "But she's of no importance now."

Ha. Of no importance. Like she was right at about the level of a nasty, crunchy palmetto bug. Okay, probably had no reason to, but I believed him. Anyone who would openly admit to being a devious bastard . . . there was something reassuringly trustworthy about that. Didn't answer the bigger question, though.

"But why?"

"It wouldn't have been right for you, Ali. Ultimately, what will sell this show is formulaic Latin pop and rock; spitting a paint-by-numbers album out within a few weeks, touring endlessly to support it, and when you're not touring, making shopping mall and music store appearances. Your music, your talent, would suffer and I think you would ultimately wither away. You're different, Ali—your gift is different. For someone like Guille or Tonio, it would work, but this format . . . it's not your natural milieu."

"Milieu"? Was he kidding? Who used words like that anymore? Then I thought about it. The same people who used words like "den of iniquity," I suppose. Great—like I didn't already have one father type who didn't think this show was right for me. Papi must be so jazzed. A voice of knowledge and experience to back him up. Even though I'd made my peace with the whole mess, it didn't mean I couldn't be a *little* burned up over being played like some damn chess piece.

"You're telling me this whole thing has been a big sham, then? A big waste of time on my part?"

He laughed. Just threw his head back and let loose. He really was a bastard. Honestly, if he wasn't such a kick-ass producer . . .

"*Ay, mi vida,* a waste of time?" Setting his beer aside, he propped his elbows on his knees and leaned forward. "After the fan mail and the websites and the autograph seekers and the audiences? Don't you understand? I wanted to get you some exposure and get you into the public's mind, create demand, before you go record your album."

Yeah. Right. Websites run by fifteen-year-olds and sure, I'd gotten fan mail, but not compared to say Tonio and Guille and even Brunhilda, and record my album?

Say what? Record my album?

My mouth opened and closed a couple of times, but damn if nothing but a squeak came out. Just like Sosi.

"Some of the contestants who finished far below you have already signed recording contracts, Ali. Surely it had occurred to you?"

Call me the biggest, most naïve, most gullible—okay, what else could I go with besides maybe idiot?

"No . . . actually, outside of the context of winning, recording hadn't occurred to me." But—*You've already made enough of an impression that someone's going to snap you up for a recording contract.* Out of the memory banks, Jaime's voice making another appearance.

Here I'd thought he was just trying to make me feel better. But for crying out loud, even the Venezuelan beauty queen had signed a contract. I'd been so fixated on winning, though, or at least not letting Brunhilda run me off. If I *didn't* win—well, hadn't thought much beyond that except that I *had* to perform.

Stupid, stupid, *stupid.*

"Don't be embarrassed, Ali." Señor Braga reached out and patted my knee. "You're savvy and confident in your talent. The fact that you're so unaffected by the rest of it—it's to your benefit, provided you don't get taken advantage of, which we're going to do our best to prevent."

Another pat to my knee, then he eased back into his chair, still looking relaxed, but something about his overall demeanor changed. Sharpened, sort of, like he was zeroing in on his objective.

"Yes, I want to record an album with you. My label, your music, your style, which we'll continue to work on developing. I think your evolution as an artist is going to be a remarkable thing to watch and I want nothing more than to have a part in it. If you'll have us."

If *I'll* have them? Breathe. Must breathe. Which got harder as he dropped his next bomb.

"There's a catch, however. You have to come to New York."

"Oh, going to New York to record? That would be cool." I wasn't getting it, quite yet.

"No, Ali." His voice, his eyes, everything softened as he looked at me. "Not just to record. To live."

Breathe. Still needed to work on this breathing action while he kept talking. "While we work on developing material for you, I want you to get some live performance seasoning that's outside the *Oye Mi Canto* experience. *Mira,* Miami has a vibrant, exciting music scene, but for what I'm envisioning, New York is *it.* Difficult to top the jazz clubs and it's a quick hop up to Boston or down to Philly if we want to broaden your scope a bit."

"But—" Okay, it was tough, but I had to think this through. "My father can't leave his job at the university. And Elaine—" Papi couldn't leave her. Not now. Besides, she didn't want to move back to New York. She'd said that a million times. I'd done a lot of selfish things the last few months, no *way* I was doing this.

"Alegría, I—*we* wouldn't be going."

"Huh?"

I looked from Papi, to Elaine, to Señor Braga. Oh. Color me slow on the uptake. They'd already talked about this. This is why Papi had been so quiet through all of this while I was having a minor freakout. He already knew.

"Go alone?" Elaine and Señor Braga faded away as I met my father's gaze. Just him and me. Like it had always been. And maybe . . . for the last time.

He brushed my bangs aside. "Such a beautiful girl—beautiful woman—you've become, *mi niña.*" Taking my hands in his, he looked down at them. So did I. So similar, with the long fingers and nails manicured just so, for playing.

"Such a tremendous gift you have. I always knew you had talent, but you showed so much more, especially the last few weeks. What you've done, your determination to perform and the ability—" We both looked up at the same time, our gazes meeting again, his eyes shiny and bright green-brown behind his glasses. "It's what you're meant to do. If you want to."

If I wanted to. He was leaving this up to me—like I was an adult or something. "But Papi, I'm not even eighteen yet. And what about school?" The nuns and and graduation and everything?

He smiled again and shook his head, like, no big deal. "Señor Braga's already explained his label owns some apartments in New York. You'll live in one of them with a guardian I get to approve of," he said with a wink. "And as for school, they intend for a tutor to help you complete your classes—you might even be done by December, how does that sound?"

Oh, now *that* I could so get behind. But . . . leaving everything I knew? Not getting to hang with Sosi or get to see what happened with Elaine and Papi?

But . . . getting to play in clubs, collaborate with Señor Braga and all the nifty people in his Little Black Book, be a professional musician. My dream. Coming true in big, glorious Technicolor.

Still looking at Papi, I nodded. "Yeah, it's what I really, really want, Papi. But only if you're okay with it." Knew, though, even as I said it, that he was okay. We wouldn't be sitting here with Señor Braga having this discussion at *all* if he wasn't okay.

28

Contracts being messengered over in the next day or so. Tentative dates for travel plans. Names of entertainment lawyers if we didn't know any who could look over the contracts. Names of possible managers. Names of possible guardians.

"Oh, I think I've got that one covered, *mija,*" Elaine had said. "I've got a cousin just graduated with a psych degree from SUNY, and she's going to be going to grad school at Columbia. I'll bet anything she'd rather hang with you than get up at six in the morning to say 'should I leave room for cream?' at Starbucks. Plus, you know my mother will bird-dog you."

Lots of names. Lots of details. All of it washing over my head as I sat there, sort of dazed. Until an assistant director knocked on the door and said they needed me out onstage—they were about to announce the winner. We had to be out there, pretending to be happy.

Oye, no pretending on my part. I was giddy as a schoolgirl. Well, you know what I mean.

But could they draw this out any more? They'd even come up with some schlocky song for the announcers to sing, sort of like some Miss America thing, while Guille and Fabiana paraded across the stage, holding hands like they actually liked each other. Once again, I sent a silent prayer up to *la virgen* that I'd been spared that experience. Hearing Fredo sing was bad enough. Hearing him sing while having to hold Fabiana's hand had to rank right up there with Chinese water torture.

"And in the search for the next great Latin superstar, the winner is—"

"Y el ganador de Oye Mi Canto, tu superstar latino es—"

Beat of silence, tympani roll, and then—

"Guillermo Correas!"

There *is* a God.

I started crying as Guille dropped to his knees, crossed himself and just sat there looking stunned as balloons and streamers and confetti poured over him. Like we'd scripted it, Tonio and I ran to him and helped him up, all three of us hugging and screaming and hugging some more.

"You did it, Guille!"

"I did it! *¡Lo logré!"*

"You did it, man!"

The three of us jumped up and down and hugged as Gabriel led the band in a crazy-wild version of the theme song. Even after Guille bounded down into the audience to hug his parents, Tonio and I hung onto each other while Fabiana stood off to one side and managed to look pissed even as she cried, shaking off the few people who tried to approach her.

"Once a *sangrona,* always a *sangrona,"* Tonio whispered, making me choke. I tried to feel sorry for her, trying to keep the bad karma at bay, but man, I couldn't. She'd *never* get everything she deserved.

The last few minutes of *Oye Mi Canto* just flew by, with more balloons and streamers and popping champagne, and people onstage and in the audience dancing as Gabriel had the band absolutely scorching like they never had before. But as soon as I saw the lights go off on the cameras, signaling we were off the air, I snuck offstage. Had something I needed to do and it couldn't wait anymore.

"Esperanza."

"Ay, Ali, *mi vida,* how're you doing? I've already seen Pancho, *felicidades, mija,* I'm so happy for you and he's completely full of himself that he's managed to sign you and you know, I live in New York, so we'll totally have to get together, I'll show you all the good out-of-the-way clothes stores—"

I laughed. Now that the show was over, the psychotic, motor-mouthed pixie was back.

"Espie—" I broke in somewhere in the middle of her saying something about shoe shopping. We'd have to get back to that. "Where's Jaime?"

"Oh." Everything about her stopped. "The little *pendejo,"* she sighed. "I guess he really meant it when he said he wasn't going to talk to you before he left. Didn't want to upset you anymore."

"Left?"

As in, *gone?*

She pulled us from the wings and toward what was now a quiet corner since *everyone* was out partying hearty in the club. "He went back to New York yesterday, *mija.* Wanted to get ready for school."

I felt like I'd been punched in the gut.

"And one day was going to make a difference?"

Esperanza had that look. I knew that look. That half-sympathetic, half-exasperated, totally "what I wouldn't give to knock both your heads together" look. Clearly, she knew at least some of what had happened, if not all of it. "His responsibilities with the show were pretty much finished, Ali, and he seemed anxious to go." Lifting several sheets of paper on her clipboard, she pulled something free. An envelope—with my name on it—that she handed to me.

"I honestly thought he was going to change his mind and speak to you before he went." Another sigh. "At any rate, he asked me to give you this."

Silently, I took it. Reaching up, Esperanza kissed my cheek. "Let me know what I can do to help, okay? I'll make sure you get my number and e-mail."

"Thanks."

I turned the envelope over and over, almost afraid to open it, but more afraid to not open it and yeah, well aware of what a cliché that was. Finally, I lifted the flap and pulled out the piece of lined paper—fresh from a spiral-bound, raggedy edges and all.

> *Ali,*
> *Sorry for the coward's approach.*

My heart jumped up into my throat. *He* was apologizing for being a coward? *Ay Dios mío,* did he ever have that *all* wrong.

> *I just couldn't stay and watch Fabiana possibly win, knowing I might've had some part in it. I know that sounds stupid, because what could I have done to change anything, right? Except I could've kept you from feeling like you made a fool of yourself. From feeling quite so betrayed. I know on the scale of apologies, this one probably sucks, but it's heartfelt. I hope that one day you can forgive me and that maybe, we can be friends again.*
>
> *Love,*
> *Jaime*

Oh, was I going to have myself a good cry over this tonight. I returned the note to its envelope and slipped it into my pocket. A nice long one, maybe with a box of Mallomars. And I'd have to wait a while, maybe a year or two, before I said anything about this to Sos. Just didn't want to deal with the "I told you so's," no matter how right she might be about them. I should have called him, should have left a message, should have done something. I suppose I still could, but—oh God, that he'd left still blaming himself . . .

It was more than enough to knock me back down to slime status. And I wasn't at all sure how to fix it. Except—Elaine. I could talk to her—she'd have good advice. A cup of tea, a box of Mallomars, and some of her no bullshit wisdom and maybe I wouldn't have to cry. Could just figure out what to do.

"Where is she?" The loud and really pissed-off shriek echoed through the near-empty backstage area. A very large, very scary-looking chick was barreling down the hall, shaking off Derrick's arm and snarling, "*Oye,* gringo, get your hands off me before I bite them off. Now, where's that skinny ho? I got some ass to kick."

Damn, whoever this large-and-in-charge chick was looking for I felt sorry for, because she looked good *and* ready to throw down with anyone who stood in her way. But, you know . . . Derrick wasn't trying all *that* hard to keep her from going out onstage, kind of following a pace or two behind, saying, "Ma'am, you really can't be going out there. Ma'am—"

Remember when Willie Wonka—Gene Wilder edition, not Johnny Depp—said, "No. Don't. Stop" in that really bored voice? Right. Kind of like that.

Sure, curiosity killed the cat, but come *on.* Derrick hadn't let anyone anywhere they weren't supposed to be the entire run of the show. Something was definitely afoot. I followed him and the ticked-off chick out to the stage where—

Oh.

My.

God.

It was *Jerry Springer* meets *Laura en America*; all we needed was a trailer, some married first cousins, and maybe an alien baby.

"*Ay, mi dulce,* I didn't know you were coming down, why didn't you say anything—" It was one of the cameramen, cowering behind his rig as he tried to combine sounding pleased with not peeing his pants. The short, skinny, crater-faced, oily-haired cameraman. *Ew.* Then I noticed. Camera One. Lead camera.

Talk about *sad,* man.

"You miserable, low-down, dirty dog of a *pendejo.* Did you really think you were gonna mess around with her and I wasn't gonna find out?" she yelled, launching herself at him with a war cry, pounding on him once, twice, *dang,* three times, before turning and scanning the crowd, breathing hard. And like radar, she found who she was looking for just before she was able to make her escape offstage.

"You skanky, cheap, man-stealing *whore.*"

And in one of the most beautiful moves I've ever seen, slapped Fabiana absolutely stupid. It was almost graceful, the way Fabiana spun full around on her spiked boot heel and fell straight onto her ass with a nice atonal screech as the cameraman's wife dove after her. That's when Derrick and the rest of security got in on the action, lifting the wife off Fabiana with no problem, even though she was still kicking and hissing how she was going to rip every bleached hair out of Fabiana's head.

She'd best get in line. I had dibs on that move. But wouldn't need it. Like Señor Braga had said, she was of no importance to me anymore. Didn't mean I wasn't enjoying every last daytime talk show moment of this.

Across the stage, I caught Esperanza's eye. Nodding at the wrestling match and the cheering crowd, she winked at me.

There is a God. And he clearly loves me.

Epilogue

"Sí, Papi, of course, I'm being careful."

"You don't need to sound quite so patient and long-suffering. I'm a father. Worry's a requirement. How's trig? Still suck?"

I smiled into my cellphone. "Yes, trig still sucks, but I did fine on my last test. Listen, let me talk to Elaine, okay?"

After a couple seconds between phone transfer, I heard Elaine pick up.

"Hey, *mija*. Everything good?"

"Hi, yeah, everything's great, just wanted to warn you, your mother is sending another batch of recipes and a box of ingredients. She seems to have this demented idea that you can't get authentic Puerto Rican ingredients in Miami." I could almost *feel* Elaine's eyes rolling.

"And that you have to fatten Papi up because *'está muy flaco y yo quiero nietos fuertes, mija.'*" I held the phone away from my ear and laughed at Elaine's outraged screech. Her mother was bound and determined to get herself a grandchild by hook, crook, or *arroz con gandules*.

"Doesn't she get it?"

"She's *your* mother, what do you think? I told her, *again*, that you guys are just enjoying living together for the time being, but she just raises her eyebrows at me in that '*niña*, what you don't know about men and women' expression that she does."

Elaine kept spluttering and screeching in the background as Papi came back on the line.

"Her mother?"

"Yeah."

"You're a good girl to go over there for dinner every week."

"Yeah, well, she scares me. She'd probably hunt me down if I didn't." Truth was, though, I really dug spending time with Elaine's family. Made me miss Papi and Elaine less—and more at the same time.

"She scares me, too," he laughed. "Okay, *mija*. I need to go take care of Elaine before she ruptures something. We'll see you next week."

"I can't wait. Bring good presents."

"A recording contract and fabulous apartment in Manhattan aren't enough?"

"New iPod? Pretty please, with sugar on top?"

"Incorregible." Amazing how affection and exasperation made it even over fifteen hundred miles of cell towers.

"You wouldn't recognize me if I wasn't."

"I'd recognize you blindfolded in a dark room, *mi vida*." His voice softened. "Miss you, Ali."

"Miss you, too, Papi. Both of you." Had only been six weeks, but had that six years feeling. I was really happy my birthday was next week. Not just 'cause of the prezzies, which would, of course, be of the cool, but because Papi and Elaine were coming up, along with Sosi, for a long weekend to help me celebrate. As I played my first professional gig at a small Village club. Couldn't order a drink, but I could play a kick-ass seventy-minute set.

"Love to you both, okay?" I flipped the phone closed and slipped it in the outside pocket of my backpack as I walked.

Could've taken the subway, but it really wasn't that far and couldn't have chatted as easily with Papi. Also wouldn't have gotten to enjoy the weather. The guy on TV had talked about stuff like Indian summer, whatever that was—all I knew was that there was a nip in the air this morning that felt completely foreign to this Miami girl. Highs in the low sixties. That qualified as a January cold snap for South Florida.

Papi had bought me this full-length quilted number for winter that made me look like the Abominable Snowman, especially with the matching hat and scarf set, but today was perfect for jeans and the leather jacket Elaine had given me. Adjusting the strap of my gig bag over my shoulder, I slowed down, touching a leaf on a tree. A leaf that was just beginning to show a hint of red.

Another reason to walk. Got to cut through Washington Square Park on my way to the studio on Broadway—see the trees, the crazed chess players who reminded me of the crazed domino players back home, the college kids lounging around. Couldn't lie. There was one college kid in particular I kept hoping to see. What was it Billy Crystal said in *When Harry Met Sally* about accidentally running into his ex-wife and her new husband? Something about a city of eight million people, he was bound to run into her sooner or later?

Figured my chances were upped exponentially since I was living in the Village, in an apartment about which Elaine had said, "You do realize, girl, that real people in New York don't live like this?"

To which I'd replied, "Hey, Elaine, real people in *Miami* don't even live like this."

It was a completely sweet place, turn-of-the-century building with a doorman, which had reassured Papi beyond belief, and located near absolutely everything, including Señor Braga's—

whoops, Pancho's—offices and Cutting Room Studios, where he'd booked time for us to rehearse and begin recording. Also located pretty close to NYU.

Now I didn't have to wait to run into him. I'd already had lunch with Espie a few weeks back and before she'd even kissed me hello, had handed me a card with his e-mail and local cell. But I was still a chicken. Just a' cluckin' as I strolled through the park and made the turn onto West Fourth.

Had a feeling this was when I was going to think about him most—as the weather eased into autumn. I'd even held off visiting Central Park since I'd moved here. Told myself it was because I was waiting for Sosi's visit, so we could do the touristy stuff together, but let's get real. Another week or so . . . might have a nice blaze of color going. Be cool to see it for the first time like that, wouldn't it?

Wonder what excuse I'd come up with for holding off on Rockefeller Center until Christmastime?

Pushing the door into the building, I made my way up to Studio A where Pancho was already in one of the lounges.

"Hey."

"Hola, mi vida." He looked up from his notes. "How's everything?"

Easing my gig bag off and setting it in the corner along with my backpack, I answered, "Good. Trig sucks. My father says hello."

Kissing my cheek, he sat back down on the sofa. "You'll be done with trig soon enough and tell your father I said hello back. They're coming up next week?"

"Yeah." Flopping down onto the other sofa, I reached for my gig bag and unzipped it.

"I'll have my assistant make some reservations."

"Nothing too spicy," I reminded him. I had so lucked out. My producer and I shared a thing for spicy food. Made for easy decisions with the takeout during the evening rehearsals.

"I remember," he laughed. "We'll do Chinese—something for everyone." He nodded at what I was pulling out of the bag. "The new axe settling in?"

Smiling, I ran my chamois over the spruce front of my new Bernabé Especial. "We had some words last night when it kept trying to go out of tune, but I think we're beginning to understand each other." We'd better understand each other. There was no one else this bad boy could belong to—not with the mother-of-pearl "Ali" inlaid in the headstock.

I'd about died last week when Pancho had come into the studio with the padded case and opened it up. I'd known it was coming, of course, because you couldn't go out and just buy one of these instruments as a general rule. Luckily, there had been one in a late stage of completion and I wouldn't have to wait that long. In the meantime, I'd been using one of my old guitars, but it just wasn't the same, y'know?

But this one . . . every bit as beautiful as my old Bernabé and with the added surprise of the inlaid "Ali." A little surprise I'm sure Pancho regretted after I nearly ruptured his eardrums with my squealing.

I set to work on tuning it up. "So what's on tap for today?"

"More rehearsal, of course, laying down some demos, and a surprise, *mija*."

"Hm?" I was getting used to Pancho's surprises. The guitar. Or bringing Guille in to rehearse a couple of songs for the new album—he was going to come back in a few weeks when we got ready to actually lay down the tracks. We'd turn Rocker Boy into a jazz crooner yet.

Or when Rob Thomas had been in the studio, talking to Pancho about maybe producing a couple of tracks for his next solo album and we'd wound up jamming on a few charts. Me. Jamming with Rob Thomas and yes, we'd played through "Lonely No More" and it had totally kicked ass and Pancho had done this out-loud musing thing about maybe, just maybe . . . I mean, can you imagine?

"Yeah, surprise?"

"Well, the main producers for *Oye Mi Canto* had to field so much fan outrage on your behalf, they felt I owed them, especially since we're keeping you so low profile right now."

"Um-hm?" Why wasn't that settling into tune?

"So they're going to have a film crew follow you around as you prepare to record and perform. They plan to show it in installments along with features on Guille, Tonio, and Fabiana, when they air the show next season."

I looked up, what he was saying having finally penetrated. "Because they had to field outrage on my behalf?"

"A lot. What can I say? I underestimated you." He threw his hands up in the air. "At any rate, they're going to start today. Just a skeleton crew, because I don't want it to be too much of a distraction, so just a cameraman, a sound man, a director, and one assistant, and here they are right now," he said in response to the knock on the door.

Weird. More cameras. Thought I was done with those. But if Pancho said it was okay, I would go with it. I trusted he wouldn't let anything bad happ—

"Hey, Ali."

Now see? *Not* nice of my mind to play tricks on me like that. Because, of course, the words "director" and "assistant" . . . and then the weather and the leaves and students . . . all conspired against me, sure, but to conjure him up—and so vividly? So much like I remembered? Okay, so the red-brown hair was a little shorter than it had been and he maybe looked a little thinner, but the eyes—*ay Dios mío,* they were still that brilliant streaky green and still doing the crinkly thing at the corners as he stood right here in front of me and smiled, almost as if I could touch him.

Not nice at all. But I was professional now. I could play along. "More nepotism?"

"Espie told me you were living here now. About your record deal—and the documentary. But because I worked on the show, I didn't even need her help getting the interview." He smiled and sat down next to me. "So more Cuban Grapevine than nepotism. Even if I hadn't gotten the gig, I was going to come see you—soon. Just didn't want to overwhelm you considering all the changes and new stuff going on."

My hands were shaking so badly, I couldn't even trust them enough to set my guitar aside. But I could trust Jaime to take it from me and carefully prop it against the wall before he turned back and took both my hands in his.

He was real. Or my imagination was a *whole* lot better than I ever gave it credit for. Couldn't be. It just couldn't be. Maybe if I bit my lip *really* hard—nope, he was still there. And now my lip stung like a mother on top of it.

"No, Ali, *por favor,* don't."

"I've been wanting to see you—talk to you—so much, but I've been scared."

He smiled and squeezed my hands gently. "You and me both."

Amazing, now that it was here, and I was convinced he was real, I wasn't even nervous anymore, and it came out so easily. "I'm so sorry, Jaime. I shouldn't have gotten so mad at you."

Oh boy, not nervous, but cue the face flameup. This next part couldn't go without saying, though, almost more than anything else. "And I sure shouldn't have slapped you." I freed one of my hands and touched his cheek. Knew *this* was just my imagination, but I could still see my hand print there and it hurt.

He held my hand against his cheek before bringing it down to rest on his knee. "Hey, I screwed up, Ali. Not that I think you should've slapped me." He laughed, then looked past my shoulder with a sigh. "I should have said something, or at the very least, had the guts to stay and talk to you one last time. That's what I'm most sorry about. That I didn't have the guts to stay."

His gaze shifted, looking into my face, like he was searching. "Can we maybe . . . I don't know, start over or something?"

I did my own searching, looking into his eyes—looking into myself, too. "Yeah, I'd like that."

Just that easy. Both of us had apologized and it felt right and okay. We both wanted to see each other and that felt right and okay. But it was different. We'd gone from the surreal atmosphere of the show and the McMansion on the island to the slightly less surreal atmosphere of my living in New York and working on recording my first album. And after that, who knew?

Okay, now was there any law that said we had to know right *now?* There was a reason cheap expressions like "day by day" and *"poquito a poquito"* existed. I was here, he was here, and we had another shot. And it wasn't just that I'd gotten kind of used to having a boyfriend. I'd gotten real used to having a friend and I'd missed him.

"You know, I turn eighteen next week."

The corners of his mouth turned up. "I seem to remember something about that."

My hands steady again, I reached across him for my guitar, settling it in my lap. "You interested in helping me celebrate?"

"Well . . ." Leaning forward, he made this face like he was trying to think, but his eyes were bright and the corners of his mouth just wouldn't stop twitching. "Rumor has it you have your professional debut."

"So you'll be there." A sweet, easy run on the strings. "Bella Luna," because it would be my good luck song, natch.

"Wouldn't miss it."

"You'll come to dinner with my family?"

"It'd be an honor."

"Jaime?"

His breath was warm on my neck as he leaned his head against mine. "Yeah?"

"Will you show me the trees in Central Park?" Another run.

"I'll show you everything, Ali."

The sound of the door opening made us look up. Pancho poked his head through, smiling at us.

"Ali, we're set up and ready to go. You?"

I took Jaime's hand in one of mine and stood, holding my guitar in the other.

"Absolutely."

Printed in the United States
By Bookmasters